A FUREVER HOME

FRIENDS OF GAYNOR BEACH ANIMAL RESCUE

KAJE HARPER & GABBI GREY

Edits by ELF

Cover by Leanne Clugston

ELF
Leanne
Wendy

*To all the readers who have stuck with Gaynor Beach all the way
through. We thank you.*

CHAPTER 1

ARTHUR

I sat behind the counter at Safe Haven animal rescue, listening to my shelter manager calling me from across the ocean. "Did you see the video?" The happiness in Shane's voice made me smile. "Was that cool or what?"

"Hang on." I swiped my phone over to where I had a waiting text from Shane's boyfriend, Theo. Sure enough, there was a video attached. When I hit play, I saw Shane with his little white cat Mimsy doing their routine of Mimsy-tricks with the iconic architecture of Paris behind them. In this short clip, Mimsy jumped from the ground up to Shane's shoulder, then balanced on his head and raised one paw in a salute.

I said, "Did you just *busk* in front of Notre Dame?"

Shane had lived off his wits and Mimsy's skills for a long time, but Theo was rich enough he no longer needed to.

"Not busking," Shane told me. "I didn't put the hat out. Wouldn't risk breaking the law here. But Mimsy was riding on my shoulder and these two kids asked if she was a real cat, speaking English with the cutest French accents, and I couldn't resist letting her show off a bit."

Of course he couldn't. Shane would deny it till he was blue in the face, but he was a sucker for kids, and for that little cat. Letting her shine while making kids laugh was his favorite thing. Aside from being with Theo, of course.

The newfound brightness of Shane's voice warmed me, even as I pushed aside an unworthy pang of jealousy. Shane had lived a much harder life than I had—forced to leave his family as a teenager, going homeless, sometimes going hungry, so independent it'd taken Theo months to persuade him love didn't have to come with strings.

My own family might've lost interest in me long ago, but I'd never gone without a meal. Now Shane and Theo had a relationship so solid even Shane was willing to trust it. I should be happy for my friend and stop thinking about how I was ten years older and far more alone. "Sounds like fun."

"France is something else." Shane laughed. "The history's just everywhere, the food's amazing, and the cafés all let me bring Mimsy inside." His tone became less animated. "Are you sure you're okay without my help? We'll be out of touch for a week, once we hit Africa and get out in the bush. I feel guilty—"

"Don't," I cut in. "The shelter's doing well. I have Neil on the office side and plenty of volunteers to help with animal care. Safe Haven will get along just fine without you for a month. Not that you aren't super valuable," I hurried to add, because it was the truth. "But we'll survive. I'm counting on some pictures of the charismatic megafauna when you get to Kenya."

Theo had a photo safari planned for them, and Shane had researched every wild critter they were likely to see and a few they weren't. His latching onto the scornful term *charismatic megafauna* for the big popular critters hadn't masked how eager he was to see them all.

Unless we were hit by a tornado here in SoCal or a plague wiped out all our volunteers, I wasn't going to ask Shane to cut their trip short.

Shane added, "And how's Foxy doing?"

"Hah. The ulterior motive," I teased. "You really only called me to talk about your dog. Nina's doing great with her, you know that." I'd offered to dog-sit, but Foxy didn't really like the hustle and bustle of the shelter. She was happier with one of the volunteers, and I'd visited her at Nina's where she was getting thoroughly spoiled.

"You are checking up on her, right?"

"Yes, Shane——" The chime of an incoming call interrupted us.

Kevin.

"I've got to go," I told Shane. "Our favorite thirteen-year-old is on the other line."

Shane chuckled. "A voice call from Kevin? Yeah, better find out what limping otter or mangy raccoon he wants you to help now."

"I'll send you Foxy pics." I ended that call and switched over. Shane wasn't pulling examples out of thin air. Last time, Kevin had wanted me to figure out how to get thirty-dollar flea-and-tick chews into a wild fox with mange... "Hey, Kev. What's up?"

Kevin's breathless tones came sharp over the phone. "There's a dog and I think it's hurt and this guy's going to shoot it!"

"Whoa. Wait." I jumped to my feet, waving at Vicky, today's volunteer who was straightening up the store, to gesture that I was heading outside. "If someone has a gun, you get yourself out of there *now*, kid."

"He's not pointing it at me. He's pointing it at the dog."

"I don't care. Get well away from him, you hear me?"

Kevin's voice sounded distant and muffled, as if he was speaking away from the phone. *"She's just scared, sir. She's not going to hurt you. I swear. Don't shoot her."*

"Kevin! Leave the man with the gun alone." I jogged to my elderly pickup in the shelter parking lot, digging in my pocket for the keys. "Where are you?"

I heard the bass rumble of an adult male voice, the words inaudible. Then Kevin said, "Culver Street. 3027. Hurry."

"Get yourself to safety. Call 9-1-1 and then call one of your dads."

"Got it." And the damned kid hung up on me.

Praying he was actually calling emergency services, I slammed the truck into gear and peeled out of the lot. Kevin was an awesome kid for thirteen, but he had a terrifying amount of faith in people and the universe. For a boy who'd faced his share of bullying, he still somehow believed everything would work out for the best if he just threw himself into helping.

As I took the back route around to Riverside East toward Culver Street, trying to dodge traffic, I called on fate or karma or whatever to *please* make it so. Kevin had a lot of good karma saved up. It would take the fingers of both hands to count the number of stray cats and injured wildlife the kid had saved, but none of that would protect him from a bastard with a gun and the willingness to use it.

If I'd had a hands-free phone set-up, I'd have called Kevin's dads myself, but the truck was too old to make that easy. I concentrated on driving fast.

That address was less than ten minutes away. As I cruised down the three-thousand block, I didn't see any cop cars or crowd. Hopefully that meant nothing bad had happened. Yet.

3027 was the last house before the ravine that led down to Gaynor River where it cut the town in two. That maybe explained why Kevin was there because he liked to explore the parkland along the riverbanks.

I parked and got out, listening. Raised voices came from behind the house, and then, before I could head back there, the sound of a shot rang out. I froze.

Kevin!

A tall blond man who was approaching down the sidewalk stared at me, then as one, we turned and sprinted up the lawn at the side of the house. I didn't know this dude from Adam, but if he was the kind to run *toward* a gunshot, I wasn't going to turn down help. "Call 9-1-1!" I shouted at him as we ran, and his steps slowed as he fumbled out his phone.

I rounded the corner of the house with blond dude a couple of steps behind me and there was Kevin standing in an untidy yard. *Alive. Not bleeding.* At least as far as I could see. He had his arms out at his sides and his back to a rickety wooden structure the size of a kid's playhouse raised up on legs, backed by a chicken wire enclosure.

"Arthur!" he called.

At his call, the man standing across from him whirled my way. This guy was short and skinny, at least ten years older than me although I couldn't tell fifty from sixty from seventy. Bushy gray hair, a weathered face, and work-worn hands holding a gun. A pistol of some kind. Handgun. Despite growing up in rural Minnesota in a family that loved their hunting and fishing, I'd never liked guns, so I had no clue.

I raised my hands. "Hey." My tone automatically fell to

the soft, low one I used to soothe frightened critters. "No need to get excited. The boy means no harm."

"There's a coyote under my henhouse and I aim to shoot it," the man growled.

"It's not a coyote," Kevin said, because the kid never knew when to keep quiet. "She looks like some kind of pittie-golden mix. Definitely a dog."

The man swung back to him, gun raised, which was what I'd been trying to avoid. "I don't care if it's a fucking show dog. It's killing my chickens and I got a right to shoot it."

"Kevin," I said calmly. "Go stand over by Mr.—" I waved at the blond stranger who'd caught up to me, phone in hand.

"Brooklyn," the guy said softly. "Come on over here, son."

"No." Kevin crossed his arms and didn't budge. "He'll shoot her."

Well, dammit. I was definitely going to have words with the boy's dads. As it was, I hoped the cops would show up soon. *Any time now would be good.* With my hands raised high, I edged forward toward Kevin.

The gun dude watched me but said nothing as I reached the boy.

"Go on." I gave Kevin a nudge. "I'm here now. You go out to the road and watch for the cops."

"Don't need no cops," the gun guy said. "This is my property, and a man has a right to defend his property. You're trespassing. I could shoot you all *and* the dog. This is my land."

Kevin turned a pale face up to me, then finally scurried out of range although he stopped behind the Brooklyn guy instead of heading to the street.

I faced the older man, trying to project *calm* and *helpful* and *friendly*. *Treat him like a feral cat*. I took my eyes off him, though it was hard, but a stare could be thought of as a challenge. Instead, I turned to look at the henhouse. "Did you build this coop? Looks like a solid bit of work."

"Uh, yeah."

"I'm Arthur. That's Kevin and Brooklyn over there." I'd read it was harder to shoot someone whose name you knew.

"Frank," he mumbled.

"How many chickens do you have, Frank?"

"Six. Now. Was seven." The growl in his voice made me regret the question and I scrambled for something else.

"What kind? Are they good layers? I was always fond of Plymouth Rocks. Consistent producers and easy keepers, but my mom swore by Rhode Island Reds."

"I have Reds."

I turned back a little to offer a friendly smile. "My mom would approve of you." Maybe not so much for pointing a gun at me, although it'd been so long since I'd seen my family, she might not even recognize me, or care.

The man huffed and I searched for another topic. *Come on, Gaynor Beach PD. Where the hell are you?* I said, "I'd worry about stray cats, myself. They like the park along the river, and that chicken-wire run in back would keep out dogs but not cats."

"My rooster would make mincemeat of any cat—"

Our bonding moment was destroyed by the dog deciding this was the moment to make a break for it. She burst out from under the side of the coop and bolted right past me toward the underbrush along the river.

The man yelled and a shot rang out.

"Aaah!" A flash of red-hot agony lanced through my thigh. I fell. Something hard smacked me on the back of the head like a two-by-four to the skull as I landed. Waves of pain slammed into me from my right leg, making my stomach cramp. I gagged against a flood of bile in my mouth, and the motion sent shooting pain through my skull. Dimly, I heard shouting, but no more shots.

A hand gripped my shoulder, too big to be Kevin's. A face peered down into my watering eyes. It was a nice face though only vaguely familiar—straight nose, determined chin, worried hazel eyes... The guy from the street. *Brooklyn.* I found enough focus to say, "Protect Kevin."

"He ran for help."

"Oh. Good." I tried to sit up, but Brooklyn pressed me into place on the ground.

"Don't move."

"It's just my leg." *And maybe my head.* I was too dizzy to even know.

"You were shot. There's no *just* about it." I heard a tremor in Brooklyn's voice, so maybe he wasn't as calm as he was pretending.

Fair enough. Neither was I. "Were's the, um, gun dude? Frank?" I blinked and tried to turn my head, but the fire-hot lance of pain up my skull made me freeze and just breathe.

"He ran into his house."

"With the gun?"

"Yeah."

"Crap. Let me up."

"I don't think..." But when I pushed determinedly, Brooklyn didn't fight me.

I sat up and looked around. Not down at my leg. I don't mind blood—heck, I was going to be a nurse, once— but I wasn't fond of seeing my own. Especially when the world was already whirling like a tornado in Oz.

Sirens wailed on the other side of the house, approaching fast.

"Thank God," Brooklyn said, which was exactly what I was thinking.

"As long as Frank doesn't do anything stupid."

"Stupider." Brooklyn gave a nervous chuckle. "Shooting you was pretty stupid."

Another wave of nausea clenched my gut. "Right." As the sirens came to a stop out on the road, I had to look down at myself. *Oh, that's not good.* Bright blood welled out of my thigh in a steady stream. I clamped my hand over the spot and hissed through my teeth. *Not the femoral artery, I don't think. That's on the inside, right?* This hole was more on the outside of my leg. I wasn't thinking straight.

Brooklyn said, "I'm going to go get—"

I grabbed his wrist, harder than I meant to. "Don't go!" Through my tunneling vision I saw the bloody handprint I'd smeared on his fair skin. *Blood. Skin.* "Don't worry. I'm negative." I knew what mattered as a thirty-eight-year-old gay man. *Right?* The pain thudded a drumbeat in my head that made it hard to form words.

Two cops in uniform skidded around the corner of the house, guns drawn. "Hands up! Where I can see them!" the woman yelled.

Brooklyn raised the hand I wasn't holding but called, "The man with the gun's in the house."

Two steps closer, the male cop said, "Arthur?"

I recognized him from somewhere, the shelter maybe. I repeated, "In the house," my voice setting up shrill echoes in my skull.

He waved urgently at us as they headed for the back door. "Stay down."

Sagging to my back on the grass was all too easy.

Something crashed over by the house, and Brooklyn launched himself to lie over me, tucking my head against his neck. Like he could cover me and protect me, though I was twice as wide as he was. *Should be me protecting him.* But I *hurt* and there was something so safe, so warm despite the chills racking me, in that moment, in having Brooklyn blanket me away from the world. I lay there through several people shouting and another crash, but no gunshots, with the clean shampoo-scent of Brooklyn's short straight hair in my face.

Another voice, this one female, snapped, "Who's injured?"

Brooklyn scrambled off me. "He is. Arthur."

"Damn it, Bjornsson, what did you do?" The paramedic knelt by me. Her face was familiar. *Lori? No, Lauren. I think.* I was crappy at names. She'd adopted a pair of male tuxedo kittens, that I did remember.

"Got shot," I told her without moving. I didn't want to know.

"So I see." Her tone gentled. "Max and I are going to take care of you, okay? Just lie still and let us help. Anything else, or just the leg?"

"Kevin," I remembered. "He's probably scared. You should help him."

"Is he injured?" she asked.

I couldn't remember. *A gun was pointed at him, right?* Before I could stress out, I heard Brooklyn say, "No, Kevin's fine. Just, like Arthur said, probably shocked at seeing him get shot."

Lauren began cutting up the side of my jeans with shears, starting by my ankle. They were a favorite pair, but I'd probably never get the blood out anyway.

My head spun. "Brooklyn, you'll take care of Kevin, right?" I didn't know the guy at all, but he'd run with me to find the gunshot. He'd covered me with his body. That made him a good guy, didn't it? "Call his dads, and...

and… yeah, the shelter. Tell them I'll be late for evening feeding."

The guy with Lauren chuckled at something, not sure what. My vision swam as he felt around my head and neck with gloved hands. "Can you move your toes? Your fingers?" I think I did, but they wrapped a padded collar around my neck anyway. Then they said more stuff and began lifting me from the grass to the lowered stretcher beside me. *Damn, new and exciting levels of pain.* I tried to breathe through it, tried to think. All I came up with was, "Kevin. And my dogs. They'll need a walk." A thought came to me through the pulsating darkness. "Brooklyn, the dog. The yellow one? Is she okay?" I tried to sit up to look for her.

Somehow, even though I'd barely moved and my eyes had drifted shut, I recognized his hand on my shoulder. "Hey, stay put and listen to the paramedics. The dog's fine. She ran away at top speed."

"Have to catch…catch her," I mumbled. "Ask Kevin…"

Then the paramedics raised the stretcher with a swoop that almost made me lose my lunch, and I was rattling over the grass, clinging to awareness and clenching my teeth not to scream. Screaming was bad. It'd scare Kevin and Brooklyn and the dog. I repeated that thought over and over in my head, till I was safely in the ambulance and the doors closed behind us.

There were things that needed to be done back there, but all I could do was breathe and answer the paramedics' questions and trust that Brooklyn, whoever he was, would figure out what those things were.

CHAPTER 2

BROOKLYN

So many flashing lights.

I'd let go of Arthur—albeit reluctantly, though he was in good hands—and come to find Kevin. Because that felt like a vaguely logical thing to do.

Smart kid had finally run when Arthur ordered him to. Well, after multiple attempts, but yeah, when the shot went off, the kid ran. He'd apparently sent the sheriff's deputy and her partner around to the back. While she and the other officer dealt with Frank, Kevin had then flagged down the paramedics and, once Frank was secured, they'd hustled to get to Arthur.

Now the teenager paced back and forth on the sidewalk, phone in hand, glancing from the side yard to the house behind us. "I can't believe the guy shot Arthur. Did you see that? Arthur has to be okay. Right? That Frank guy would've shot the dog, too. That dog was *not* a coyote. Sure, they sometimes come to the river, but they mostly stay in the forest over by the base. And there was a fence. I doubt the dog was even attacking his chickens. Something else probably did, so he had *no reason* to shoot at her. Or him. I didn't get a good look. Did you?"

Before I could answer, he drew in a breath.

"I still can't believe—"

I held up my hand. "Have you called your dads?" Dads...right? That's what Arthur had said? I'd been a little focused on the man who was putting himself between the gun and the kid with the dog. "How old are you?"

"Thirteen. And yes, I've called my dads. Well, I called Alec because I hoped he'd be a little less angry. When I realized I'd miscalculated, I hung up and called Dad."

"Did you hang up on him too?" I eyed his phone with the suspiciously dark screen.

"You'll be okay." At the female paramedic's voice, I spun to see her and her partner wheeling the stretcher.

Arthur looked deathly pale against the white sheet, and panic surged within me. I wanted to stalk over and demand to know if he was going to be okay.

Except they appeared to be very focused, and anything that might delay the trip to the hospital would be bad.

I heard shouts of, "Kevin. Kevin!"

The young man and I pivoted to see two men being held back by a female police officer from one of the four patrol cars now parked haphazardly along the street.

"You can't go down there, sirs." The woman couldn't be more than perhaps twenty-four...so a couple years younger than me. Not much of a force to be reckoned with, against two determined guys a decade older.

"Dad!" Kevin waved.

The officer glanced at us as I encouraged Kevin to move toward two rather harried-looking men. The shorter and slimmer of the two kept running a hand through his straight brown hair. The taller and broader guy waved agitatedly at

Kevin. And despite Kevin being skinny and not tall for thirteen, he really did favor the bigger guy with matching snub noses and wavy hair and something about the shape of their eyes. *Dad, I presume. And the other one must be Alec.*

"Officer—" I called.

"Branson."

"Right." I tried to smile even as the ambulance pulled away, siren blaring.

Using that momentary distraction, Kevin's fathers slipped past Officer Branson to snatch the young man into their arms, the likely bio dad sweeping him into a hug while the shorter guy hugged them both and clutched the kid's sleeve like he wasn't ever going to let go. After a moment, the bio dad said, "Let's get you home."

"Hey—" Branson shouted, striding toward the huddled family.

"Officer Branson?"

She met my gaze.

"He just saw someone get shot—"

"Which makes him a witness. We've got officers who'll need to take his statement."

"I'd prefer you start with me. I saw what happened." Whether I could be a great witness was an entirely different story. Everything had happened so fast.

"And you are?"

"Brooklyn. Brooklyn West. I was walking down the street, and I heard a gunshot, and—"

"Sir." She held up a hand. "I'll need to take your statement as well, but perhaps not at this exact moment." Even as she said the words, the front door of the house opened.

The sheriff's deputy and the other officer guided a handcuffed Frank down the driveway and to their car.

Frank whined, "Someone's got to look after my

chickens. That damn coyote will come back and eat them—"

"It's not a coyote!" Kevin actually yelled the words. "That's what I was trying to tell you. The dog's a pittie—"

"Kevin." The dad who had his arm protectively around the boy squeezed his shoulder. "Maybe let's let the police do their job. He had a gun."

"He shot Arthur. But he didn't have to shoot him. We could've caught the dog—"

"Damn coyote probably has rabies." Frank tried to angle himself toward the deputy propelling him by the arm. "Kathleen—"

"That's Deputy Olson to you. You can't shoot people. I'll see about your chickens, but you've been advised of your right to remain silent, and I suggest you do that." She tucked him into the car with way more gentleness than I would have, had our situations been reversed.

"Is that blood?" Officer Branson pointed to my hand.

"Well, yeah—"

She yelled at a burly young cop down the block, "Quakenbush, call another ambulance."

Quakenbush? Unfortunate last name. I waved my hand at him. "It's Arthur's blood. I'm okay, I swear. Although if I could get something to wipe it off..." I took a good look at my wrist, remembering the feel of his hand on me. I'd bet he was normally a strong guy, but he'd felt weak as he'd asked me to stay. As he'd listed off all those things that needed tending to.

"I've got a first aid kit with disinfectant wipes." Quakenbush gestured for yet another police officer to help hold back the gathering crowd, then strode off toward one of the cop cars.

A thin voice that was meant to be strong echoed in my

brain. *"Call his dads, and…and… yeah, the shelter. Tell them I'll be late for evening feeding."*

Arthur's instructions for me flashed back in an instant.

Call his dads. Check. Well, I hadn't actually been the one to call them, but Kevin had. And I'd have offered him physical comfort while he waited, if that's what he'd needed. Along with Kevin's fear, though—appropriate given Arthur getting shot—I'd sensed a whole pile of righteous indignation and independence from the young man that didn't invite a hug from a stranger.

Kevin's dads kept murmuring things to him.

I couldn't hear, which was probably their intention, but I was impressed they were keeping it together. If my baby sister Cheyenne had pulled this crap? I'd be hollering my head off at her stupidity. Bravery…and stupidity. Kevin could've got himself killed. For a dog. My sister likely would've done the same thing.

Call the shelter.

"Uh…?" I was about to stick my hand in the air to get their attention when Quakenbush approached wearing gloves and carrying a first aid kit.

He laid the zippered kit on the patrol car trunk and started rummaging through it. While he was busy…

"Hey? Kevin?"

"Yeah?" He eased out of his dad's hold and stepped toward me, straightening his shoulders and jerking his chin up although I could see his face was flushed and his eyes glossy.

A protective hand landed on his shoulder. The slimmer guy I assumed was second dad Alec met my gaze. "You said your name was Brooklyn, right? And you helped?"

How much I'd helped, I wasn't certain. Questionably, I'd run *toward* the gunshot. Still… "Yeah, I tried to help."

"You kept our son from getting killed." The taller dad offered a tiny smile. "Thank you."

I cleared my throat but then the police officer grabbed an alcohol-wipe and set about cleaning my wrist. I spoke past him. "Really, no thanks necessary. I'm just sorry—" An image of Arthur's jeans going dark with blood filled my mind. "I wish things had ended differently. Oh, meaning that *no one* got shot." Lest they think I'd somehow meant their son should've been killed...

"Well, we're grateful," the big guy said.

"I might need your help." Frustration welled within me. I would've been happy to clean myself—given there wasn't any injury—but Quakenbush seemed determined. As long as that meant he finished quickly, I was okay with that.

"Whatever it is, you just ask." The dad winced. "I should introduce myself. Apologies. I'm Joe, and this is my husband, Alec."

I waved with the arm not being tended to. "Better circumstances, right? I'm new in town, and this wasn't how I envisioned meeting people."

Joe offered a sheepish smile. "That's true. How can we help? Is there something you need us to do?"

"Arthur said something about a shelter? Did he mean Safe Haven Animal Rescue? I've heard about it, of course, but I haven't had time to go there myself." One item on my long to-do list was to take my brochures there and see if they would stock them. Once I *had* better brochures for my doggie daycare. A redesign was even higher up on that to-do list.

"Oh, of course, Arthur's dogs will need to be fed and walked. And all the shelter pets too." Kevin grabbed his father's arm. "We can go, right, Dad?" His gaze passed between his two dads—almost like he figured if one said no then the other might agree.

"I promised Arthur I would go." I eyed Quakenbush. "If you're done with me for now."

"Statement." That came from Officer Branson.

"Surely you can take my statement at the shelter." I glanced over to Frank's house. "And what about the chickens?"

Officer Branson pursed her lips. "They'll be fine for a few hours. I can call Pam. She organized fosters before Safe Haven opened. I'll see if she can take care of the chickens. And I'll call Shane. He's the manager of the shelter—"

"Shane's in Europe with Theo and Mimsy." Kevin jutted his chin as if daring any of us to argue.

I, of course, had no idea who any of these people were. "Arthur said something about the evening feeding. I want to help him out." That felt super important to me. He hadn't asked for much. And given how much pain he'd likely been in, the fact that he focused on the shelter suggested it meant everything to him. Well, along with the young man before me whom Arthur took a bullet for.

Quakenbush said, "We'll take a statement from you now. The shelter can wait half an hour. Give me your ID, and I'll make sure we have your address so we can follow up later." He met my gaze with dark-gray eyes. "You're going to want to wash your hands and arms well with soap and water, but the blood's gone."

"Thanks."

"Sure." The cop's dark-brown hair shone in the late afternoon California sun. A very different shade from Arthur's red-tinged light brown. Clean-shaven too, where Arthur had a full beard and a long curling mustache I'd thought a bit comical, until the man turned out to be a damned hero.

Ridiculous man, letting himself get shot, standing in front of a gun like he was invincible. God, I hope he'll be all right. I couldn't recapture the disinterested amusement I'd felt as I approached down the sidewalk, noting a tall, broadly built stranger with a wild beard, in the moment before that shot rang out. Arthur wasn't just some stranger now.

Alec said to Quakenbush, "I suppose you need Kevin's statement, too." He didn't look pleased.

"We'll make it as easy as possible."

Officer Branson smiled and, for a moment, I noticed she was attractive. "In fact, why don't you take the boy on home? We know who you are and where he lives, and the perp's in custody so there's no huge urgency. Quakenbush can get Brooklyn's statement now, then drop by and get Kevin's. No sense having the boy waiting around on the scene—" She gave Kevin a compassionate look, which he didn't seem to appreciate if folded arms and a raised chin were any indication. "—or dragging everyone down to the station."

"I'm not a child—"

I interrupted before Kevin could antagonize a friendly cop, asking Branson, "You got Frank's gun, right?" I couldn't remember any deputy having brought the gun out with them. "The bastard won't get out on bail and come right back and use it?" The quiver in my stomach told me I had some shocky anxiety waiting to pounce, the moment I stopped finding things to keep me busy. *I hope the shelter needs me for hours.*

Branson told me, "We're waiting on a warrant, and we'll do a search of the entire house and confiscate any weapons. He certainly shouldn't have been waving one around his backyard. Plus, he won't get bail till tomorrow, if then."

"Dad, if Mr. Brooklyn's going to the shelter, we need to find the loose dog. She's probably scared." Again, Kevin looked back and forth between his fathers. The closeness between fathers and son touched me. So unlike my own upbringing.

"Kevin, I understand you want to help. I really do. But for tonight, we should go home, have some dinner, speak to the nice police officer, and then call it a night. If you want, I can spend some time with you tomorrow looking." Joe caught my gaze. "I'm a writer, so my schedule's flexible."

I wouldn't have asked, but writer sounded cool. I didn't, to my knowledge, know any writers.

He kept his attention on me. "Do you need a ride? We've got our car..." He waved down the street.

"Thanks for the generous offer. I don't live far from here... and I know where the shelter is. As soon as Officer Quakenbush is done with me." My gaze passed between the two police officers.

"Let me clean up and then we'll get to your statement." Quakenbush disposed of the gloves and cloths in a plastic bag he sealed. Then he set about tidying up the first aid kit. He hadn't needed to take care of me personally. I was appreciative and offered my hand. "Thank you."

He shook it. "I'm glad you were here." His gaze settled on Kevin. "Things, although they're bad, could've been much worse.

Not going to get any argument from me. "How's Arthur doing? Does anyone know?"

"That's confidential medical information." Officer Branson gave me a stern look.

I held up my hands. "Innocent question."

"You'll have to take it up with him." Her cell phone

rang. She glanced at the screen. "Excuse me." She stepped away as she swiped to accept.

"Hopefully I won't need a key to get into the shelter." I yanked my own keys out of my pocket, almost like a talisman. I had a home to get to and an SUV to drive to the shelter with, and—I glanced at the old beat-up truck. "Is that Arthur's?"

"Yes. I wish I could drive it home for him." Kevin nearly vibrated with tension.

"Still a few years until you turn sixteen." Joe appeared relieved at that statement.

Although Kevin tried to appear responsible, he also had an impetuousness that couldn't be hidden. *I bet he's a handful.*

Like Cheyenne. She was thirteen years younger than me, and had been wild and demanding from the day she'd been born. Brave and defiant and never willing to keep her head down. Now, she was a senior in high school, and I despaired of her focusing enough to get a college scholarship, her escape if our parents would even let her go. She was brilliant...but undisciplined. Which was ironic, coming from a household where rules were of paramount importance. She understood that—and then broke them all anyway.

"We should call James." Alec gazed first at Joe and then at me. "Arthur's best friend. He'll want to know what happened. He lives in Marina Park, and he might have a key for the truck."

Joe nodded. "We probably should've thought of him first. If my best friend were shot, I'd want to know. I'd be at the hospital in a heartbeat."

"Don't forget he and Colin are super busy fostering," Kevin put in.

"A dog?" If I didn't run a doggie daycare, I might've

considered fostering. As it was, with my growing business, I had plenty of furry chaos every day.

"Uh, no. Colin and James are fostering three young children. The kids' single mom is going through a rough patch, and so they're helping out." Joe pulled out his phone. "I'll make the call." He wandered away.

The sun was starting to set, and I still had no idea how long my statement would take or what I faced at the shelter. I met Kevin's gaze, and told him, "I'm proud of you. Thank you for sending the cops around back to us. I was…busy." *I'm not going to think about the gun and how easily Frank could've turned my way. That's for another day.*

Alec rested his hand on Kevin's shoulder. "You always try to do your best, son, and I'm proud of you too. We're going to have words about going onto strangers' properties, though, okay?"

"Yeah." Kevin didn't sound thrilled, but he looked down. I got the sense, fleeting as it might be, that he'd at least listen to what his dads had to say.

Joe returned. "James is heading to the hospital. When things calm down, he said he can get his brother Danny to drive Arthur's truck back home to the shelter."

"Arthur lives at the shelter?" I asked.

"Yep." Kevin beamed. "Isn't that the best job ever?" Then his smile slipped, and he glanced between us. "He's not hurt that bad, right? Just his leg, and he'll be back running the shelter soon?"

Joe put an arm around his son's shoulders and hugged him close. "I sure hope so. He seemed awake when the ambulance left, and that's a good sign. Come on, I think you've had enough excitement for one day."

"Should we go to the hospital and make sure? There was a lot of blood." Kevin's lips quivered, despite how adult he was trying to seem.

Alec said, "Remember when the snapping turtle bit your finger and you shook blood all over the kitchen? That's not always a terrible sign."

Joe added, "And James will be at the hospital, and Colin, probably Neil from the shelter, and more. They'll let us know how Arthur's doing. Come on, let's get out of the way and let the police do their job." He held out a hand to me and engulfed my fingers in a strong clasp. "Thanks again, Brooklyn. If you need anything as you get settled here in Gaynor Beach, let us know."

I watched them walk off, the boy between the two men, already talking and gesturing. When I was a kid, I'd never had anyone who listened...

"Right. Time for your statement," Quakenbush said. "My body cam is active, so you are being recorded while I make notes. Do you give consent to that?"

"Uh. Sure?"

"We're going to start from the beginning. Where were you an hour ago?"

"I was home, I guess." I had to check my phone. *Only half an hour since I walked out my door?* Felt like a lifetime. "Yeah. At home."

"And when did you leave?"

Quakenbush led me through the events of the last half hour. When he focused on *Did I know I was on private property?* and *Had the homeowner asked me to leave?* I began to wonder if I should have a lawyer myself, but then he moved on to the shooting. I was priding myself on how calm I sounded until my breath stuttered and came short. *So much blood. And Arthur fell.* I choked on the words and squeezed my eyes shut.

"No rush, sir." Quakenbush's voice came deep and steady. "Take your time."

I can do this. I counted backward from thirty, listened to

23

the sounds of a seagull overhead and voices to my left. *I'm fine.* I opened my eyes. "Sorry, where was I?"

Quakenbush wrapped things up fairly quickly and closed the case of his tablet. "One of the detectives will call in the next couple of days to bring your statement by for your signature, and to ask any follow-up questions."

"Right. Of course." I sucked in a deep breath. "Is that all?"

"Yes. You're free to go. Drive carefully, now."

I nodded, turned my back on the scene, and walked slowly and calmly—*ha, who was I kidding?*—I hurried home. The sooner I got into my SUV and busy taking care of things for Arthur, the less time I'd have to worry.

As I drove the short distance from my home in Riverside to the shelter in the tonier Marina Park neighborhood, I considered Kevin's words. *"He lives at the shelter. Isn't that the best job ever?"* I thought I had the best job. A run of bad luck had landed me where I was—good coming out of bad. I'd have given the money back if it meant not going through the shit I had, but I'd come out in one piece—more or less—and I had a new home, my doggie-daycare business, and a fresh start in an LGBTQ-friendly town. What I didn't have were friends, or any kind of support system here. What I also didn't have was a familiar routine, that sense of knowing where I was and how I belonged. Seeing Kevin with his dads, hearing them talk about all of Arthur's friends, made me feel alone.

Of course Arthur has friends. A guy like that, what would he need with me? But a promise was a promise, and I'd do my best for him.

I parked in the front lot, exited my vehicle, and headed to the door beneath a cool mural of cats and dogs that spanned the upper story. I stepped inside the airlock entry, pushed open the inner door, and stopped short. *Not what I expected.*

The floor under my feet looked like expensive marble, or the best fake I'd seen. The lighting fixtures overhead were chandeliers dripping with sparkling crystals. *This is a shelter?*

A woman hustled out from the back area. "We're closed. Sorry, I was about to lock the front door. We open again tomorrow morning at nine."

"My name is Brooklyn. Uh... Arthur asked me to come by, and—"

"Arthur? Do you know where he is? He tore out of here, and I haven't been able to reach him, and Mario's out sick. I'm done with my shift, and I have to get to my night class, but I can't just leave. But I'm writing a big exam. I *can't* be late…" She bit her lip.

"Well, then my timing's perfect. Arthur asked me to do *evening feedings.*"

"Oh, thank goodness!" Her eyes brightened, looking so happy that I choked back the words *"Arthur got shot,"* Someone else, someone closer to her, could pass along that news. After all, she'd want to know if Arthur was okay, but I had no clue, and there was nothing she could do right now. Let her write her exam.

He has to be okay…

"Do you know the routine?" she asked.

"No. I run a local doggie daycare though, so I'm good with the critters."

"Cool! Come on, come on." She hustled me down a hallway. "It's all written down, but I'll show you quickly. I'm Vicky, by the way." She gestured for me to follow her.

So, I did. And she took me through everything with such speed that I was breathless. Kitchen, food, feeding list, bowls, runs, cat room.

Then she handed me the keys and was gone.

I couldn't blame her for leaving, although I did wonder about her giving keys to a stranger. She must've really been stressed about that test. Although probably there wasn't much to steal, unless I wanted to take off with a mixed-breed pit bull. And, as I'd said, Arthur sent me. It seemed like "Arthur" was a magic word to earn her trust.

I carried the list with me as I fed the various animals in the kennels. Each dog got their meal. I took time to read the chart on each door, focusing on the *behavior notes* like "Escape artist" and "He will jump on you" and "Very timid. Don't approach." I smiled at one that said, "Super friendly but will shark-bite for treats; watch your fingers." *This* I understood. This I was good at—runs full of dogs with their tails up or down, wagging or still, ears pricked or flattened, approaching or hanging back, eyeing me or looking away.

Running a doggie daycare meant I'd had to get adept with dog body language. For the first time in an hour, I felt grounded and competent. While the dogs ate, I did the cats. Not my area of expertise, but the instructions were clear. Food, water, each cat litterbox required an evaluation and, in a few cases, fresh litter. The place was cleaner than I expected. Clearly Vicky had taken care of everything to this point.

I wondered if I should try to walk the dogs, and was out inspecting the exercise yard when a battered pick-up with a topper drove up to the side door.

Is that Arthur's truck? I hadn't paid enough attention.

The man who swung out was a few inches shorter than me with a shock of red hair. He came toward me, eyeing me with assessing green eyes. "Brooklyn?"

"Yes. Brooklyn West." I held out my hand and we shook. He looked familiar.

"I'm Colin Reynolds. We met when Phillip picked up Wally, remember? You took care of the little Yorkie back in the summer. My husband, James, is Arthur's best friend. He's at the hospital with him now."

"How's Arthur? Is he okay?" I demanded.

Colin frowned. "I wish we knew. He's getting a cat scan or something. They won't say anything even to James. He sent me here to take care of evening chores, because I hate hospitals."

I did too, so I knew better than to ask him why. "I made a start. Everyone's fed. But not walked."

"What about Arthur's dogs?"

"Uh? Arthur's?"

"Come on." Colin led the way back into the building. "Let me introduce you to his menagerie. Up these stairs." He headed toward the second floor up a narrow steep flight of stairs. "This is Arthur's apartment, and these are..." He pulled a key out of his pocket and opened the door. "The drama brigade."

A big black lab galumphed over and tried to leap on Colin, then at the last minute swerved to land huge paws on my chest.

I caught those bear-sized front feet with the ease of long practice, aiming the dog back to four on the floor.

"Ebony, off," Colin ordered.

A beagle, sitting by the doorway into a small kitchen, howled in our direction with flop-eared pathos.

"That's Twain, lying about how starved he is. The little chihuahua mix is Chili, and the cat—" Colin spun in a circle, then pointed at the top of a bookcase.

A longhaired Siamese-like cat peered down at us with scornful pure-blue eyes.

Like Arthur's. His dazed, imploring gaze rose in my memory.

"That's Xandra," Colin finished. He addressed the dogs. "Sorry guys, your daddy won't be back for a bit. But this nice guy Brooklyn and I are here to do dinner and walkies and maybe some butt-scritches, till we find out how your daddy's doing and how soon he'll be home."

Resisting the temptation to look around Arthur's home, I focused on cleaning water bowls and opening cans and bags to fill food dishes. Working with Colin, forced to guess since there was no helpful list of directions here, we got everyone fed and he located the pill he knew Xandra needed, and convinced her to take it in some minced tuna. Then we walked every canine in the building, except one poor shepherd-mix too scared to come out of the run.

It was good to keep busy, to be productive. The beat of worry in my head was muted as long as I had things to do. But by the time we reluctantly locked up for the night, with Colin taking a bag of clothes for Arthur and promising he'd come back to meet the morning volunteers, we still hadn't heard if Arthur was okay.

I went home and scrubbed my house within an inch of its life—even though it was already spotless—until I was finally tired enough to sleep. But my dreams were haunted by hospitals and gunshots, blood, and nebulous anxiety where I tried to prevent a disaster and always arrived too late.

CHAPTER 3

ARTHUR

My mouth tasted like the bottom of a birdcage, all papery-dry but slimy too. A bit of plastic pressed against my nose, like a giant, dried booger. Someone had poured sand in my eyes and—oh, hell—in the middle of discovering those minor discomforts, someone stabbed me in the thigh with a hot poker, then jammed it up the back of my skull. I groaned.

"Waking up, are we?" said a cheery voice.

"No," I muttered through gritted teeth. My next couple of breaths sounded embarrassingly like whimpers. *Damn, that hurts.*

"Come on, big boy," the voice urged. "Show me you're awake and aware, and then I can give you a bit more painkiller."

Now that was incentive. I blinked my stinging eyes open.

The guy bending over me wasn't familiar—at least, not to my currently half-offline brain. Blue scrubs, red curls, pale skin, a face like a teen popstar…but I didn't think they let teens do patient care.

I licked my chapped lips. "Who?"

"I'm your floor nurse, Dylan. Welcome back. Can you tell me your name?"

"Arthur," I managed. "Water?"

"Sure thing, honey." He picked up a cup and tapped my lips with the straw. "Tiny sips, now. Head trauma makes some folks nauseous."

"Head…" The water was a blessing on my tongue. I had to force myself not to gulp too fast. Something pulled along my cheek as I swallowed and I raised a hand toward my face, but Dylan caught my wrist. "There's something on my nose," I protested.

"Oxygen cannula. Leave it alone."

"Oxygen? My chest's okay."

"Oxygen's good for bruised brains. Sounds like you gave yours a bit of a bouncing around."

How bad? But I was thinking and talking, despite the blinding headache, so this couldn't be much worse than getting hit by a two-hundred-pound lineman in high school football. "My leg?" I asked. That burning pain was unfamiliar.

"What's your birthdate?" Dylan asked, instead of answering me.

When I told him, he chuckled. "You don't look thirty-eight. Good skin. What city are we in?"

"Gaynor Beach. Town not city."

"Hey, we're growing. Who's the mayor?"

"I'll tell you when my head isn't killing me."

"Good answer."

"Painkillers?"

"Any second now. I need to finish the neuro assessment and check your vitals and then we can push the magic button."

I held still through having the thermometer in my mouth, and various things checked. A bright light aimed into my eyes hurt like a squirt of lemon juice and I grunted. Dylan said, "Sorry. I'll try to be quick. Pupils are looking good."

"Didn't we do this before?" My brain was hazy, my thoughts like sticky cotton candy, but I remembered the light torture, maybe more than once.

"Honey, I hate to tell you, but we'll be doing it all night long. At least you're looking fine. Real stable. So the doc said I can give you a little dose of the good stuff. I'll be back in five minutes. Let me know if you feel woozy or nauseous as the relief comes onboard." He tucked a plastic device into my right hand. "There's your call button."

"Wait," I said as he moved out of my flat-on-my-back line of sight. "What happened? What's next?" I didn't want to put my worries into words.

"You'll have to ask your doctor," Dylan said unhelpfully.

"When will he be here?"

"You mean she. Dr. Ranjan will stop by when she has a break. The painkiller should take effect soon. Try to get some rest."

I lay flat, breathing shallowly, trying not to move so I wouldn't stir up the hornets nesting in my right thigh or the fireworks behind my eyes. *What happened? Did I fall?* I had a vague impression of Kevin and a dog, and a light-haired stranger who met my eyes in a moment of shock. Pretty greenish-gray eyes, I thought, and parted lips surrounded by a short-cropped light-brown beard. Startled...*Gunshot.* Memory came flooding back, of the sound of a shot, running, Kevin, the dog, the damned chickens. "He shot me. He really shot me!" I could hear the shock in my own voice even as I squeezed my eyes at the volume.

"Sure did," a familiar deep voice drawled from over by the unseen door. Footsteps approached. I blinked and then James's face came into view, with an unfamiliar tight-jawed frown. "What were you thinking?"

"I don't remember?" The morphine or whatever it was seemed to be hitting. My brain felt fluffy as tangled cotton wool, but the pain had backed off to something nasty instead of excruciating. *Thank you, modern medicine.*

"That's fair. You've been through a lot in the last couple of hours." A scraping sound and then James hauled a chair over so he could sit where I could see him.

"But they let *you* in?" I was teasing. Having James there was a comfort.

"Since I came back with your medical power of attorney, yeah. And a good thing too, because they insisted you couldn't have visitors otherwise."

"Thanks." I was glad he was there, even though I wasn't managing any stellar conversation. "Did the doc tell you what's wrong with my leg?" I remembered a pulsing flow of blood and felt sick.

"Other than being shot?" James held up a big hand. "Sorry. They said you had a penetrating wound and muscle damage. Nothing broken."

"So it's going to heal?"

I'd tried to sound casual, but James reached across and set his hand over mine where I clutched the call button. His dark skin was a warm contrast to my pasty white. "As far as I know, you'll heal just fine."

I sighed and didn't bother to ask about my head. I'd had a concussion before. The signs were familiar, and I knew what the docs would say. *Give it time.*

James let go of my hand and sat back. "Why don't you

get some sleep, and I'll wake you when the doctor comes in?"

"You won't leave?" I begged, the painkiller loosening my tongue. "I know you have Colin and Widget and now the kids to get back to, but...stay? For a bit?" James was a good friend. Although now he had a husband and so much on his plate, I shouldn't ask for his time.

"I promise. I'll be here when you wake up."

I wouldn't have expected I could drop off, but I was exhausted and trusted James to keep me safe. The woozy warmth of the drug sucked me under.

———

When I woke to the dual throbbing of my head and leg, some time had passed. How much, I wasn't sure, but a middle-aged, dark-haired woman in blue scrubs was standing over me. "Mr. Bjornsson? Arthur?"

"Arthur, please." I licked my lips and squinted my eyes against the halo of the room lights behind her.

"I'm Dr. Ranjan. I'm here to do an assessment and then talk about your ongoing care."

James said at her shoulder, "Do you want me here, Arthur, or should I wait outside?"

"Get yourself some coffee," I told him. "Or a snack. Thanks for staying with me." If the doc had bad news, I didn't want James to hear it.

He made a sound as if he wasn't pleased, but disappeared from my limited view, and I heard the room door open and close. James was a really good guy.

"On a scale of one to ten, how's your pain?" Dr. Ranjan asked.

I wanted to say eight, but I could imagine much worse

things, like falling in boiling water or having my leg blown off, so I said, "Six."

"Is your head or leg worse?"

My brain was fuzzy enough it took me a minute to think that through, and then I said, "Same? But different?" I closed my eyes because the lights weren't helping.

I felt a touch on my shoulder that was probably Ranjan's hand. "I promise, it will get better soon. You were extremely lucky. The wound to your leg was from a small-caliber bullet, and it went straight through. An inch to the side, and it would've broken your femur. As it is, you have a couple of wounds we're letting heal by second intention with just bandaging, but they will heal. Some muscle damage that you'll want physical therapy for, but I anticipate a nearly full recovery."

"Nearly?"

"Some scarring is inevitable."

"And my head?" I asked into the darkness.

"A bad concussion. We'll do an MRI tomorrow before we discharge you, but both CTs were essentially normal. Nothing surgical. Just time and rest. Have you had a concussion before?"

"Yeah, at sixteen. Playing football to please my father." *Crap.* Painkiller or trauma was fuzzing my brain, because I didn't tell people that little detail. Didn't reveal the pathos of being a beefy six-foot-tall teenager so eager to please his daddy he spent an entire summer working like hell to get fit, only to ride the bench in the fall. I made the team, but wasn't on the field enough for our games to be worth my father's time.

"Well, a second concussion's a bit riskier than a first, but I'm pleased with your status so far. I'm going to do a full assessment now." The doc proceeded to ask me questions and make me remember a series of words, and move my fingers and curl my toes. I messed up some of the memory stuff, the pulsing pain in my head making it hard to concentrate, but when she was done, Dr. Ranjan said, "You seem stable, which is good. We can get that oxygen off you now." She eased the cannula free herself, and I sighed at the loss of one irritant.

"Thanks."

"Try to get some sleep, and I'll look in again tomorrow before you're discharged."

I'd been trying to tough it out, but then, part of the reason I quit football after the first concussion was because I didn't buy into stupid macho nonsense. So I asked, "Can I get a little more painkiller?"

"Let me look at your chart." A pause. "You can have another dose of Tylenol. I'll have the nurse bring it by."

"Tylenol."

She must have heard the flatness of my tone, because her voice went gentle. "Sorry, Arthur. We limit the amount of opioids we give head-trauma patients. I'll put in an order for some ice packs too."

I managed to say, "Thanks," from behind closed eyes.

The door scuffed open, clicked shut. I let my eyes water unwiped, and lay flat and deflated on the pillow, focusing on my breathing.

When James murmured, "Hey, Arthur," I jumped and yelped. "Sorry!" he added.

"Not your fault." In case he got the wrong impression, I rubbed my damp face and told him, "Everything's fine. Puncture wound and a concussion. She said I'll make a full recovery. I'm just feeling sorry for myself."

"You're allowed."

"Doesn't help anything, though." A thought floated to the top. "The shelter. Vicky had to leave early. Did anyone take care of the evening chores?"

"Colin volunteered."

"But your kids." I couldn't remember how long they'd been fostering, but I knew they were dealing with some emotional issues with their new brood.

"They can handle Danny babysitting for an hour. He brought his kids along as a buffer, and it went fine."

"Oh. Oh, good. Thank him for me. I might not be out in time for morning chores, though."

James chuckled, the bastard. "No shit."

"Watch it, Mama might hear you swearing." James's mother was the reason he rarely used that kind of language. So he must've been really worried about me. "What day is it? Is Neil working?" I put the heels of my hands on my temples and squeezed. Didn't help the throbbing.

James's warm fingers ringed my wrists. "Hey, your brain is already bruised. Let's not make it worse." When he'd guided my hands down to my sides he said, "Colin will let the volunteers know you're out. It's Sunday, by now."

"So, no Neil."

"That guy Brooklyn was already there when Colin arrived," James told me. "Colin said he was real helpful."

"Brooklyn?" For a moment the name meant nothing, then those hazel eyes floated into my mind. "The gunshot guy? I mean, not the shooter. Him? Why?" As far as I knew, I'd never met him before.

"He said you asked him to."

"I did?" Maybe so. I remembered lying on the grass, scared to death, with the stranger a comforting presence I clung to. *That's not embarrassing at all.* "You should tell him he doesn't have to."

"I don't have his number. But he told Colin he runs a

new doggie-daycare business, so he understands dogs. Even Chili liked him."

"Colin's probably lying about Chili," I muttered because that chihuahua-mix barely tolerated me.

"Maybe." James chuckled. "But it means he thinks Brooklyn is a good guy."

"I hope I can pay him back by sending business his way."

James squeezed my shoulder. "Arthur, you don't have to pay everyone back for helping you. People like you."

Maybe so, but it was always safer to reward that. A doggie daycare would be an asset to the community, and I could recommend him to clients—after I checked him out, of course. Win-win.

The nurse Dylan came in with a tiny cup of pills and an ice pack.

James pushed up out of his chair. "I'll let this guy get you comfortable."

"You should head home," I told him. "It must be late, and Colin will be home alone with the kids. I'm just going to sleep anyhow."

"All right," James said. "I'll be back in the morning."

"No, don't do that." I'd no doubt feel like crap in the morning and look it too. "I'll have them call you when I'm being discharged. Probably afternoon." Especially if they were going to do another scan of my throbbing head. Nothing happened fast in a hospital unless you were dying. "Okay?"

He hesitated, looking down at me, then said, "Okay. Sleep well." He told Dylan, "You take care of this guy. He's one of the good ones."

After the door closed behind him, I told the nurse, "He's biased. But a great friend."

"I can make my own judgements, and I agree with him." Dylan raised the head of my bed slightly.

That set off some fun swoopy dizziness, but I didn't complain.

"I have some Tylenol for you, and an ice pack. Yes?"

"You're a god among nurses," I told him, and prayed that there was some magic in those little capsules in the cup.

CHAPTER 4

BROOKLYN

"He's probably going to be cranky." Colin chuckled. "Don't say I didn't warn you."

I didn't know Arthur well enough to be able to judge how *cranky* he might or might not be. When I'd arrived at the shelter that morning—to find Colin and Vicky already hard at work—I'd considered turning around. Except, honestly, I didn't have anything else to do on a Sunday with no clients scheduled, and, just as clearly, my help could be used here.

I'd put in a good day's work so far, and felt useful doing it. That'd helped stave off my worry about a man who was essentially a stranger. But who didn't feel like one. "You said they were doing another brain scan this morning, and along with getting shot, he has a concussion. I think a little crankiness might be allowed."

Another chuckle from Colin, his Long Island accent a little heavier. "I should record you saying that, for after you deal with him."

Who knows how long I'll even be here? Arthur might send me on my way. Hell, I couldn't even be certain he'd remember he asked me to help. "You said you told James to tell him that I'm still here, right?" *Wow, that sentence confused even me.*

"James told him. I didn't hear what the response was, but Arthur's always grateful for volunteers, so you're good. Vicky gave you an orientation, and you took care of Arthur's babies. That was the most important part."

Chili had been particularly pleased to see me when we arrived that morning. I'd worried about leaving the three dogs and cat alone last night while I'd gone home, but they'd all been fine. And I'd known Ebony would try to put his massive paws on my chest, and was ready to thwart his efforts to knock me over. "They did great."

A newer-model SUV pulled into the parking lot.

Almost as soon as the engine cut, a bald Black man with a bushy beard leapt from the driver's side and hustled around to the passenger rear door. He had that door open and was pulling out a crutch when the front passenger door opened. "I asked you to wait," the tall man holding the crutch scolded.

"That's James." Colin beamed with clear admiration for his husband in his gaze.

The passenger grumbled, "I told you, I don't need you hovering." And that would be Arthur whose frown really marred his handsome face as he emerged. He accepted the crutch, then looked up and caught my eye.

Our gazes held.

After a moment, he broke away to glare at James.

"Cranky." Colin grinned as he headed toward the SUV.

After a moment, I followed.

"You're looking…" Colin cocked his head at Arthur. "Rough."

"Thank you." Arthur's frown didn't lessen. "You have three kids you should be with."

James rolled his eyes. "A few hours with Danny and Rob, as well as Hallie and Thomas, will be good for them."

I wracked my mind. Colin had told me a bunch of proud foster-dad and close family stories as we worked. Danny was James's brother. Rob was Danny's fiancé. Hallie and Thomas were their kids.

See? I could do this.

"May I help?" I gestured to the bag James carried.

"That would be lovely." The big man handed it over. He topped me by a couple of inches, and I was six-two. A bit of a height difference between the husbands.

I grinned at Colin. "All good."

Arthur nodded to me. "Thanks." He pivoted back to James. "So you can stop hovering. See? I've got a minder."

Okay, yeah, a little cranky. I didn't blame him. Gunshot wound? Knock to the head? Guy was probably in pain— even if they were giving him *the good stuff,* which I had a vague impression they couldn't with a head injury. Poor guy. "I'm happy to be a minder. Nothing else to do." And since Arthur intrigued me in a way few men had recently, I was determined to prove myself useful.

Arthur hobbled toward the shelter, and I hustled ahead with his bag to get the door for him.

I tossed a *nice to meet you* at James before following Arthur into the grand lobby space. Colin had explained how this used to be a wine tasting room. That made all the majestic marble tiles and mirrors and chandeliers understandable.

"Do you want to go straight upstairs to rest?" I held up the duffel bag. "I need to run this upstairs, right? And do you want to see your dogs? Or do you want me to bring them down here? Because those stairs are steep but, I have to say, your dogs are super adorable."

"Is Vicky here?" He glanced around. "She usually works Sundays."

"She had to take off early. She apologized and was relieved when Colin said you were being discharged from the hospital."

"Not a moment too soon." He winced as he rubbed his forehead. "Hospitals are expensive."

No shit. Expensive, stressful, scary. But I pushed those memories aside. "I think resting is a good idea—"

"I'm fine. Really." He tried to grab his bag from my hand. "I can take care of things from here on."

I cocked my head. "We haven't done evening feeding yet. Your dogs need walks. How are you going to manage all that?" I held the bag away from him. Clearly he thought he'd just nab it and, what? Head upstairs on his crutch, then hobble back down and feed a shelter full of pets? *Stubborn man.* "Let's get you up to your apartment."

"Fine." He said the word with annoyance. "We'll make it fast."

Apparently my hovering wasn't any less annoying to him than James's. *Is he always this…cranky?* I could completely see where he was coming from, but he wouldn't be able to do everything himself. "I bet these marble tiles are a little slippery, but then you're familiar with them, I guess. I thought the upscale look was weird, but Colin explained about the winery. Looking fancy probably helps adopters believe you take great care of the pets, right?"

"Yup." He managed to crutch through the hallway to the stairs halfway back.

I shuffled behind him. Trying not to rush him, and yet trying not to seem like I was holding back and babying him. *I'm so confused.* Which was weird. I was a pretty confident guy who could tackle just about anything. This guy had me word-vomiting and unsure of myself.

We were about halfway up the staircase when he stopped.

I waited.

He swayed dangerously and started to lean backward.

I dropped the bag and was at his back in an instant—countering his momentum and pushing him forward. Banging our knees landing upward onto the steps was one thing. Both of us crashing backward was a catastrophe in the making.

The crutch slipped from his hand as he grabbed the railing. "Fuck."

"It's okay. I've got you." Which I mostly did. The guy was solid—and probably had a good thirty pounds on me. Still, I had us both upright and balanced.

For now.

"What's wrong?" I asked, bracing at his back.

"Dizzy." His fingers were clenched white on the railing. "Head's spinning. Damn."

"Do you want to sit down?" I wasn't sure how, but we'd figure it out.

"No. Not moving. It's okay. Just…keep your hands where they are?"

"Sure. Of course." I pressed both palms firmly against his spine while he pulled in slow, deliberate breaths.

"No offense if I puke on your feet," he muttered.

"None. Um, is that likely?" I didn't flinch. The muscles of his back were taut under my hands.

"Maybe. Damn." He swayed, then straightened again. "Whoo. Merry-go-round."

"I can't catch you if you fall," I admitted. "Lean forward a bit."

"Smart man." Arthur added his other hand to the railing, hunched his shoulders over, and bowed his head, shifting his center of gravity toward the wall and the steps in front of him.

For what felt like an hour but was probably five minutes, we stood there, me braced against disaster, him breathing in a forced rhythm, sweat breaking through his shirt. Then he said, "Easing off a bit. Hang on."

"Take your time," I told him, not moving my hands. Digging out my phone to call for help would be smart, but not letting both of us go backward down the stairs was smarter.

Inch by inch, he straightened, then took one hand off the railing. "Okay, that was fun. Not. But I'm better, thank you." He shifted his weight away from the wall. "Yeah, better."

"I'm going to bend and get your crutch, then we should gently go back down the stairs. I saw a staff lounge where you can rest while I call the ambulance."

"No ambulance. No more paramedics or doctors or scans or any of that crap unless I'm dying."

"Let me drive you, then," I offered. I was pretty sure a dizzy spell was a bad sign.

"No!" He sighed. "My deductible's six grand. Between the ride yesterday and the hospital, CTs, everything, I already owe that much. My copay is still twenty percent out of network. There's no way I'm getting near the ER again."

"A doctor, then. Just to check you out."

"It's no big deal!" he snapped. Then mumbled, "Sorry. I've had a concussion before. Dizziness happens the first few days. Anyhow, I was probably just woozy from stressing this stupid leg on the stairs. Getting shot hurts. Zero out of ten, don't recommend." He sighed. "Could you grab my crutch now?"

With one hand still on his lower back, in case the dizziness or whatever came back, I snagged the crutch.

He took a deep breath as he slid it under his arm. "Right. If we can get upstairs, I'll be fine. I just need to lie down for a bit."

I frowned. "And then what? You'll go back and forth on these steep stairs by yourself whenever your dogs need to go out? You'll manage the animals down here as well?"

He twisted to eye me over his shoulder.

I considered glaring, but he looked so bleak with sad eyes and a downturned mouth under that extravagant mustache, I didn't have the heart.

Overhead one of his dogs whined, loud enough to hear through the closed door. Down the aisle below, one of the shelter dogs barked in response. I *couldn't* leave him in a dangerous situation where he'd almost certainly hurt himself. I'd left behind one person in my life that way already. *Not this time.* But the problem felt almost insurmountable until the obvious answer hit me.

"You're coming home with me."

"What?" That frown was back. "What are you talking about? My home is here."

"Well, until your head and your leg are healed, your home is with me. I mean, I suppose I could move in here—"

"I have a one-bedroom apartment."

"With a couch that won't fit me. I noticed." Because I'd scoped the place out this morning while I fed his dogs—even as I warned myself I was snooping. So sue me. "I have a three-bedroom rancher. No stairs. You can have an entire bedroom to yourself. We can bring all your dogs and even Xandra would be welcome. I'll admit I've never had a cat live with me before. Is she a Siamese?"

"Blue-point Himalayan." He eyed me.

I gestured for him to back down the stairs one step at a time. Best I go first—in case he lost his balance. I'd be better able to break our fall. No way was I leaving him here to go back up and down multiple times a day. And there was nowhere for him to sleep on the main floor of the shelter, so that was out. "The shelter animals did just fine overnight. But I suspect you'll want your four with you. I have room."

"You honestly think I'm just going to…" He gestured his hand in some weird way I didn't understand.

"Move in with me?" I grinned. "Well, I have Colin's number. I'm certain he and James will come back. You can stay with them. And the three foster kids. And Widget." Colin had waxed poetic about both the foster kids and his French bulldog. "Plus, I think Danny, Rob, Hallie, and Thomas are there as well. Apparently they brought Trouble as well." Trouble was their husky who had a penchant for taking off when she could. "Shouting and barking and crying."

The furrow between his brows deepened. His eyes looked bloodshot and glazed. Yeah, a busy household was no place for a man with a concussion.

From what Colin had said, Arthur knew everyone—but shied away from events with lots of people. He'd stood up for James when he'd gotten married and that had, at least to Colin's telling, been a big deal. "Plus, Danny and Rob are getting married next month. Your attendance is apparently mandatory, so you need to heal up."

"Oh my God." Slowly, Arthur made his way back down the stairs—with me guiding him. "How long have you been here, to know all this?"

"Since Colin unlocked the door at nine. He's…a chatty guy." Apparently he hadn't always been—by his own

46

admission. Meeting James and the six other Reynolds siblings—along with Mama and Daddy—had taught him to be more assertive in large gatherings. To not be bowled over by massive amounts of love directed at him. By marriage, he now had five sisters-in-law, five brothers-in-law, and apparently—by last count—fourteen nibblets. His word for nieces and nephews. His own family, back in Long Island, had abandoned him when he'd become ill. He'd come west, met James through Arthur, and the rest was, according to him, Reynolds family history. "He got me up to speed."

Arthur groaned.

I smiled. "Why don't you sit in the staff lounge and figure out how we're going to move three dogs and a cat as well as your stuff to my place?"

"I can call my shelter manager, Shane, for a place to stay. He and his boyfriend are out of town, and their house is empty."

"I guess." I wasn't sure why that disappointed me. "Although I'm pretty sure you shouldn't be driving back and forth tomorrow." I could give him a lift easier if he stayed with me.

Arthur pulled out his phone, then stared blankly at it. "Except. Damn." He squeezed his eyes shut.

"What?"

"I can't."

When he just stood frozen, squinting down at his phone, I prompted, "Why not?"

"Because if I tell Shane why I need their place, they'll cut short their trip, no matter how much I say not to. They'll worry. It's the first time Shane's ever travelled anywhere for fun. He's really into it, and they're leaving for Africa any time now. Oh hell." Arthur tipped his head to look at the ceiling, and I saw moisture at the corner of his eyes. "I don't want to spoil things for them, just 'cause I messed up and got shot."

I didn't think this situation was in any way his fault, but there was an easy answer. "Then come home with me."

He blinked. "You're serious?"

"Or I'll call Colin. I don't really care which option you choose."

Totally lying to yourself. You really want him to come home with you because, as grumpy as he is, you like him. You want to take care of him. And if we're going for honesty here, you're also attracted to him.

When I'd mentioned to Colin how much I loved Gaynor Beach's LGBTQ-friendly vibe, he'd shared that he'd heard the town was friendly before he moved here and, after his real estate agent, Arthur had been the first person he'd met and wasn't it great that his first friend was gay? He said the words casually, assuring me Arthur was out.

Just as casually, I might've mentioned to Colin that I was bisexual. I certainly hadn't been in the closet since making my pronouncement at eighteen. Like I'd expected, coming out had been an unmitigated disaster.

But now at thirty, I was still out and bi and proud, and Gaynor Beach looked like a good place for that. Especially with kind, welcoming queer men like Colin and James around. *And Arthur. Who's looking way too good, even pale and sweaty and, oops, swaying.* I grabbed his elbow, steadied him, then let go.

Arthur stared at the floor as he mumbled, "Don't call Colin."

"Great. So you rest in the lounge while I do evening feedings. Yell loud if you start feeling worse. We'll figure out what stuff you need, and then we'll determine the logistics of moving your menagerie." I followed him as he hobbled to the staff lounge then hovered as he plopped into a padded chair.

He glared yet again, stretching his leg out stiffly, and grunted.

"Wow. And Colin told me you were a super friendly guy." He also said shy and reticent. Better with animals than with people. Colin probably had no idea just how much he'd talked about Arthur.

Of course, that might've been because I was gently peppering the man with questions. Because as much as me being here was about helping the animals—and possibly drumming up business for myself—I was also here because this man had put himself between a gun and a kid yesterday. That...piqued my curiosity. Had he not been there, would I have found the courage to do it? I couldn't answer that question. I certainly didn't fear death the way many people did. I'd faced it down once. I'd come out the other side. But I also had a healthy dose of respect for mortality and I was no hero.

Arthur pursed his lips. "I'm sorry. This...isn't me. I just want to take care of the animals. We have a couple of prospective foster parents to interview tomorrow. I *need* to be here for that."

"So I can drive you over here in the morning and pick you up. I have four dogs tomorrow at the daycare but we can make the trip before they arrive. I don't mind early mornings."

"I can't ask you to do that."

"You didn't ask—I offered. And I'm happy to do it. I'll drop you off here, then give your dogs a good walk tomorrow morning. I might as well keep Eb, Twain, and Chili with me for the day so you don't have to worry about them."

"They're *my* dogs."

49

"Well, isn't it convenient I run a doggie daycare? All four of my dogs tomorrow are well socialized and do great with other dogs. Now, if Maisie were coming, things might look a little different. But she's not. If she does, we'll adapt."

"Maisie?"

"Mastiff with an attitude. She needs slow introductions to other dogs. I've got Hiro, Jett, George, and Poppy tomorrow." I scratched my nose. "Poppy will run circles around everyone—she's an eight-month-old goldendoodle. George is a bit more reticent. He's a senior rat terrier who's more comfortable with people. Hiro's an overweight Japanese chin who stays with us during the day so his owner's mother-in-law doesn't feed him treats when she thinks no one's looking. Jett is a young lab-pittie mix. He plays with Poppy and they get into all kinds of mischief."

"That sounds like a handful." He scratched his chin. "Eb and Twain get along with everyone. Chili..." He sighed.

"She likes me." I grinned, feeling rather pleased. Even Colin had been surprised how quickly the chihuahua warmed up to me.

"That's unusual."

"I'm an unusual guy." My grin only grew. "Right, now I'm going to do feedings." I grabbed a pen and a piece of paper and passed them over. "You write down everything that you need from upstairs. My SUV can fit two crates, and I have a harness tether system in my back seat." I looked him over.

He was still pale but the sweat on his forehead had dried. His eyes were still reddened but less glazed, and he seemed to be sitting up straight. And he was coherent. Hopefully that meant he wasn't about to crash.

"Let me put my number in your phone," I told him.

"If you get dizzy or nauseous or, well, anything, call 9-1-1. And if you won't, call me. I'll be around the place."

He wrestled his phone out of his pocket. "Cracked the corner of the screen." But he held it out to me, and it still worked.

I entered myself under "Brooklyn," skipped the selfie, and sent myself a text. "There. All set." With a jaunty wave, I headed off toward the dog runs.

Two hours later, Arthur sat in the front of my SUV with Xandra in her carrier buckled into the back seat. Her food and litterbox were safely stowed along with all the other food and dog beds in the back footwell. Eb kept all their stuff company tethered to the harness system on the opposite side. Chili and Twain were secure in their crates in my cargo area.

I sighed. "I can't believe we fit them all in."

Arthur eyed his overnight bag at his feet.

"The suitcase with your other stuff is packed, and I'll bring it home when I drop you off tomorrow. You've got enough for tonight. By this time tomorrow, you'll have all your things, and you'll be completely settled. Just you wait."

He gave me what I could only call a deadpan look. "If you say so."

"I do." I put the SUV in reverse, pulled out of the parking spot, put the vehicle into drive, and headed to the street.

Arthur gazed out the side window. "If I forget to say this later, because my head is killing me...thank you."

"You're welcome. We'll get through this, I promise."

I had no right to make that promise—and yet I did it anyway.

Because I was just that kind of optimist.

CHAPTER 5

ARTHUR

"What the *hell* are you doing here?" Neil demanded, striding into the shelter reception area next morning.

I looked up from the cash register where, admittedly, what I was mostly doing was gritting my teeth and counting the minutes to my next ibuprofen. "I run the place. Remember?"

"You got *shot*. And have a concussion." Safe Haven's funding-and-volunteers coordinator glared at me.

"I'm well aware." I resisted the temptation to squeeze my head between my hands, and returned the glare.

"Which I had to find out about from Hilary when I arrived this morning."

I figured part of his anger was being kept out of the loop. I hadn't meant to insult him. "You told me you and Sawyer were headed to San Francisco for the weekend to see a show. I didn't want to bother you."

"Bother me?" Neil ran a hand through his dark hair, tugging on the back. "I'm the volunteer organizer. When something affects staffing, that's literally my job. And may I repeat, shot?"

"A flesh wound." That wasn't as satisfyingly macho to say as I'd imagined, back when I was a lonely teen holed up in my room watching cop-show reruns. Maybe because the flesh wound still hurt like hell. "I was only out one day. My friends handled it with the regular volunteers. Mostly Colin, and this guy I met. Brooklyn. And I'm back now. I'm just moving a bit slow."

I eased my tall stool back so I could stand, and Neil set a hand on my shoulder. "Oh, hell, no."

"No what?" I shrugged off his grip.

He pushed his glasses up his nose. "No, you're not running around the shelter working today. You look like shit."

"Aww, thanks."

"What? It's true."

"The docs wouldn't let me shower." I could tell my tone was bitter, but damn, I hated being dirty. And they'd said *two weeks* of sponge baths and shampooing in the sink. I'd tried that this morning, but bending my head low had brought on another bout of the powerful dizziness and nausea. I was lucky I'd told Brooklyn to expect my hair wash to take some time in the bathroom. I'd been able to stagger round and collapse onto the toilet seat, and huddle there and not move until the worst of the effects wore off. I don't think Brooklyn noticed when I emerged, otherwise he might not have been willing to drive me to the shelter. He was kind and overprotective, something I didn't need.

"My hair's more comfortable loose right now," I added. I usually wore my long ashy-red hair back in a ponytail, but I'd taken the elastic out hours ago, hoping that would ease some of the pressure in my skull. "Sorry if you think I'm not up to your promo standards at the front desk."

"I didn't say that." Neil sighed. "I'm worried about you, okay?"

"I'm fine." I sat up straighter and tried to look fine.

"Tell you what. You stay here, man the till if customers come in. Let me and the volunteers do the animal care."

"That was actually my plan. Mostly."

"No *mostly*. Sit." He pointed a finger at me. "Stay. So when do we expect Shane back?"

"Huh? Three weeks. You know that." Neil had fixed the volunteer schedule to cover for Shane's absence and was chipping in more than his normal time on the main floor, in between writing grant proposals and chasing sponsors and all the stuff he did to keep the shelter in the black. I'd already felt guilty about making him clean litterboxes. He shouldn't have to cover for me too, but there was a reason I didn't stand when ordered to sit. The move wouldn't look so powerful if I hit the floor a minute later. I fought the urge to squeeze my eyes shut.

"You mean he's not cutting his trip short to come back here for you? I don't believe it."

"I didn't tell him. And you can't either." I pointed my bigger, stubbier finger back at Neil. "You hear me? No tattling. I told him I had a fall but was fine, and to enjoy his trip. And he's going to." I wouldn't have said even that much, but I worried someone else might spill the beans.

"He won't thank you for keeping him in the dark."

"Theo will. He planned this trip for months and paid all kinds of deposits and tickets."

"Theo can afford to lose a few deposits." Neil held up his hand. "Okay, quit trying to glare a hole through my skull. It's your personal business. Until it affects the shelter."

"It won't." I didn't repeat *I'm fine* because I could feel a band of pressure creeping up around my head, and nausea turning my stomach. *Not now.* I waved Neil off and snapped, "Go do your job."

That got me a look with some real hurt in it, but I didn't want him to hang around to watch me puke so I didn't apologize. He left the lobby, and I was relieved to see his back disappear before a wave of pain rolled over me and the stool I was sitting on decided it was part of a merry-go-round. I grabbed for a wad of tissues and dry-heaved. Luckily, breakfast was enough of a memory that my stomach was empty. I wiped my lips and clung to the edge of the counter as the world spun and dipped.

"Excuse me?" Seconds or maybe hours later, someone stood in front of me.

I blinked hard, reached for my water bottle, chugged a mouthful, and plastered on a smile. "Yes? How can I help you?"

The white-haired old woman across the counter tilted her head and eyed me. "Are you all right, young man?"

"Ate the wrong thing for lunch." *Is it lunch time yet?* The morning seemed unending. "I'm better now. What can I do for you?"

"I was hoping to look at cats. Maybe an older cat? I don't have a lot of years left myself, but I can give a good home to some nice quiet senior."

"Oh yes, perfect." I glanced around but didn't spot any volunteers. *Because they're in back doing your job for you.* I pushed the buzzer button. "Someone will be here in a minute. Have them show you Lucy and Spritz. Lucy's fourteen and she's in great health. Sweet cat, pretty much a lap potato. Spritz is more aloof but he's gentle when he gets to know you. Might need his teeth done next year— Oh, Jeff." I waved to the retired gentleman who appeared down the hallway. Several of our mid-day volunteers were seniors who couldn't afford a pet or lived in no-pet housing, but loved being around the fur-babies. Jeff wasn't up to walking the bigger dogs, but he adored the cats.

"Show our client Lucy and Spritz, please, and any other older friendly cat she might like."

"Can do." He peered at me. "Are you okay, Arthur?"

"I wish people would stop *asking* me that!" I closed my eyes and pinched the bridge of my nose. "Sorry. Didn't mean to yell."

"I'll go show the lady some cats."

I heard their footsteps click away across the marble tiles and sighed.

"Okay, that's it," Neil said from my elbow.

"What?" I barked, then pinched my nose harder as my head vibrated from the noise. *You dumbass.*

"That." Neil's tone was gentle. "You look like you're about to fall over, and you've yelled at three people so far this morning."

"I don't yell at people."

"Not usually, no. Which is why I'm sending you to your bed. Or wherever you're staying, I guess, since the dogs aren't upstairs."

"With Brooklyn." Who didn't deserve to deal with my cranky self either. "I'll just go up and sack out in my apartment for a while." I pushed to my feet using my good leg, bent to retrieve my crutch from where it leaned against the counter...and dizziness swamped me until I puked right on Neil's foot. Luckily just a little yellow bile. I followed that performance by staggering into the counter, grabbing it for dear life as I hit my bad leg on the edge and yelped like a bee flew up my thigh. With a red-hot poker. *Owowowowowie.*

Neil caught my arm in a strong grip. "Do you need a doctor?"

"No! Damn. Just my ibuprofen and stretching out in bed for a bit, I guess." I swallowed my pride and asked, "Can you give me a hand getting up the stairs."

"No can do." Neil shook his head. "I'm not leaving you alone at the top of the stairs, and I don't have the time to stay with you."

"I'll call when I want to come down."

"Uh-huh." He eyed me. "What was the name of the new volunteer I introduced you to this morning?"

I was better with pets' names than humans', and I barely remembered the intro. I'd been focused on staying upright. "Brown hair, short, about thirty." I searched my aching brain. "Said she had to go to work at ten. Has a dog named Chloe." Or Cleo, or something like that.

Neil nodded. "Yasmin. As I told you three times."

"That's not much of a test. I'm crappy with names at the best of times," I grumbled.

"Which is why I'm not sending your ass to the ER. But I am giving you two choices. Either I drive you to this Brooklyn's place, or you let me send you in a cab."

"You can't spare the time. If we're open to the public, one of us has to be here."

"I'll call a cab, then." Neil crossed his arms and gave me a hard stare.

"You're not the boss—" I cut off "of me," before I manage to sound like a toddler.

Neil pushed the stool up against my butt. "Sit down, stay put."

I lost the energy to keep arguing. "All right."

"Good." Neil hesitated. "You know it's because we all want you to get better, right?"

"Yeah, yeah. Go do your things." I flapped my hand at him.

Neil went and did whatever, and I stewed in my own irritability, which was better than taking it out on a friend.

Thirty minutes later, my taxi pulled up in front of Brooklyn's peach stucco house. My head was much better.

Of course, recovery happened ten minutes *after* I left. I thought about turning around, but Neil would probably kick me back out, and I couldn't deny I was beat and still aching everywhere. Just without the debilitating levels of vertigo.

I was still humiliatingly glad when the friendly driver, Carlos, hurried to open my door and helped me to my feet with a hand under my elbow. He waved off my thanks. "I know who you are. The shelter's a good thing for Gaynor Beach. You heal up quick, now."

Kind words were welcome right then, and I made sure my tip was generous.

Once the taxi had pulled away, I hobbled up Brooklyn's front path and rang the doorbell. A whole bunch of barking answered me, including a warbling howl I recognized as Twain's.

"Coming!" Brooklyn opened the door, grinning, and I was struck like a two-by-four to the brain with how attractive he was. Not model-pretty, but totally boy-next-door, his hazel eyes warm, smiling lips framed by his neatly cropped beard, a deep dimple carved in his right cheek and a shallow one in his left. He was taller than me even when I wasn't leaning on a crutch, and lanky with legs that went on forever in snug-fitting denim. He had competent-looking long-fingered hands and big feet in black sneakers—

I dragged my thoughts back to why I was standing here on his front step, leaning to one side like a drunken clown. "Hey, Neil thought a half day was long enough for me to work."

"Neil?"

"My funding-and-volunteers coordinator, and my left hand at the shelter."

One tidy eyebrow arched. "Left?"

"With Shane as my right." I sighed. "Can I come in before I fall down?"

"Of course!" Brooklyn pulled the door open and stood back, a hand out in an offer of assistance.

"Thanks." I tried to put sincerity into that. I didn't have to be a jerk, and I had a feeling that sometime during the ten hours since he brought me home, fed me, helped me clean up, got me into sweats to sleep in, gave me a bed, and then did the same in reverse in the morning, and drove me to work, I'd probably been rude to this kind man. Maybe more than once.

When he'd shut the door, I said, "I don't know what's wrong with me, but if I'm irritable or short with you, I don't mean it." My face flushed but I made myself admit, "It's not about you. I yelled at a seventy-year-old volunteer today."

"Ouch." Brooklyn's expression showed only compassion.

"I feel like crap."

"You know what will make you feel better? A cup of tea, your pups and kitty, and some furry tail wagging. Come on."

He led the way toward the back of the house. I'd only seen the kitchen, bathroom, and my bedroom so far, but when we reached the rear, I could see why he'd bought this place. What had maybe been a family room was now a wide-open space across the back half of the house. Patio doors opened to a shady backyard with three spreading trees, two fenced areas, and a row of big, covered kennels along the side.

Inside the house, four smaller dog pens lined one wall of the main room. The floor was some kind of rubbery tile, and a solid baby gate blocked the doorway. Brooklyn let us in, then made sure the gate was double latched.

I spotted Chili in the farthest pen amid a collection of toys and two beds. I called, "Hey, Chili baby." She was chewing on some rubber Kong toy and barely lifted her head to glance at me before going back to her gnawing.

In the open indoor area, two other small dogs lay sprawled on big stuffed beds. The Japanese chin wagged his tail at me without getting up but the rat terrier with a graying muzzle came over to greet me, rising stiffly to put his front paws on my knee. Luckily the good knee.

"George, sit," Brooklyn called. When the terrier dropped his butt to the floor, removing his paws from my leg, Brooklyn said, "Good job," and tossed the elderly dog a treat. That got the chin out of his bed in a flash, and he was willing to run through his tricks, his rounded little body wriggling in eagerness for the tiny bite Brooklyn gave him.

"Come on out and see your other babies," Brooklyn told me. "I let the bigger and more active dogs play outside unless the weather's too hot or too wet."

I crutched over and greeted Chili. I always made sure she knew she was my special girl, even if I wasn't sure she cared. Then I followed Brooklyn into the yard.

He urged me to sit in a sturdy chair, then hauled over a patio table. Behind the inner play-area fence, Eb and Twain leaped and barked alongside two unfamiliar dogs who'd caught the excitement. Brooklyn set the table in place overlapping my chair. "Protection for that leg, you think?"

I watched Ebony bouncing his fool head off and said, "You're a smart man."

"Brace yourself." Brooklyn opened the gate a crack and with the ease of long practice, let my two squeeze through and shut the gate on the disappointed golden and black duo. Before I could suggest they come for pats too,

Brooklyn reached into a tub of toys by the gate and began throwing them across the exercise yard.

The two dogs yelped in glee and gave chase. Even Eb paused, looking wistfully over his shoulder at the flying rubber, before finishing his charge my way.

I said, "Sit," before he could do me any damage and pulled his head into my lap, rubbing his silky ears and cheeks. Twain danced, clearly thinking about jumping up. I didn't want twenty pounds of beagle to hit my aching lap so I said, "Sit pretty." The begging position put his head in reach and I fondled his even silkier ears as he braced his feet on the side of the chair.

Nothing soothed a man's soul better than petting a fur-baby. I murmured to these two how special they were, how pretty, such good boys, such sweet boys, while I rubbed their heads and soaked in the love. After a long time, when my head hurt less and my body felt settled, I looked up.

Brooklyn was gazing at us with a soft expression on his face. Well, everyone loved these two dogs, of course. Our eyes met and I smiled for what felt like the first time since I saw that gun in Frank's hand.

"Thank you," I said, meaning it. "For having me and my menagerie in your space. For taking care of us."

"My pleasure." He gestured at the other two dogs playing tug-of-war with a rope toy, their ears up and their body language playful. "The more the merrier."

I leaned back in my chair, raised my face to the sky, and patted Eb and Twain. The pain was still there, but the ibuprofen I'd taken at Safe Haven was beginning to kick in. The bouts of vertigo were scary, but with my last concussion, any dizziness had gone away fast. I was alive, Brooklyn was alive, Kevin was fine. The dog... "Did Kevin find that lost dog?" I asked without taking my gaze from the blue overhead.

I expected Brooklyn to tell me he didn't know, but he said, "Yep. His dads told James who told Colin who told me that they caught her yesterday—apparently by luring her with their dog—and took her to the vet. She had a microchip, and now she's back with her owner who's building a taller fence."

"Oh, good. Then everything worked out. Now I just need to quit spinning." I could feel a bit of the vertigo hovering. If I ignored it, no doubt it would go away.

"Spinning?"

I was surprised to hear myself admit, "Still a little dizzy." Usually I tried not to burden other people with my weaknesses, but somehow Brooklyn disarmed me.

I held my breath, waiting for him to make a fuss or ask intrusive questions, but the only one he asked was, "Have you had lunch?"

"Not yet."

"Some of the dizziness might be low blood sugar. You think you can keep something down?"

I turned my attention inward, but patting Ebony apparently was good for stomachs too. "If it's simple."

"Grilled cheese?" Brooklyn said. "Would that work?"

Some of the flutter in my stomach turned into a grumble of *yes, please*. "Perfect. You're amazing."

Brooklyn's loud huff of breath made me drop my gaze to check his reaction. He looked surprised, but maybe pleased too. "You keep on petting," he told me. "That's your job for now. Eb told me so. Two grilled cheese lunches coming up."

I watched him head back into the house, heard him speak to the small dogs as he passed through to the kitchen. I sat with my dogs at my side and the two boarders now chasing each other around the yard, and something in me settled for the first time in…I don't know. Years? This little house with the retrofitted dog spaces felt like my old place that I'd sold months ago, but somehow, even better. Homier. Warmer.

I pretended not to know that it was the presence of Brooklyn, someone I already liked and trusted, that made the difference.

CHAPTER 6

BROOKLYN

A WEEK LATER, EB AND I WERE IN A STARE OFF.

"This is my cheese and I'm not sharing."

He gave me puppy-dog eyes.

"You don't beg with Arthur because you know he won't give in. Well, I'm not giving in." I held the slice of Swiss cheese in my hand. "Shouldn't you be guarding Arthur or something?"

The light from my fridge was the only illumination in the kitchen. We were in the early hours of the morning— or was it the late hours of the evening…? I glanced at the microwave clock.

12:57

Too early for morning…so late, late evening.

Normally I would've turned on the television in the living room, but I didn't want to wake Arthur. *Should've bought a television for your bedroom.* Yeah, except I'd be tempted to watch it all night, and that was bad for sleep hygiene. My therapist had given me lectures on how to sleep properly. As if that could somehow keep the lingering nightmares at bay. The fear of—

Nope. Not going there. Long in the past.

I surveyed my already-beloved home in my mind. Paid for by nightmare money, but my home nonetheless. I'd made a fresh start and wasn't going to think about all the shit that had—

"Are you going to close that refrigerator?"

I spun to find Arthur, leaning on his crutch.

The fridge door alarm was binging.

Sunk deep in my memories, I'd totally missed that. "Sorry." I slammed the door shut.

Thereby dropping us into darkness. I had a habit of closing all the blinds to try to keep out the light pollution from the streetlamp by the house, but that resulted in pockets of deep shadows and near obliteration of illumination. I knew my way to the fridge—okay, late night snacks were not an uncommon thing—but I wasn't used to someone else sharing the unlit space. I froze.

Arthur, clearly accustomed to this quirk of mine after eight days in my house, knew where the light switch was, and he hit it.

The kitchen filled with light.

I blinked, dazzled, and found myself staring right at him.

He held my gaze with those fathomless blue eyes that so resembled Xandra's.

The cat had settled nicely here over the last week. She'd found a perch in my living room that allowed her to survey all who lived here—as well as the street beyond—without her having to interact with anyone she didn't wish to. More and more, she was interacting with me. That felt good.

And now here I was with Arthur standing in my kitchen, his solid body clad only in gray sleep pants and a snug T-shirt, also interacting… "Cheese?" I held the slice aloft.

Ebony barked.

"Eb." Arthur's voice was clipped. "He knows better." He eyed me. "Are you giving him treats behind my back?"

"Of course not." Well, except that little bit of tuna juice—which he might've shared with Twain. I'd saved the actual pieces of tuna for Chili and Xandra. "Okay, maybe a bit of tuna juice. They'd just…they'd been so good with Maisie today."

"That mastiff with attitude. I wondered how that went. Sorry, I should've asked."

"You were tired when you got home from the shelter."

"I ate your tuna melts—which were delicious. Nice touch with the sweet pickle."

I preened at the compliment.

"And then I went to lie down, and I fell asleep. Like every day this week."

"Dizziness still?" We hadn't spoken much of his health, even though we encountered each other constantly and I drove him to work early each morning. He'd made it *abundantly* clear he wanted his space—so I'd given it to him. I'd noticed, when he wasn't looking, how he still struggled with both his leg and his head. I just didn't know how bad he was suffering.

"It's better."

Which wasn't the same as gone.

He pointed to the kitchen table.

I gestured for him to sit. *Should've offered that right away.*

He eased himself onto the chair and tucked his crutch against the wall. "I'm hoping to move to a cane soon and then be okay completely. I can't wait to be free of…" He ran his hand up and down his body.

That big, solid dad-bod I'd noticed on more than one

occasion. But lusting after someone in such obvious distress was a hard *no*. He didn't want me to see his pain—but I did.

Lamely, I held up the piece of cheese. "I don't suppose you want—"

Eb's eyes never left the cheese.

"No, I'm good. Not a fan of Swiss."

"I have orange cheddar, white cheddar, gouda, cheese curds, Monterey Jack, Pepper Jack, or mozzarella. Although I'll warn you—I plan to use that on a homemade pizza tomorrow. Well, tonight." I'd cooked every night and he ate without complaint. Perhaps even with grudging gratitude, as he muttered thanks at the end of meals. I'd given him a lot of leeway because I was well-aware how much he struggled with the headaches and nausea.

He regularly offered to clear up and do dishes. I regularly turned him down with a nod at his crutch. So then he started bringing me things from the shelter store every day—leashes and dog toys and chew treats and more. He'd hand them over with "You're cooking and all," and crutch off to his room when I protested. Like no one ever told him you could accept a favor without payback.

"You really love cheese." He offered a small smile.

"Yep." I shoved the whole slice of Swiss in my mouth —only then realizing I'd gagged myself. I chewed quickly and swallowed. "You never told me what you'd like…"

"Did I see you had a bag of potato chips?"

"I didn't figure you for a junk-food fan, but yes, in fact we do have three bags of potato chips. I've got barbecue, rippled, or salt and vinegar. Which would you prefer?"

He scratched his elbow. Which flexed his biceps. Which I couldn't help noticing because his T-shirt was a little tight. And his sleep pants hung low on his hips.

"I love salt and vinegar." His smile was shy and tentative—but definitely there.

"As do I, obviously. But we'll need something to drink."

"Water's fine."

"You're always so healthy." I laughed as I made my way to the sink and filled two glasses of water. Then I snagged the potato chips from the back of the pantry cupboard, poured them into a bowl—because yeah, I could be a good host—and put the bowl on the table. I plopped down onto my chair as well.

Eb dropped to his belly on the floor—clearly ready to assist us if any chips were to fall. Xandra stalked into the kitchen and eyed us, then gazed around.

"Not on the counter, fuzzy girl," Arthur told her.

She wandered over, rubbed her face against the hand he held down to her, then meandered out, doing her own thing.

"Where are Chili and Twain?" I asked.

"Asleep on their beds. Chili glanced up, decided her beauty sleep was *not* going to be interrupted, and went right back down. Par for the course. Twain didn't even lift his head, although he would've if a hint of cheese had reached him." He eyed his black lab. "Eb, as you can see, made his way here. He must've snuck out when I went to the washroom."

I glanced at the dog and arched an eyebrow, even as I ate a chip.

The pooch blinked back with absolutely innocent eyes.

I completely believed Arthur trained him to behave—but that he saw me as an easy mark. In my work, I followed the owner's instructions *to the letter.* With Arthur's dogs, I was a little more lenient. Especially Chili, with whom I truly was developing a strong bond.

Arthur crunched a chip. Then he took a sip. "Those are salty."

"I love how strong they are. But if they're too much—"

He waved me off. "All good."

"How's the shelter going?"

"We've found homes for seven cats and four dogs this week, so that's good."

"Sounds productive."

"Although of course, we took in just as many new ones. Still way more than I could help when I was fostering."

I took a sip. "I want to get a dog of my own, but I'm busy getting the daycare up and running. Oh, I had some flyers printed. Do you think I could leave a few at the shelter? Scott at the library said he'd take a few as well. And the community center said they have a wall of posters from local businesses."

"Absolutely!" Arthur looked thrilled that I'd asked him for something. "We'll be happy to have some handy at the shelter. Leave us a bunch. Access to doggie daycare might be the deciding factor some prospective owners need."

"Cool. Thank you." I had room for four large dogs and four small, right now, and I was almost never at capacity. That mortgage wasn't paying itself, and every little bit would help.

We munched chips in quiet companionship that I didn't feel the need to fill.

For once, Arthur seemed really relaxed. As the bowl emptied, he said, "If you don't mind my curiosity, why doggie daycare? I suppose I should've asked before now."

I waved off his concern. "You've had other stuff to deal with. My story's pretty boring. I love animals. I wasn't allowed to have pets growing up. When I left home, after I came out as bisexual—" I wasn't sure Arthur knew, so hey, chance to get that out there. "—I rented a room in a house with a guy who literally trained animals for a living—for the New York theater and movie business. I was enraptured. He taught me tons of stuff and was even grooming me to work with him in the business and then—"

"Then?"

"Well, he got married and moved out of town. He couldn't afford to pay me full time, and I couldn't afford to move with him. So, then I tried going to school at night, but I got derailed, and—" *Do I really want to go here? With a guy I barely know? Keep it simple.* "—I came into some money and decided I wanted to spend my days with dogs. Hence." I waved at the darkened downstairs.

"Why out here in Gaynor Beach, though? You said New York?"

As far from home as I could get. "I researched California, found Gaynor Beach, a gay-friendly town, and discovered no one had opened a dedicated doggie daycare. I found this house and snapped it up. That back family room is amazing. And the yard?"

"Doggie heaven."

"Yep. And with enough shade that I'm good out there for long stretches even when it's hot. I hung out a shingle, and within two days of my first ad, Hiro's owner had me on the phone. He's lost two pounds since he started coming here. The mother-in-law still tries to sneak him food, but her daughter has explained that too many treats will shorten the dog's life and wouldn't that be tragic? How much of an effect that's having is debatable, but he's more active when he's here, and Dr. Louisa at the animal hospital is happy with his progress." Which made me feel all warm and fuzzy inside.

"You've done well with him." Arthur examined a chip. "Although him getting stuck under the chair was…"

I burst out laughing. "The look on your face."

"His antics were...unexpected."

"He's a character. All dogs are, in their own way. I didn't know I'd have so much fun with this job. I need to drum up more business, though. Jett and Poppy are regulars, but Maisie and George are only occasional visitors. You were very sweet to George, by the way. I appreciated that." George had decided Arthur was his god and followed him within tripping range every chance he got.

"You thought I wouldn't be patient with a loveable, older dog who just needs attention and affection?" His eyes shone with amusement.

Good Goddamn, he's making fun of me. Hallelujah! I loved seeing a lighter side of Arthur. "I hadn't thought of it like that. More that not everyone wants a shadow underfoot—especially when they're first home from work and exhausted."

"Home." He appeared to turn the word over in his mind.

"Well, your home for the foreseeable future. When do you see your doctor for a follow-up?"

He sniffed. "Supposed to go the day after tomorrow. Nothing's infected and I'm fine, though, so I don't really need—"

I decided to bite the bullet and admit I was watching. "Didn't you almost pitch over this morning while trying to tie your shoes?"

"Uh...is there a right way to answer that question? Something that won't get me a stern lecture?"

I frowned. "You were seated and you almost lost your balance, likely because you got a bout of vertigo. You're nowhere near healed. And you came home with a bad headache tonight. I know that's why you crashed as soon as you arrived. And now you're awake in the middle of the night—"

"So are you." He tried to tip his chin up and glare at me. With his bushy beard and rounded cheeks, though, it probably didn't have the effect he was hoping for.

I found him cute—not intimidating. "My doctor's aware of my insomnia. I have coping mechanisms. I would've had my cheese and gone back to bed. Some deep breathing exercises and mediation and I would've been back to sleep in no time."

He arched an eyebrow.

I pursed my lips. "Okay, well, I would've tried." I wasn't going to tell him how sleep sometimes terrified me. How I worried about not being able to breathe, about my chest clamping down and my hands going limp while alarms rang, and all the other madness that kept my nights broken and disturbed.

Breathe in, breathe out. In. Out.

My therapist said I was a *work in progress*. Truthfully, I just wanted a good night's rest. "Are you going to be able to get back to sleep yourself?"

"I need to take some ibuprofen."

"For your head or your leg?"

"Leg, this time." He glanced away as if he hadn't meant to reveal even that much.

"Ah." I pushed the last of the chips toward him. "You need food in your stomach first. More than chips. Would you like some milk? Milk's good when you're taking anti-inflammatories, right?" I wasn't going to tell him all those painkillers—the NSAIDs, as I'd learned to call them—were permanently off my permitted list.

"I'm going to pass on the milk." He picked up another chip. "I don't see the two mixing."

"Oh, you'd be surprised the foods I've combined."

"Like tuna, melted cheese, and pickles?"

"You bet. I didn't see you complaining. Oh, I love mustard and peanut butter."

His eyes widened. "On a sandwich? That's…" He wrinkled his nose in evident disgust.

"Want to know what else is super good? Dill pickles and peanut butter. You can dip them. Oh, tuna with olives and mayo—"

"Okay, I think we need to have a discussion about your culinary habits. Are you sure you're not pregnant or something?"

"Isn't that pickles and ice cream? Honestly, I can't speak to pregnancy cravings. I just like what I like. Do you need me to grab your pills?"

"I can—"

"Sure, but I'm already up." I popped out of the chair.

"They're on the dresser. Chili might get upset."

"She'll be happy to see me." At least I hoped she would be. When I got to Arthur's room, she certainly tracked my movements as I grabbed the bottle of pills, but then set her chin back on the bed like I wasn't a threat. Twain slept the sleep of the dead—which I desperately envied. He was a good warning system during the day, but apparently passed out cold at night.

Eb's tail swished as I returned.

"You're still not getting any." I wagged my finger at him as I handed the pill bottle to Arthur. I snagged his mostly empty water glass and refilled it, set it in front of him, then plopped back in my chair and munched away happily while he downed his pills. "You know, you're an easy guy to be around."

He placed the pill bottle on the table. "I'm not certain how to take that."

"As a compliment. I've been a bit isolated lately—

although I aim to change that. Any interesting events coming up in Gaynor Beach that I might take advantage of?"

"There's some stuff around Halloween. That's just a few weeks away." He rubbed his temple.

I snagged the empty chip bowl, pleased to see how many he'd eaten. I popped up and set it on the counter. Then I spun back, planning to clear the glasses.

Arthur was trying to grab his crutch.

I reached for it just as he ducked down.

Our heads collided.

"Oh God, I'm so sorry." I pulled back, crouching before him so our gazes were level. His blue eyes were wide and startled, inches from my own. "Your brain's already bruised, and I'm making it worse. I really should be more careful. It's just that I wanted to help. You're always trying to be independent, and there are so many little things I could do to make your life easier, but I don't offer because you're prickly—which is totally understandable, given the circumstances. And I think I'd be a little cranky too if—"

He grabbed the back of my neck and crashed our lips together.

Well, that's one way to shut me up.

CHAPTER 7

ARTHUR

I HADN'T MEANT TO KISS BROOKLYN. TOTALLY NOT. No matter how many times I'd thought about it in the last few days. Until the moment our lips met, dry and soft, the salt and tang of vinegar chips between us, I didn't realize what I was doing.

I let go instantly and lurched back. "Sorry! Wow, I didn't mean—My bad. Do you want me to go? I should go." I scrabbled for that damned crutch but Brooklyn went to one knee and leaned close, his eyes on mine.

"Hey, Arthur, slow down. Take it easy. Breathe." He set a hand on my shoulder, urging me not to stand.

I could've pushed free, but a couple of oxygen-containing breaths would be a good idea. I squeezed my eyes shut and sucked air into my tight chest. "Tell me I didn't just kiss someone who didn't want me to." *Please.*

Brooklyn's chuckle held a dark heat. "No. Definitely not that."

"It's not funny. Consent." I made myself look into his face, trying to read his expression. "You did say you were bi, right? But that's not consent."

Even if it had blasted the lid off the mythical "but he's straight" box I'd been trying so hard to keep Brooklyn in. Suspicion wasn't evidence. Colin talking like Brooklyn was one of us wasn't evidence. I'd made "straight guy" a useful barrier between me and a man I liked way too much for one week of…of him cooking for me, and helping me out, and driving me places, and charming my ornery little chihuahua. Okay, maybe I had excuses for liking him. "All the more reason not to assault you."

"Arthur, that wasn't assault. I've been trying hard not to flirt with you, but I think I failed. You wouldn't have kissed me if you weren't pretty sure I wanted it."

I wasn't so certain. He was so perfect and I'd gone a damned long time with just me and my hand, just me and my dogs, while James and the others found their forever guys. While I felt more and more certain I'd be alone forever—

"Quit thinking so hard." Brooklyn set one long-fingered hand against my bearded cheek, leaned in and brushed my lips with his.

I met his gaze, saw his pupils dilate in those hazel-green eyes before he leaned in again with purposeful intent. This kiss wasn't dry or soft. Brooklyn took possession of my mouth and I welcomed him, let my lips part, let my eyelids drift shut, and took everything he gave me. His tongue raided my mouth, then teeth nipped my lower lip and his hand shifted from my cheek to thread into my long hair, tugging a little as if he knew I loved that.

I hadn't gotten fully hard since the hospital, not even when I'd been imagining laying Brooklyn out on my bed like a gift while telling myself I was being a fool. But now my dick stirred at the heat of his mouth on mine. Relief and desire made me frantic, and I pressed toward him, driving the kiss. I took his head in both hands and held him still as I changed the angle. He opened for my tongue and we traded leads. Brooklyn's kissing was as generous as the man himself.

When we paused, drawing back a little, Brooklyn ran the back of his hand over his chin.

"Beard burn?" I asked. "I'm sorry. We don't have to—"

Brooklyn gave my hair another tug. "Hush up and kiss me again."

So I did.

Seconds, minutes, hours later, my leg throbbed in deep displeasure at the way I was leaning. The pain jolted me out of the haze of need and want, glorying in a universe that was all Brooklyn West's mouth. I managed to turn my yelp into a grunt but I had to sit back.

Brooklyn let go of me. "Head? Leg? What can I do?"

"Leg. I just need time for the ibuprofen to kick in. Stretch it out a bit."

Brooklyn's smile brightened his eyes. "Like, say, on a bed?"

"Um?"

"Only if you want to." His grin faded. "I know you're hurting."

"Not that bad," I told him. "I want to. If you don't expect too much."

"More kissing?"

"I can do that." I let him get up first, then used the crutch to lever myself out of the chair. My thigh rebelled against the first few steps, but it was just pain. I forced my thoughts away from the vertigo and nausea that still sometimes hit out of the blue. Tonight was a good night. *Don't think about that and it won't happen.* I switched off the kitchen light and followed Brooklyn down the dim hallway with Eb dancing ahead of us.

At the bedroom doors, Brooklyn paused. "Your room

or mine?" The tiny nightlight plugged in the wall didn't let me read his expression.

"Yours." I loved my dogs but I didn't want Eb-nose or Chili-paws landing in naked places at the wrong moment. "Let me put Eb away." The big dog gave me a betrayed look when I ushered him into my bedroom with the other two, but settled for an ear-rub before I closed the door. "Lead on."

Brooklyn hovered in his doorway. "It's not that clean. I wasn't expecting this."

"I really don't care. You can't work with animals and be too picky."

"Right. Sure." He hesitated a moment longer, then gestured me in.

The room was dark enough that I paused. "Is there a lamp, maybe? If I whack my leg on something the game's over."

"Of course." Brooklyn hustled past the end of the bed and switched on a small lamp.

I was glad to see he had a king-sized bed, to suit his height, I guess, which would also suit my size. Most of the room was tidy, but the covers were twisted and askew off one side, the pillows disarranged. Looked like he'd been having a restless night.

No kidding, since he's up at almost one in the morning.

Brooklyn tugged at the comforter and picked a pillow up off the floor. "I could change the sheets."

I don't mind if they smell like your skin. Not something I could say, but I hobbled to the bed and eased myself down to sit on the side. Brooklyn came and looked me over. "You want your leg raised?"

"If you'll lie down beside me, yes." I scooted around and grabbed my pants leg in my fist for leverage, but

Brooklyn was there faster, holding my ankle in his hands, helping me raise my foot onto the bed. There was nothing sexual about his touch, but his hands on my skin made my heart race. I patted the bed beside me. "Come lie down."

"Turn on your side and I'll put a pillow under your knee."

I wasn't stupid enough to turn down some comfort, especially since my dick had gone soft with the walk from kitchen to bedroom. I rolled obediently onto my left side, and he got me settled before walking around the bed and getting in beside me.

Brooklyn stretched out, pushed up on his right elbow, and looked at me. "How are you doing?"

"Peachy," I lied, because movement was still bad, but even as I said it the worst of the ache backed off a bit. "Meds will be kicking in soon." I reached out to trace the line of his arm from his wrist up over his lean biceps to the curve of his shoulder. "You want to tell me what made you turn the bed into a disaster zone?"

"Not now. Not at all sexy." He reached out in his turn to touch the tattoo sleeve on my forearm. "Why don't you tell me what this means."

Someday I'd give him the details, maybe. Sometime that wasn't the first night I had Brooklyn's fingers dancing on my skin. "Places I've been, things I've done. It was all separate bits and then when I hit Gaynor Beach and decided I was staying, I found an artist to turn the sections into true sleeves with the Celtic knotwork to tie it all together."

"Must've taken a while."

I shivered as he traced the loops of the knots above my wrist. "Yeah, it did."

"I like it. The detail suits you."

I wasn't sure how he meant that. I was a pretty simple guy. But my leg had settled down some, and when Brooklyn raised his attention from my tattooed arm to my face, I leaned forward and kissed him.

He met my lips, then scooted closer and wrapped his arms around me. His warm, bare chest pressed against mine through my T-shirt. He took my mouth, fast and hard, and I liked letting him set the pace. I was a big guy and I sometimes worried I was overwhelming the man I was with, but not now. Brooklyn took control and I was happy to accept his kiss and his tongue, the clutch of his arms around my shoulders, the tug of his hand in my hair.

He groaned into my mouth and I echoed him. My dick charged back onboard, rising hard and eager, mashed up against Brooklyn's thigh. I arched my back, thrusting against his leg and he grunted. "Yeah, that's good."

I wrenched my mouth free to say, "I want you naked."

"You too." He rolled away from me to tug off his sleep pants, and I paused, hand on the hem of my T-shirt, to watch. His cock sprang free from his waistband, long and slender and uncut, a little curved, the head ruddy and already rising from the foreskin.

My mouth watered, thinking about tasting him.

He slid the pants down his thighs and off over his feet and paused, looking my way. He had runner's legs with long lean muscles, and a flat, tight ass with those dimples that begged for a kiss. What little hair he had dusted between his nipples down to a thin treasure trail, neatly trimmed pubes, and a little more fur on his thighs. Nothing like my ginger pelt.

Brooklyn eyed me as he folded his pants and draped them over the foot of the bed. "You waiting for an engraved invitation?"

"Just enjoying the show." I felt my cheeks heat, because sexual innuendo, or whatever that had been, was not my comfort zone. I added, "You're hot as hell," because compliments I could do.

"Thanks." He sat against the headboard and ran a hand down his chest to thumb the head of his cock. A little slick already glazed his fingertip. The groan that left my lips when he sucked his finger clean made him smile. "Come on. Your turn."

I was comfy lying there, so I tried stripping off my T-shirt without sitting up. I got tangled in the second sleeve, but Brooklyn reached over and got me free.

He laughed as he tossed the shirt down the bed. "Your hair's a mess."

I blew some long strands out of my face and tried to pat the rest into behaving. "I have hair ties in my room."

"No, I like it. My wild ginger." He kissed my temple and then my nose.

"Lips," I suggested.

"Let's get your pants off first. No—" He pushed down on my shoulder, holding me in place as I tried to sit up. "I'll do the work."

"Just shove them down far enough. That's easier." I didn't want him to get a good look at the padded bandage and the bruising I still wore on my thigh and decide I was too hurt to sleep with. Slipping my waistband below the curve of my ass and under my balls was easy and barely twinged my leg. The bunched fabric covered my bandage and left me feeling sluttier than if I was fully naked.

Brooklyn hummed as I freed my erect dick. "Mm. Nice."

"Pretty average."

"I have a thing for gingers." Brooklyn reached over and

delivered a slow stroke down my shaft that had my cock sitting up and begging.

"I could blow you," I offered. "If we can figure out a position." My thigh had almost stopped throbbing, and in that miracle, I was hot and hard and eager, unwilling to move and lose this moment.

"Nope." Brooklyn eased his long legs down the bed, stretching on his side facing me. "Nothing fancy, nothing that might twinge your leg or your head."

"I'm fi—"

Brooklyn kissed the second consonant off my lips. "You're definitely *fine*. You're also going to be holding still. Let me do the work. Start with kissing." He tapped his lips with his forefinger. "Right here."

I didn't know if that was just how Brooklyn was, or if he'd figured out I liked to be told what to do in bed. Didn't really matter right then. I kissed him, right where he wanted it at the outer corner of his mouth. The faint hint of growing scruff prickled my lips.

He chuckled and turned his head to find my lips with his. With a light tug on my beard, he changed the angle, deepening the kiss. Then I felt his palm press over my nipple. I moaned. I was always stupidly sensitive there.

"Oh, yeah." Brooklyn went back to kissing me while he rolled and pinched and tugged at my nipples.

My hips tried to punch forward of their own account, and a flash of pain up my thigh made me wince.

I thought I hid it, but Brooklyn leaned away from our kiss. "You have just one job, Arthur. Hold still and let me take care of you."

That didn't feel fair. He'd been taking care of me all week. But when he slid lower and closed his mouth around my nipple, all I could do was gasp and try not to move.

I cupped his head in my hands, his short, straight hair

silky under my fingers, and tried to guide him to the other side. He resisted, long enough to make me whine, then turned his attention to my other tight nub. I gasped at the edge of teeth, fighting to keep my touch on his head gentle. Then he licked where he'd bitten me, soothing sensitized skin with the flat of his tongue.

Brooklyn moved down my body an inch at a time, stroking and licking and nipping—a gentle bite on my stomach, a kiss pressed to my hip bone.

In the past, I'd been self-conscious about my soft pasty-white stomach. What muscle I had was hidden in a layer of cushioning, but Brooklyn treated every bit of me as if it was worth exploring. Then he reached my cock and slid his hot mouth over the head.

I looked down and all I could feel was need and wonder, as Brooklyn bobbed up and down and took me apart with his mouth and hands. It wasn't so much technique as how attuned to me he was. How he'd clamp a hand on my hip if I was about to move, or pause, open mouth hovering around me, too much and not quite enough, as I teetered on the brink.

After getting me almost there three times, he backed off and started *again*, kissing my stomach, my hip, then lower. He cupped my balls, rolling them, but when I tried to raise my thigh to give him room, I flinched and he let go. "Maybe not this time. Hold still, Arthur."

"You have someone sucking your dick like a graduate from cock-sucking college and see how well you hold still," I muttered, my breath rasping in my throat.

"Not an excuse." He nipped my stomach. "And thanks." He sucked my dick down again, this time almost reaching my curls with his lips.

"Goddamn *graduate* degree," I said. "Please, Brooklyn. Come on. Don't stop now." My pulse pounded in my throat, and all my nerves were strung tight, vibrating. I'd never in my life seen anything hotter than Brooklyn West with my cock between his pretty pink lips, while controlling my movements with those long, strong fingers. "Please!"

He sucked me harder, faster, with less variety and more sloppy, wet, tight perfection. Heat rose in my belly, in my groin, in my face and chest. My balls ached, climax boiling just below the surface, and I wanted to thrust down his throat but I obeyed the grip of his hands. "Yeah, that, God, yes, God!" Orgasm hit me in an avalanche of heat. My cock jumped and spurted in Brooklyn's mouth.

He laughed, a low choked sound, even as he drank me down. Then he pulled me closer, deeper, his fingers digging into my hip, his mouth full of me.

"Oh God." An aftershock ripped through me, perfect white-out pleasure rocking me one more time. Then I sighed, long and hard, and my body rolled down the other side of that exquisite climax mountain. My breathing steadied. My heartbeat slowed. Other sensations came back online, including a sharp ache in my thigh that I ignored, because nothing was allowed to make this moment less than perfect.

"That was incredible. Thank you," I murmured.

Brooklyn eased off, letting my softening cock sag against my thigh, and grinned up at me.

Look at that man.

I asked, "Can I blow you now? I want to."

He eyed me up and down. "Some other time."

I liked the confirmation that he wasn't thinking of this as a one-time hookup, but I could see he was still rock-hard. "My hand, then. C'mere." I beckoned. "Up here. I want a kiss."

Brooklyn raised an eyebrow, but scooted up the bed and found my mouth with his. Tasting myself on his tongue made me wish I was ten years younger and a bit less battered. I reached for his erection, and he arched into my grip.

That long slim cock was made for me, a perfect fit in my palm. And he was uncut so we didn't need lube to let me jack him, hard and smooth. I took up a rhythm, and he gasped with each motion of my hand. Precum welled under my palm as I swiped over the head. Then I added one long, tight stroke, tip to base and back up, and Brooklyn cried out and arched, shoving his dick through my fist. Thick spunk jetted between my fingers, hitting my chest and dripping onto Brooklyn's stomach and thighs.

He groaned, his eyes half-shut, his face flushed. *God, he looks good coming.* I used the jizz to lube my strokes and kept going till he grabbed my wrist.

"Enough. Wow. Fuck, that was embarrassing. I came in, like, fifteen seconds."

"After fifteen minutes of blowing me," I pointed out.

"True. You were unfairly hot." He delivered a hard, off-center kiss to my mouth. "Hottest I've ever seen."

I laughed, feeling floaty and happy. In the glow of the moment, I almost believed he really meant that. Me, nearing-forty Arthur Bjornsson, who'd never been anyone's first choice, was his tonight. No one's preference, until this kind, cute, sexy, determined man invited me to his bed.

We shuffled closer together, sticky and messy but unwilling to stop kissing long enough to do something about it. I clasped his shoulder and he draped an arm across my hips.

Slowly, the need to get our mouths on each other ebbed into a quiet exchange, lips brushing lips, breath mingling. I sighed and closed my eyes.

"Here," Brooklyn murmured. "Let me grab some tissues and get us wiped up."

"I should go to my room." But I didn't move as his gentle touch patted and wiped me, cleaning the sticky aftermath from my skin, then pulling up my sleep pants.

"You'd just wake the dogs," he said.

"Point."

"Stay here. Morning will come soon enough. And I feel like I can sleep for a change."

From the dark circles under his eyes as we'd sat in the kitchen, I suspected he needed that. If I could help him sleep, that would be something I could give, for all the things he'd done for me. A reason to stay in Brooklyn's bed.

Face it, you don't want to leave.

I decided it was too late, or too early, to deal with the angel on my shoulder. Or devil, whichever. Once Brooklyn had tossed the tissues, turned off the lamp, and lain down beside me, I told him, "Roll over. I can't, and I want to hold you."

He sighed, but the soft breath sounded more content than exasperated. He turned over and eased his bare ass against my flannel-covered dick. I was far too wrung out to get hard again, but I liked having him there. I hugged him lightly, my arm across his waist, and breathed in the scent of the back of his neck.

Sleeping with a stranger had never been something I was good at. Mostly I hadn't tried to spend the night after getting off with guys, but if I did, I'd lie awake, rigidly holding still so I wouldn't wake the other guy, worried I'd snore, or fart, or something. If I dropped off, my sleep was light and fitful.

And at first, in Brooklyn's bed, I tried to control my movements, my breaths, hoping to lull him to sleep. But as I heard his breathing deepen and even out, I relaxed. I didn't feel that familiar tug of anxiety, the need to be perfect, to not do anything wrong. Being with Brooklyn was different, and I drifted into deep, restful sleep. Best I'd had all week.

Until, of course, I was woken from that deep sleep by repeated chimes of Brooklyn's doorbell and a chorus of barking from my dogs.

CHAPTER 8

BROOKLYN

"WHAT THE FUCK?" I JOLTED AWAKE WITH THE NOISE.

Door chimes. That's just your doorbell.

Yeah, but who the hell would be here at…

I squinted.

3:37

Well, okay then.

A voice groaned from over my shoulder as the hand on my thigh tightened.

Right, Arthur. He stayed.

My heart did a little pitter-patter.

He stayed.

More ringing.

More barking.

I slipped out of bed and fumbled in the dark for my sleep pants, bumped my shin getting out the wrong side of bed, then realized I'd left the pants somewhere at the foot and worked my way around.

The bedside lamp flicked on. Arthur grunted, a pained sound as the stretch clearly tweaked his sore leg, but said, "Can I help?"

Pitter-patter.

"I swear I'll get this sorted. I'm so sorry they woke you." I yanked on the pants and found the T-shirt I'd abandoned earlier today from my hamper. "Uh, stay put." I didn't look at him as I headed out of my bedroom. I couldn't conceive of who might be ringing my bell like that. The police? A neighbor? A client who had an emergency and needed daycare immediately?

Twain continued to howl as I made my way to the front door, the tiles cold on my feet.

Without checking the peephole, I threw the deadbolt, and then opened the door wide. "Jesus Fucking Christ." My jaw dropped.

"No. Cheyenne Fucking West." She put her hand on her hip. "You going to let me in? And what's with the noise? You get a pack of dogs since you moved here?"

"Yes, come in. No, they're not my dogs. What the fuck are you doing here?"

My baby sister flounced in with a tiny overnight bag and a determined look on her face. She wore faded denim jeans ripped in just *that* way. She'd paired them with a yellow cotton top that matched her blonde hair, an oversized pale blue checked chambray shirt, and cowboy boots.

Yep, cowboy boots.

As soon as she was securely inside, I shut the door.

About the same time, the howling ceased.

I was one-hundred percent certain the two actions were not connected—which meant Arthur had his dogs under control.

Oh yeah, this isn't going to be awkward at all. "I repeat… what the hell are you doing here?" Not to be taken wrong —I was thrilled to see her. Just, how she'd made it from upstate New York to Gaynor Beach, California was a little baffling. I was positive Mom and Dad would not have let her have a car, or a plane ticket.

"Hitched." She toed off her boots. "God, my feet are killing me. And I've been living in the same two sets of clothes for a week. I'm gross."

Gross? Don't think about the dried cum on your skin that you might've missed while you were wiping yourself down with tissues. Don't think about Arthur—"Hitched? What the fuck?" I shook my head.

She met my gaze with intense hazel-green eyes so much like my own. "Hitched. As in, I stuck out my thumb in New York City and found rides all the way across the country. Wasn't as hard as I thought it would be."

"You mean aside from the fact it's illegal and you could've been murdered?" Images flashed in my mind of her being left on the side of the road. In a ditch. Her head bashed in or shot or strangled or—

"Do you have food? I'm hungry. The last woman who drove me here was nice, but she had to ditch me just inside the city limits and get back on the highway. She only had a couple of hours to get to San Diego. Some kind of…" Cheyenne waved her hand around. "You know, I didn't really listen. She said she could drive me to Gaynor Beach, and here I am."

"You walked from the highway exit ramp?" That was a long enough distance at any time. At three in the morning? Wearing cowboy boots and tight jeans?

"Yes. Food. Then chitchat. Is the kitchen this way?" She pointed down the hall.

I redirected her. "Nope. Bedrooms are that way. Bathroom if you need it. I'll put your bag in the spare room because I'm working off the assumption you don't have a hotel to go to, and you're not going to hitch back to New York at three a.m." *I don't want to make you go, but you can't stay here long.* Being seventeen and all. "Kitchen's through here." I led her through the living room, formal dining room, and into the kitchen.

She headed straight for the fridge.

I hovered behind her. "Why don't I cook you something? You must be starving. When did you eat?" She didn't look any skinner than I remembered. She was always more coltish than curvy. Lanky, like myself.

"A trucker who brought me from Vegas through to LA bought me dinner."

I didn't like the sound of that.

Cheyenne elbowed me in the ribs. "Nice woman. Strong as an ox, and wouldn't put up with bullshit from anyone—"

"Language."

"You can say *fuck* and I can't say bullshit? What kind of bullshit is that?" She opened the fridge door. "But LA was a while ago. Took a bit of time for me to find someone heading down I5 who was willing to give me a ride."

I said a prayer of thanks to the woman who'd done just that. I hated the idea of my sister hitching on the side of the road. "The cops didn't pick you up?" I tried to elbow her aside. "Grilled cheese? Tuna cheesy melts?"

Arthur had really liked those.

Arthur! Shit! Clearly, he'd gone back to his room since the barking had ceased. How the hell was I going to introduce him to my sister? Or her to him? We just got started. *Is this going to wreck everything? Will he freak out? Will she?* My sister could have no doubts that I was bisexual, after hearing that last blowout fight with my parents, but knowing was different from seeing.

Oblivious to my moment of panic, Cheyenne was still checking out the fridge. "I love your tuna cheesy melts, but I'm hungry *now.*"

"Tuna sandwich?"

"Mayo but no olives?"

"That works."

She grabbed the bread and the mayo from the fridge while I grabbed a tin of tuna from the cupboard. I snagged a bowl while she opened the tuna. She was about to drain the tin when I stopped her.

"What?"

"Ebony really loves—"

Crap.

Cheyenne arched an eyebrow in a way only she could really pull off.

"It's not what you think."

"You don't know what I think. I know you're bi. So I'm assuming Ebony is—" She glanced around. "—where, precisely?"

"Drain the tuna and let's get this done."

She put her hand on her hip. "You've got company."

"Tuna." I snagged the tin and, with a heavy heart, drained the juice. I didn't have time to sort out four saucers anyway and only giving some to Eb wouldn't be fair.

I dumped the tuna into a bowl, added several heaps of mayo, some pepper and celery salt, and stirred. "Do you want butter on your bread? I use it so infrequently that I keep it in the fridge."

"This is fine." She opened a random cupboard, located a plate, and put it on the counter. She had two slices of bread ready for the mix and I dumped a pile of it on the slices. Her preference was always more mayo than tuna.

"Milk?"

"Do you have Coke?"

I arched an eyebrow.

She glared back. "You know I never get to drink it at

home. Well, they're not controlling me now, and I want a fucking Coke."

"Seriously, Cheyenne, you don't have to swear all the time."

"Why not?"

"Because it's crass and beneath you."

"You swear." She mashed the bread together and started peeling off the crust.

Good to see some things never change. She'd always hated crusts.

"Look, I'll grab you a pop. Why don't you sit at the table like a civilized human being?"

"When did you ever care about that?"

"Hey. That's not fair. Just because I didn't believe in our parents' philosophies on—" I waved my arm about.

"Everything," she helpfully supplied.

"Well...okay." She wasn't wrong. Coming out hadn't just been a repudiation of their beliefs—it had been a middle finger to their plans for me. *Go forth and multiply* was the name of the game where we came from. The more children the better, despite the fact that meant more mouths to feed. After the globalist attack they were sure was coming, all hands would be needed. My parents had three other kids between Cheyenne and me. All were, as far as I'd ever perceived, also true believers.

Why Cheyenne and I called bullshit on everything was beyond me. Something in our genes? A bullshit detector? Still... "You're underage, Cheyenne. You knew you'd be way better staying until you turned eighteen. Even better, an extra few months and finish high school. More opportunities."

"Like you?" She plopped into a chair and put her plate on the table. Then she took a massive bite.

I got a can of pop out of the fridge, added some ice to a glass, and then poured the cola over it.

"You remembered." She grinned when I presented the glass.

Truthfully, I remembered a lot about her. She'd only been four when I'd left the first time, a sweet, mischievous toddler I'd missed in the moments I had energy to spare. Those more recent few weeks had imprinted themselves on my mind, though. Newly turned seventeen, she'd made time for me, while Nevada, Austin, and Denver had kept themselves busy. Well, Nevada was married with two kids, but Denver and Austin were still single. Which didn't mean they took any notice of their disdained older brother, and I couldn't care less what they liked. My brilliant, surprising little sister, on the other hand… "I do my best. Look, uh…" I pointed over my shoulder down the hall, gesturing that I needed to duck out for a moment.

"Say *hi* to Ebony. Whoever he or she might be." She took another bite of her sandwich.

Right. "I'll be back. Don't…wander."

She made a gun with her hand and pretended to shoot my way, a "you got it" gesture telling me she'd do what I asked.

I hotfooted toward the bedrooms and, once I was certain my nosy sister hadn't followed, stuck my head into my room.

The bed was empty and neatly made. *Okay, that's super sweet. Especially since he was probably balancing on a crutch while doing it.*

I crossed the hall to his bedroom and knocked softly.

Three cacophonous barks erupted.

I rolled my eyes. Then the door opened, and I stepped in before Xandra managed an escape.

She meowed at me, perhaps smelling the tuna, and

twitched her tail, showing me her butthole in punishment for not bringing her some.

I shut the door behind me and came face-to-face with Arthur.

His hair was pulled back into an elastic. He wore jeans and a sweatshirt and even socks. He leaned heavily on his crutch, though, and lines of pain etched his face.

"What are you doing?" I might've whispered that. I straightened. "Sorry, what are you doing up and dressed?"

"Leaving, of course. I mean—" He gestured around the room. His suitcase was haphazardly half-full and he'd sort of managed to pile the dog beds, Xandra's carrier, and—

"What the fuck? Sorry, what the hell? You're not leaving. Jesus, Arthur, you can't just go. You can't drive, can't lug that stuff up your stairs. Let alone your three dogs and…"

Xandra leaped back to the bed, making herself at home on his pillow.

She blinked at me, then indolently began licking her paw. Okay, she could take care of herself. Fresh litter and food were her only requirements in life. We all lived to serve her.

"I heard you out there. Your little sister just arrived, Brooklyn. I can't stay."

I pressed the bridge of my nose with my thumb and forefinger. "First, I don't even know if she's staying more than one night."

Liar. Underage or not, making Cheyenne leave before we sorted out her shit was a pipe dream.

I forged on. "Secondly, you were here first."

"Only because—"

"Thirdly, I have three bedrooms. And, out of an impulse to homemaking I thought was ridiculous and am now eternally grateful for, both spare bedrooms have, you know, beds." I hadn't ever anticipated hosting any of my family, but I'd wanted a home, not too much of an office space.

I had a small, tidy alcove set up off the kitchen with a desk where I kept my laptop, a filing cabinet, and my paperwork for my business. Keeping everything in that small space ensured I didn't spread stuff everywhere. Having things organized, tidy, and in their place was important to me, as far as one could when dogs were the business model.

"So, I have room for both of you."

"But—"

I pressed my finger to his lips. "We don't have time this moment to talk about what happened tonight, before my sister arrived, but rest assured, we will find the time. I regret nothing, in case you were wondering. Right now, though, I need to sort out Cheyenne. Obviously, our parents have no idea where she is, or they'd be on my doorstep in a heartbeat. Well, that would mean leaving upstate New York. So…they'd send someone, one of my brothers, maybe. She's only seventeen."

Arthur regarded me. "She's underage. Deputy Olson takes her job seriously. If she thinks you're involved in something illegal without parental consent, even if you mean well, she'll nail you."

I didn't doubt it. Her treatment of Frank the gun-toting chicken owner taught me to take her seriously. "I can't just send Chey back, though. Not without learning why she's here."

"Harboring a runaway's a crime in most states."

"And she hasn't finished high school." I exhaled. "She turns eighteen in December, which makes me question why she couldn't have just waited an extra two months."

"You think it's something serious." Arthur regarded me.

"I think that as impetuous and impulsive as my sister is, she doesn't fly off the handle often." I considered. "Well, maybe that's downplaying her…hardheadedness. She's…a spitfire. She's never agreed with my parents. Never followed their rules without being browbeaten and believe me, they tried. Never showed any desire to live like them."

"Like how, exactly?" His brow knit.

Oh God, you have no idea. But I didn't have a month to try to explain my family, my childhood, or the clusterfuck that had been my life before I'd come to Gaynor Beach. *Fucking hell, I thought all that was behind me.* Apparently not. Life had just delivered an effective blow to my balls.

Speaking of balls. Totally cockblocked. I'd fully intended to make Arthur beg some more, come morning. Instead, we'd have my sister as an inadvertent chaperone. I sighed. "Will you come out and meet her? She loves animals, so if you'd be so kind as to introduce your three —" I hesitated over Xandra. "—dogs, that would be amazing."

Softly, he chuckled as he eyed his cat. "Yes, Princess Xandra likes people, but on her own schedule."

Clearly, he'd seen my second thoughts about dragging the lovely creature into the kitchen and what? Thrusting her unceremoniously into Cheyenne's arms as something warm to hug? Nope, that wouldn't go over well.

He added, "Chili might not warm up to her."

"That's okay. Just…if there are going to be three adults in the house—" *Wait. When did I start succumbing to the idea Cheyenne's staying? Fuck my life.* I went for humor. "—then the dogs will want to know who's most easily manipulated."

Arthur chuckled. "Given the way you describe your sister, that would be you."

"Yep." I beamed. "And proud of it." I held his gaze. "You'll stay?"

He pursed his lips. "I feel like…you need time with your sister."

"Can I be honest? She's a lot to handle. If you're around, that might moderate her…enthusiasm."

"I don't understand what you mean."

"Well, you'll soon find out."

"Okay." He didn't appear convinced.

CHAPTER 9

ARTHUR

I'D HAVE GUESSED CHEYENNE WAS BROOKLYN'S SISTER EVEN if I'd seen her on the street. She had the same tall, lean build, the same brown-blond straight hair, the same eyes. Even the way she tilted her head, eyeing me as I entered the kitchen, carried an echo of Brooklyn. Her nose was more snub, and I didn't see the match to his dimples. Then again, his weren't in evidence either in their strained exchange of glances.

Brooklyn said, "Arthur, this is my little sister, Cheyenne. Chey, this is my…friend Arthur. He hurt his leg and his apartment's a walk-up so he's staying with me."

"Don't call me Chey," she snapped, then raised an eyebrow at me. "Boyfriend?"

"Cut it out," Brooklyn told her before I had to come up with an answer. "You're the one who showed up here in the middle of the night. You don't get to demand details of my private life. Or do you want me to ask if our parents know where you are?"

"Of course they don't. Duh." But she dropped her gaze and took another big bite of her sandwich.

I figured I knew one way to take the tension level between the siblings down a bit. "Hey, do you like dogs?"

A smile crossed Cheyenne's face showing that in fact, she and Brooklyn did share those dimples too. "I love them. I heard barking."

"My dogs. Brooklyn's letting me keep them here until my leg's healed enough to go home."

"What happened to you?"

Before Brooklyn could lecture her again about nosiness, I said, "I got shot."

She stared at me.

I stared back.

"You can't just say that and stop there. Like, are you a cop or something? Was it a burglar?"

"Nope." Keeping a teenager off-balance wasn't a bad thing, so instead of explaining, I called, "Ebony, come!"

Eb's big paws scrabbled down the hallway from where I'd told the pups to stay, and he burst into the kitchen.

I ordered, "Sit," just in time, before those same paws would've landed on Cheyenne's lap. He plopped his butt down but gazed up at her, his big tail thumping.

"Can I pet him? Her?" Cheyenne's eyes were glued to Ebony.

"Him. Eb for short. He's very friendly but he's also a moocher, so keep an eye on your sandwich."

"Hi, Ebony." There was something odd, a tone of wonder in Cheyenne's voice as she reached to pet him that made me think of a much younger child.

I called, "Twain, come." When the little beagle mix trotted in, I gestured him toward Cheyenne too.

In a moment, she'd slid out of her chair to the floor and was laughing, stroking Twain's long ears while Ebony alternately nudged her with his nose and tried to lick her hands.

Brooklyn edged closer to me and said under his breath, "We weren't allowed to have pets as kids. Nothing useless. Our neighbor had hunting dogs, but they lived in the shed, and when they got too old to work or didn't do what he said, he'd shoot them. We weren't supposed to ever pet them or give them treats because it would make them soft."

"Oh man. That's sad." I was really curious about Brooklyn's childhood. The clues I had suggested something rigid and unhappy. Who didn't allow pets? Who shot dogs? But three a.m. wasn't the time to ask. "She seems to like these two."

"I love dogs," Cheyenne said. "I used to sneak treats to Mr. Gordon's hounds."

I told her, "Well, as long as you're here, you can give Eb and Twain all the attention you want. They eat that up." A click of smaller feet warned me Chili was about to arrive. Holding a stay command wasn't her forte. "This third dog, though—"

Chili paused in the doorway to the kitchen, spotted Cheyenne, and began barking her fool head off.

I gimped over, awkwardly stretched my leg out, and bent to scoop her up so we could hear ourselves think. She grumbled a bit, but then relaxed in my hold. "This is Chili. It's probably best if you ignore her. Let her come to you if she wants to, leave her be if she doesn't. She doesn't like most people."

"She loooves me," Brooklyn sing-songed. The smugness in his tone was probably due to the presence of his sister. I might not've seen my family in years, but I remembered the one-upmanship that was part of having siblings.

Chili has excellent taste. I didn't say that out loud at the last moment, realizing that I didn't know what role we were playing in front of Cheyenne. Or even if there would be an *us*, going forward. *Maybe best not to sound too besotted.* "He's right," I told Cheyenne. "She likes him the most."

"He probably bribed her with tuna sandwiches."

"Is it working on you?" Brooklyn asked.

That made her laugh, looking up from the happy greetings of the two dogs. For the first time, she seemed like a young seventeen, and I realized how much strain she must be carrying. "I didn't come here just for the tuna sandwich, big brother, but it helped."

I could see Brooklyn fighting not to ask her why she did come, except a yawn split his face. Of course, I did the same, and then Cheyenne and Eb followed suit.

Cheyenne stared at Eb's furry black face as he gaped his jaws. "Are yawns contagious to dogs?"

"I think so." I couldn't help setting off another round.

Brooklyn sighed. "It's late. Or early. Whatever. Finish your sandwich, Cheyenne, and then I'll show you your room."

"Can I shower?"

"If you want. If you can stay up for it. Otherwise, sheets wash. Do it in the morning."

Cheyenne pushed away from Eb and stood, stuffed the last bite of sandwich into her mouth, then rubbed her eyes. "Bed sounds awesome. I slept on a bench last night."

I met Brooklyn's gaze and read fear in his expression, and no wonder. I was the youngest in my family, but I could imagine how scary the thought of a teen sister wandering out in the world alone was.

Well, not *just* imagine. Melissa was three years older than me, but she'd gotten herself into some hair-raising situations. Luckily, that hadn't been my problem as the baby of the family, and my parents had kept a lot of her worst moments from me. I had the impression Brooklyn felt more responsible for Cheyenne.

"I'm glad you made it here safe," I told her.

For a moment, her air of confidence wavered and she admitted, "Me too." But then she dredged up a grin. "I still want that shower, though. I'm gross."

"Follow me." Brooklyn led her off down the hallway.

Eb stretched, then before I could stop him, set his paws on her abandoned chair and licked a glob of tuna and mayo off her plate.

"Ebony!" I scolded. "Sit." Then when he did, "Down." Once he'd been a good boy, I set Chili on the floor, hobbled over, and swiped a bit of mayo with my finger. Twain happily licked it, Eb slurped his share. Chili looked at me as if I was trying to poison her. "There's tuna in it, picky princess," I told her, then gave Twain hers, before carrying the plate to the sink.

I heard the water come on in the shower down the hall, then Brooklyn reappeared.

I wanted to ask questions, to demand what came next, for her, for us, to ask if he still wanted me around. But when he came into the light, he looked exhausted, almost lost. Darker-than-usual circles ringed his eyes, and his pretty mouth was pressed in a flat line. I opened my arms and he came to me for a hug.

"Sorry," he said from the circle of my hold. "I had no idea she was coming, or staying. I know family drama's not what you bargained for."

"Shh." I told him. At least I could hold him and make him feel better. "We'll worry about it in the morning."

"I want you back in my bed, but we probably shouldn't."

"Probably not." I was gay and out and not ashamed of anything, but I wasn't comfortable coming out of a man's bedroom in front of his teenage sister.

"Damn. I had plans for us and that bed."

"They'll keep."

"Oh good. You're not going to run away?"

I loosened my hold so I could meet his eyes. "Run?"

"Get out of Dodge. Fade into the distance. Scarper."

"I know what it means." A twinge of head pain made me say that more roughly than I meant to. Then the vertigo hit, and a flash of light across my vision forced me to grab the edge of the table. "I'm going to bed."

"I'm sorry."

"Quit apologizing. It's not about you." I regretted the gripe before it left my lips. *I hate who I am these days. I don't know why he puts up with me.*

"Are you okay?"

No, I'm not okay. My head hurts, my leg hurts, I might puke on your kitchen floor, and I'm turning into Jekyll and Hyde without warning. I'm scared this is still happening, and now your sister needs you more than I do. Which is probably a good thing for your sake. I couldn't say any of that, so I mumbled, "I'm fine." Clutching my crutch in a tight grip and praying I'd make it out of sight, I trudged to the hallway, calling the dogs behind me.

Somehow, by keeping my free hand braced on the wall, I made it down the hall and into my room. When I closed the door behind me, the floor was closer than the bed. I put my shoulders to the wall, stuck my bad leg out, and slid down to my ass with a thump.

Footsteps paused outside my door. "Need a hand?"

I wanted to reply cheerfully, *Sure, on my dick*, but the last thing I wanted then was sex. Not to mention the teen sister in the bathroom. "Nope. Get some sleep." And to prove I wasn't entirely Hyde-monster, I added, "Good night."

Brooklyn hesitated, then said, "Good night."

I heard his door open, then close.

"Well, crap." I raised my good knee and rested my forehead on it, waiting for the spinnies to fade.

Eb tried to lick my face, which wasn't helpful but he meant well. Chili jumped onto the bed, as if she knew I was in no shape to remove her, and Twain stood by, tilting his head back and forth and whining under his breath. Xandra gave me a blue-eyed stare from the spare pillow.

My little family. Really, I didn't need anything more. I was a mess and Brooklyn would be busy for the foreseeable anyhow. My stomach twisted and I dry heaved, but luckily nothing else.

I heard Cheyenne come out of the main bathroom and go into her room. Heard a few thumps and sounds and then silence. Eb lay down beside me and agreed to pillow his big head on my ankle and not my aching thigh. Twain curled up against my hip.

Eventually, the bout of vertigo eased enough for me to make it to the bed and stretch out. I should've checked my bandage, since I'd skipped it, falling asleep beside Brooklyn…for a moment I *ached* for how sweet and hopeful that'd felt, lying warm and sated with a man I cared about close against me. But reality had intruded. No surprise. I closed my eyes and tried to relax each muscle one by one. My leg could wait till morning.

———

I HAD MY BANDAGE CHANGED, THE FUR-BABIES FED, THE dogs let out into the yard, coffee brewing, and bread in the toaster when Brooklyn wandered into the kitchen next morning, rubbing his eyes.

"That alarm goes off way too early," he muttered. He smiled at me, but only half wattage and he didn't cross the room to kiss me.

Well, of course not. That's not how we are.

I said, "You could sleep an extra half hour if you didn't drive me to work."

"But I'd have to get up half an hour earlier to make breakfast so it's a wash."

Cooking didn't take half an hour, but I'd take that rationale. I set juice, coffee, toast, and jam at two places and eased down into my seat. Xandra stalked in and made a leap at the table. I caught her with the ease of long practice and hid my face against her fur for a few moments before setting her down. Once she was on the floor, I gave her a swipe of butter off my toast as a reward, then finally looked up.

Brooklyn eyed me and I saw concern cross his face, so before he could say anything, I jumped in with, "You look pretty tired. Didn't sleep well?" It wasn't a lie. We could've had an eye-bags contest and he might've won.

"Not really." He rubbed his face, then sucked down some coffee. "God, that's good."

"Your coffee-maker." Keeping the focus off me, I asked, "Do you have any idea why Cheyenne is here?"

"Sanctuary from my parents, I expect." He sighed, then began nibbling his dry toast.

I kept quiet, because I knew all about not wanting to discuss family. I pushed the jam his way and got a sweet smile in return.

But somewhere around the fifth bite, he began talking down toward his plate, not looking at me. "My parents are...weird. The little town where I was raised in upstate New York has a long history of preparing for the worst. The hills around us are riddled with caves, and as far back as World War Two, the locals stocked those caves to hide out in. For resistance, when the Japanese or the Germans invaded."

"Not completely foolish," I suggested.

"No. But then…" He sighed. "The enemy changed, but the town didn't. We were going to be the last bastion against communism, the last survivors when the USSR dropped the bomb. Now it's the globalists and Bill Gates, Soros, and the New World Order. When the UN invades America, Piperston will be the loyal defense for *truth, freedom, and the American way.*" He gave me a smile that held no real humor, bared teeth below sober eyes. "And woe to anyone who doesn't see the clear and present danger."

"From the *UN?*" I had to say. "They can't even manage to keep small ethnic groups from trying to wipe each other out."

"Right?" Brooklyn ran a hand over his head. "But that conspiracy mindset is so ingrained, and there are a thousand online sites grinding out the propaganda. My parents and neighbors are true believers."

"Like a cult?" I didn't like the bleak look on his face.

"Yeah. With less God than most, though. I mean, everyone goes to the local Baptist church, but God only comes into it as a given, American as apple pie. What counts is how straight you can shoot, how well your women prepare canned goods, and how much you hate globalism and taxes."

"So they didn't kick you out for being bisexual?" I'd assumed that was why he was rejected.

"Oh, partly. Not because I was defying the Bible as much as because the queer kid was too much of a wimp to finish off and dress a terrified, gut-shot deer. Plus, me dating boys wasn't going to add to the local population. That's a bit of an obsession."

"Sex? Population?"

"Adding to the local core families. Like most small towns, a lot of the young folk leave Piperstown and

KAJE HARPER & GABBI GREY

surprise, surprise, they don't come back. There are a few new folk who show up, some of them even crazier than the locals, but the core is third and fourth generations. My folks expected me to marry a neighbor girl and raise them a bunch of soldiers for America. As a queer, I was useless to them, and they treated me that way. So, I left. For a while." Brooklyn's gaze went unfocused and distant, the twist of his lips suggesting his thoughts were not fun ones.

I didn't press, and a moment later he shook himself and glanced at me, his shoulders relaxing. "I imagine it's something similar with Cheyenne. She's smart, smarter than me——"

"Don't put yourself down," I told him.

Brooklyn waved a dismissive hand. "Nah, just the truth. She's got so much potential, and my family would only see her as domestic labor and motherhood. The question is, why didn't she wait till she was eighteen, like I did? Running while underage and without a high school diploma seems like a foolish choice, and while Cheyenne can be hotheaded, she's never been stupid."

"Makes you worry," I suggested softly.

"Sure does." He stared morosely at the last of his toast, then popped it into his mouth. "Well, nothing I can do about that till she wakes up. Which, judging by how she looked, might be afternoon. I'll get you to work, and then Poppy's arriving at seven."

"Oh good, goldendoodle zoomies first thing in the morning." I glanced over my shoulder. "Might cheer Cheyenne up, though."

"It might. I hope she'll talk to me."

"What if she doesn't? Will you let her stay if you don't know why? Will your parents be looking for her?"

"I don't know. They were glad to see the backside of me, but she's a girl and not queer. Well, as far as I know."

108

He glanced toward the bedrooms too. "This is a mess. I was gone, free and clear, didn't owe them a thing, didn't even have to think about them. And now..."

"She's back in your life, but she's your sister and just a kid, and you're going to help her." I was sure of that. Brooklyn hadn't even let a grumpy stranger climb a flight of stairs without offering to help.

"I guess."

"I know."

He cleared our plates and mugs into the dishwasher. "Let's get going. I'll leave her a note in case she wakes up."

"I'll put the dogs into the outdoor kennels till you get back." If Cheyenne hadn't been around dogs before, I wasn't going to leave her responsible for three, even while sleeping.

My lack of rest made the seat of Brooklyn's old SUV less comfortable. The sun was just coming over the horizon as we drove, forcing us to squint.

Brooklyn dug a pair of sunglasses out of the door pocket and offered them to me. "Here. You want?"

I waved for him to put them on. "You're driving."

Gold and lilac streaked the sky as I looked away from the crescent of the sun. At this point in the fall, up in Minnesota, six-thirty would still be pitch dark. Folks would already be working on my father's farm, though. Cows didn't wait for daylight to need milking. Mom would've made a light breakfast and would be starting the full meal for after morning chores...

As if he'd followed my thoughts, Brooklyn said, "You never talk about your family, either."

"Well, I don't have any younger sibs who might show up on the doorstep," I said lightly. *Nieces, maybe.* Except I'd been gone so long, they'd no doubt forgotten about me. Still, Brooklyn had given me some truth, so I owed him mine. The easy version, anyhow. "Five older sibs. Minnesota farm country. Nothing like yours, though. My brothers and sisters stayed local, started families, but they're good people. I grew up only a little older than some of my nieces and nephews, and Mom sometimes babysat them with me."

I still remembered when I was seven and had a bad cold, Mom asked my cousin Rick to watch me because she was going to take care of my sister's three and didn't want me to make them sick. Achy and feverish, I'd asked why Rick couldn't watch the littles and let me have my mom. But she said they needed her more. In retrospect, she probably didn't want to saddle a teenage sitter with three toddlers, but at the time, I'd sat huddled on the couch, numb, as she headed out to be with kids who were more important than me. And it wasn't the only time...

I shook off the mood. "I never really fit in, and my next older sister, Melissa, took up a lot of my parents' energy and money." I remembered Mom crying at the kitchen table when Mel had been gone deep into the night again. I'd tried to comfort her, but at thirteen I was just clumsy, and she sent me off to bed. They'd paid for Mel's rehab twice and an abortion I wasn't supposed to know about. That was Mel's personal business, though, and I said nothing.

Brooklyn threw me a glance at a stoplight. "You sound sad."

"I wish my folks and I were closer. I went off to college, and we kind of drifted apart."

"Do you ever go home?"

"I used to. Long time ago, now. I just got tired of making all the effort. Like, my freshman year, I used to call or text home every single Sunday morning. Then one time, I was *sick*." I gave him a crooked grin. "Meaning hungover.

I missed most of Sunday. I was going to call and apologize in the evening, but they hadn't even texted me to check up. So I decided to wait and see what they would do." Selfishly, I'd wondered if they'd worry about me like they did about Mel.

"And what did they say?"

"Five weeks later, I got a text from Mom. 'We haven't heard from you for a while. Are you okay?'"

"Five *weeks*?"

"Yeah." Thirty-nine days, to be exact. Days I'd counted first in curiosity, then with growing anger, and eventually with a thickening ache in my chest. I hurried to add, "They were busy, of course. It was planting season, and my sister Mel was having some kind of crisis."

"But still."

"I was over eighteen and on my own. I was fine. I didn't need them hanging over my shoulder, but I guess I found out they just weren't all that interested in the kid that never fit in." I'd still texted now and then through college, but those five weeks broke something in me that bound me to family and home. Something I'd never found again.

Brooklyn reached across and set his hand on my knee. The warmth of his palm reached me through the denim. My throat tightened and I kept my eyes on the road ahead, but I didn't nudge him away either. He kept his hand there till he had to make the sharp turn into the shelter parking lot.

When he pulled up out front, I turned to him. "Thanks for the ride. You really didn't need to."

He waved me off. "Hey, it gave me a peaceful, extra twenty minutes before I have to deal with my sister." As I opened the door, he said, "I'll see you tonight, right?"

I pushed to my feet, balancing with the crutch, and peered back in. Brooklyn sounded hopeful, not like I was an additional burden in his home. But then, he was a generous soul. I couldn't be sure what would be best. Still, moving out would be an effort I didn't want to make tonight, and if he and Cheyenne had a rough day, maybe I could be there for him.

"Yeah," I said, closing the door and giving the roof a little thump. "We're good. See you tonight."

CHAPTER 10

BROOKLYN

I'D THOUGHT CHEYENNE MIGHT BE AWAKE WHEN I returned, but her door was still shut. I let Arthur's three out of the back kennels and into the house.

Eb loped over to an abandoned Kong and started nosing it—undoubtedly hoping for peanut butter. He was out of luck as I'd cleaned it thoroughly yesterday.

Twain headed for Arthur's bedroom. Fancifully, I believed he was checking on Xandra. Realistically, he probably wanted more rest on Arthur's comfortable bed that smelled like him. Hell, I wanted to bask in that scent as well. The way soap and clean skin had blended at the back of his neck had intoxicated me. At once fresh and soothing. Like a warm towel out of the drier.

Unexpectedly, Chili followed me around like a shadow. I might've thought she wanted food, but she just seemed to enjoy my company. I pushed down a little ego trip about being the difficult dog's favorite person.

About ten minutes after I returned to my house, Poppy and her owner showed up at the door. The woman handed over the leash and beat a retreat to her car. She was working a daybreak shift and was grateful I was willing to take her pooch so early.

Poppy's tongue lolled as she gave me slurpy kisses. Far be it for me to turn down affection. The young goldendoodle had the greatest personality.

Chili nosed her before they trotted together toward the kitchen.

Arthur had cleaned up, of course, so no crumbs were to be found anywhere. Still, the pooches lived in hope.

"Why don't you head out to the backyard? Jett's coming, so you can run off some of your energy." Poppy vibrated with excitement as I checked my watch. "Okay, we've got some time. Let's play ball."

The goldendoodle bolted for the back room while Chili followed me at a more sedate pace. *Ball* was sometimes fun for her, but her happy place seemed to be by my side.

I wouldn't point this out to Arthur, as I didn't want to hurt his feelings. Maybe it was a sign of doggie dementia, since no logical dog would pick me over Arthur.

Eb abandoned the Kong toy as I opened the patio door, shoving past me hard enough to jolt me on my heels as he followed Poppy out into the early morning cool.

Ordinarily, I'd work on door manners, but seeing the two wrestling as they dashed into the bigger play area made me laugh and I let it go.

When they got tired of trying to knock each other over, Poppy and Eb tore across the grass as I threw ball after ball.

We weren't working on retrieving skills today—although they got tons of praise if they brought the ball back.

Jett arrived and we continued with vigorous exercise.

Then, eventually, Hiro showed up. He struggled to run on his stubby little legs with his big belly, so we played a game where I coaxed him into chasing me around the yard. Fear of missing out was real, so Eb and Poppy joined in.

Chili sat on the back deck, lazing in the sun, and watched us as if we were all a little loopy.

Xandra came and peered out at us through the glass, then yawned and wandered off to her hard job of napping on the window ledge.

Still no Cheyenne. *Do I go and wake her? Let her sleep? Is she going to bolt again? How can I keep her safe? And while we're on the topic…why the fuck is she here?*

After a solid hour of exercise and some recall training, my troop was pooped.

We trudged into the kitchen, where I doled out one small sliver of freeze-dried salmon each in exchange for a nice calm sit. Well, for Xandra that was in exchange for not jumping on the counter. Nobody looked satisfied with my paltry offerings, but when I herded us back into the family room, everyone followed.

Twain even deigned to join us—having shown up just in time for his treat.

I plopped onto the floor, then lay on my back so everyone who wanted to could lick, cuddle, and get close.

Chili was first in there, tucking herself under one of my arms.

Poppy, not to be outdone, licked my cheek before nuzzling my hair.

I giggled as Hiro tried to flop on my chest. "Uh, squishing me there, buddy." I eased him to the side opposite Chili and scritched his ears.

The cat retreated to her high perch, eyeing our messy dogpile with sleepy blue eyes.

Eb chose not to partake and, instead, found a flavored plastic bone to gnaw on.

Jett, not to be outdone, chose one for himself.

I had ten so there were plenty to go around, but I kept my eye on Arthur's dogs in case someone was toy-possessive. Sometimes two dogs wanted the same one, and we might get some snarling that would be a warning all toys had to be picked up. Eb seemed chill, though, and the other two weren't interested.

"I don't think I've ever seen you so happy." Cheyenne spoke quietly.

Chili lost her shit.

I petted her. "Oh hush, baby girl. You met my sister yesterday." I almost called her *Chey* again—my nickname for her when she'd been a baby. Well, she wasn't a baby anymore.

Eb loped over to Cheyenne for scritches, and Twain nudged her leg.

Not to be outdone, Poppy, Hiro, and Jett all ambled over to the stranger.

Eb, Twain and Hiro viewed every human as someone to manipulate into handing over treats so I reminded her— "No treats for any of them, okay? I have them on a tight schedule."

Cheyenne plopped onto the floor crosslegged and was immediately set upon by pooches. Protocols of introducing new dogs flitted through my mind, but they were doing well.

If Maisie the mastiff was here, things would be different. Same with George, who, although he loved people, still needed a gentle *hello*.

Poppy, Jett, and Hiro just loved everyone, and their easygoing nature made them great company.

Chili stayed at my side, but her displeasure subsided.

Watching my sister with the dogs, I admitted, "I'm the happiest I've ever been."

Our gazes locked.

Slowly, she nodded. "Yeah, I can see why." She waved her hand around the space. "Did the money help with this place?"

"Downpayment and renovations, yes." I didn't want to talk about the settlement because that way led to the pain of what I'd been through in order to get that money.

"Better than if *they* got it."

They meaning our parents. They'd been convinced, when swooping to my rescue after the crisis, that they could take all my settlement money. I *owed* it to them, in their books. They'd been dead wrong, of course. I recuperated at their home—as much an excuse to see how Cheyenne was doing and to remind her that I loved her as not having other choices—because God only knew if the letters I sent home were reaching her. She never wrote back and, in the end, my instincts had been right. She hadn't been getting the letters I diligently wrote.

"Yeah, I gave them what I owed them for caring for me for a few weeks, and not a penny more. And I'm not sorry." I'd left their house as soon as I was able.

I stayed with a friend until I got the settlement in my bank account. After sending five hundred bucks to my folks for their *inconvenience* in taking care of me, I bought the used SUV, packed up what little stuff I had, picked Gaynor Beach, and drove west. And here I was, with this place and the dogs, and yes, happy at last.

"Did you have breakfast?" I hadn't seen signs in the kitchen, but she could've grabbed something while I'd been in the backyard.

She shook her head. "Not hungry. In fact, a little nauseous."

My stomach clenched in memory. All the times Mom had been nauseous in the morning. *Oh God, is Cheyenne pregnant? What the fuck are we going to do? Will she keep the baby? Will she need help raising it? What about the father—*

She snorted. "Breathe, Brooklyn. I'm not knocked up."

"How…?"

"I know pure panic on your face when I see it."

For all her laissez-faire attitude, she'd also been the most intuitive and empathetic of all my siblings. "Well, you can't blame me. I have an underage sister show up at my doorstep and I'm not supposed to panic?"

She bit her lower lip—something I'd witnessed her doing a lot when I'd stayed with my family. "Oops, I need to eat."

"Cheyenne." I frowned. "You just said you couldn't eat."

"Between an interrogation and food? I'll take food every time." She rose and headed for the kitchen.

Several pooches made to follow her.

"Close the gate?"

"Am I allowed to keep any of them?" She poked her head around the corner. "I think there are enough to share."

Well, I couldn't argue. "Keep Twain—the beagle—he's been a little quiet this morning and the extra attention won't hurt. Not a scrap of food, okay? They get fed plenty."

Twain gave me a baleful look, but followed Cheyenne into the kitchen.

Hiro nearly made it through the crack as she closed the gate, but didn't manage. He yipped his displeasure at being thwarted.

"You can come cuddle with me." I used my sing-songy voice. "Ear rubs."

I had five dogs lining up for their turn until Cheyenne returned with a plate of toast and a cup of coffee.

She sat in a chair, holding the plate up, and eyed her newfound doting audience.

Xandra leaped to a closer shelf but stayed up out of dog-reach.

Twain whined.

Eb drooled.

"Brooklyn says *no*. He's the mean one for not letting me share." She jutted her chin.

I mock glared. Then considered what I could and couldn't ask. "How'd you find me?"

She snorted "It's called the internet. There aren't many *Brooklyn West* guys out there, and none in a gay friendly town with a doggie daycare business. Plus, your picture's on your website. You and a pile of grinning dogs."

Shit. The publicity shoot Anderson Michaels had done for me when I was first setting things up. Honestly, it had never occurred to me that anyone from my old life would want to find me. *Or maybe you wanted to make certain Cheyenne could if she ever needed to.* That would've been a subconscious thought at best. God knew, I hadn't deliberately left breadcrumbs. "And you just, what, hitched from Piperston?" That terrified me.

She eyed her food as if trying to determine if she could manage it, then set the plate on her knee.

"Don't force it if you're not hungry. I can make some chicken noodle soup or poached eggs—something that'll be easier on your tummy." I wanted to take care of her like I had when she was three. I wanted to be the big brother I would've been if I'd been in her life all these years.

"It's fine." She met my gaze. "I'm just wondering what to tell you."

"Whatever you can. Everything. We've got major issues to deal with here, and the more information I have, the better."

She shrugged. "I was in New York City with Mom."

"In the city? Doing what?"

"Shopping."

That sounded entirely improbable—my family loathed the bastion of internationalism and blue politics that was NYC. "Okay. Then what?"

"I slipped away. Caught a ride to the New Jersey turnpike to get out of the city. I found someone heading to Ohio, and I asked if I could go along."

I blinked. "Just like that?"

"Well, they had Ohio plates. I was counting on them being, I dunno, liberal or something. Having chosen to come to New York City in the first place."

Liberal didn't mean safe, and anyhow, I wasn't going to list all the reasons someone less *liberal* might go from Ohio to NYC and back again. "And then?"

"Some hitching here, crashing on a bench in a bus station there, cajoling rides, and eventually ending up in LA. I told you the rest." She pulled the crust off the bread and bit into the middle.

Finding a nice woman to drive her to Gaynor Beach.

"You're leaving a shit ton out of that story."

"I'm telling you what you need to know."

"Why were you in New York? Why did you give Mom the slip? Hell, *how* did you give Mom the slip?"

She eyed the rest of her toast, then dropped it onto the plate.

Hiro placed himself at her feet and gazed longingly at the discarded food.

After a moment, she picked up her coffee and sipped. "It really doesn't matter."

"Cheyenne—"

"We were shopping, Brooklyn. That's all you need to know. And I had to get away. She was inattentive for a moment, and I took that as a sign from the universe to turn tail and run. I had my overnight bag, and I decided to hightail it as fast as I could." Another sip.

"Do you have a phone they can trace?" Because the last thing I needed was the cops showing up at my door.

She rolled her eyes. "You think they'd give me a phone?"

"You might've, I don't know, bought one yourself."

Her eyes clouded. "I had thirty-six dollars in my wallet and had to make it last nine days, and…" She gazed upward as if trying to calculate. "I don't know how many states. I can say it wasn't a direct route."

Jesus fucking Christ. It's truly a miracle she's alive. "You can eat anything you want here, okay? We should buy more stuff. Why don't we do a grocery order?" I hesitated. "You don't have enough clothes to last more than a day or two, do you?"

"If I keep laundering them, I should be okay."

I shook my head. "Let's get you a couple of outfits. There's a great thrift store in town. And they donate proceeds to charity, so you'd be doing a good thing."

She arched an eyebrow.

"I won't ask if you would agree to call our parents—"

"Good call."

"—but is there someone else who might be worried? Someone you'd want to reassure?"

"Nope." She popped the *p*. She held my gaze. "I didn't have friends, Brooklyn. My one non-wacko school friend moved to Canada two years ago. I was completely ostracized by the rest because I didn't respect their crazy-ass beliefs."

Neither had I, so I understood. "But you couldn't wait until you turned eighteen? The day of your birthday, I could've been on your doorstep with a plane ticket—if that's what you wanted." Would've been a hell of an expensive gift, but if she'd asked, I would've swung it. Done whatever was necessary.

"I couldn't wait."

"Couldn't or wouldn't?" Because semantics were important.

"Couldn't." Her eyes turned flinty. "Don't ask, Brooklyn. You won't like the answer."

"We still have to deal with the fact you're underage and you ran away." I wanted to believe her when she said she wasn't pregnant, but I'd lied a time or two out of desperation back home. *What else could be that urgent?* I rubbed my face. "Maybe we'll brainstorm when Arthur comes home."

"What's the deal with the two of you?"

"Cheyenne." I injected as much warning as I could. Although I urgently wanted more from Arthur than what we'd done last night, sharing that little tidbit with my baby sister wasn't the answer to getting there. How he'd acted around Cheyenne reinforced the impression Arthur was shy, and I knew how she could tease.

"Fair's fair."

I pursed my lips. "Hardly the same thing. We'll put this discussion on hold. Before lunch, let's organize a grocery delivery."

"I can cook, you know. I didn't want to be domesticated, but Mom insisted I learn and Dad didn't make that optional. So maybe I can stay here in exchange for, like, cooking and cleaning?" She eyed my floor that had, admittedly, a lot of dog hair in the corners.

Cleaning hadn't been the priority this week. When I wasn't doggie-sitting for my clients, I was trying to take care of Arthur without appearing to take care of him. Not hovering, of course. Watching for obstacles, moving things to where they'd be more convenient. Making sure he had something to drink if it was time for his meds. Suggesting he rest when the crease between his ginger eyebrows got deep. Stuff like that.

"I'm not going to turn down your cooking," I said. Cheyenne appeared to need to feel useful. God knew, if I was healthy and staying at someone's house, I'd want to contribute too. "I want to get you a pay-as-you-go phone first thing, though. For safety. We can put it on my credit card." Another expense, but worth it. "Even so, I'd prefer you not leave the house without me. There's always a chance the cops might be looking for you. We need to deal with all this mess."

"When Arthur gets home." She rose. "I'll check out what you've got in the pantry and the fridge, then I'll make a list of everything I need." She was at the baby gate before she turned back. "Thank you."

She looked so heartbreakingly young in that moment. Whatever it took, I swore I'd protect her. "Of course."

After holding my gaze for several moments, she nodded and headed back to the kitchen.

A long time passed before I got up off the floor to arrange midday snacks for the grateful pooches and a treat or two for the cat.

CHAPTER 11
ARTHUR

"You got *shot*!"

I held the phone farther away and frowned at Shane's small image. "Yell louder, why don't you?"

"Fuck you." Shane glared at me from across the ocean. "'I had a *minor incident*,' you said. 'Everything's fine,' you said. A bullet is not fucking minor. And I had to find out about it from Nina."

"Um."

"She assumed you'd told me, like you *should* have. She was showing me video of Foxy, and then she said, 'It's a good thing I took her, since Arthur has his hands full with being shot and all.' I dropped my damned phone."

"What kind of video?" I asked to distract him. "Was it cute?"

"Oh, no, you're not getting off that easy. What the fuck happened? Spill it, Arthur."

I reluctantly told him the basics, emphasizing that the gun was small, the wound was healing, and leaving the concussion as "rung my bell, but no fracture or anything."

When I was done, Shane said, "Holy shit. I'm glad you and Kevin are okay. Did you ever find the dog? Is it safe?"

I laughed, maybe harder than I should've from the ache in my head, but yeah, Shane, Kevin, and I were a lot alike in some ways. "Kevin did."

"That kid." Shane sighed. "I worry about him, you know? Not just walking in front of guys with guns for a dog, but in general. The way the world is."

"Me too." Every time I turned around, someone was in the news crapping on kids like Kevin. Using trans people as the scapegoat for everything, the distraction from the real evils in the world. And there was no way to protect a thirteen-year-old from seeing himself called insane and a threat to kids and a thousand disgusting names. Joe and Alec must be tearing their hair out, unable to stand between hate and their son.

"You don't think he got in that position on purpose?" Shane's voice went low. "Standing in front of a gun, I mean, risking his life?"

"God, no." I thought back. "I hope not... No, I think he was just focused on the poor dog, the same way he always protects anything helpless and scared. Admittedly, he's not the sunny kid I first met a year ago, but he's a teenager now. When I turned thirteen, I was a mess."

"We should try to get him to hang out at the shelter more often," Shane suggested. "He's safe and appreciated with us." His tone changed. "But that doesn't mean you're off the hook. Nina said you're rooming with some guy you don't even know."

"Brooklyn. He's the one I told you about, who helped me when I got...hurt."

"*Shot.*"

"Yeah. Anyhow, he runs a doggie daycare, and he's a good guy, will be a wonderful resource for our adopters who need that service. He's putting me up while my leg gets happier about stairs, and in exchange, we'll stock his brochures and cards at the shelter and recommend his business."

"We'd do that anyway."

"This way, I can say I've checked out the place personally and he's great with the pups and has a clean and safe facility. Win-win." That even sounded logical. *Is that all we're doing?* But memories of last night before Cheyenne's arrival intervened to tell me no, this wasn't just some kind of business arrangement. *God, the mouth on him. And the kind heart…*

"Hmm. Yeah, I guess the stairs to your place would be tough. You know, you're welcome to stay in Theo's house if you want." I noted Shane didn't call it "our house." He loved Theo, without a doubt, but the money difference was still a hurdle.

At least, Brooklyn and I don't have that problem—

Shush. I shied away from even imagining he and I were becoming like Shane and Theo. "I appreciate the offer, but I couldn't drive at first, and Brooklyn, well, offered to give me a ride in the mornings." I wanted to say it was on his way, but of course, it wasn't. He was just that kind. His sister had been smart to run to him.

"Theo would pay for a cab if you change your mind. If you're not comfortable where you are." Shane eyed me closely across the miles.

I was glad of the small screen, where he couldn't puzzle out what was going on in my head. Shane was a sharp guy, his skill at interpreting people's moods honed by his years on the streets. But even he couldn't do much with a three-inch picture. "I'm fine. I like his place, and the dogs are in heaven. But yeah." Of course, Cheyenne changed everything.

"Thanks. If I need an alternative, I'll take you up on that."

"You have the key and the code." He tilted his head. "Are you sure you don't want me to come home? I've done one safari now."

"Not a chance. Neil's doing a great job wrangling extra hours out of the volunteers. We don't actually *need* anyone at the shelter overnight, it was just handy, and I'll be back in my place soon."

"And you really are healing well?"

"Really," I said, crossing my metaphorical fingers, because I could feel a headache looming. They were less frequent, though. I wasn't lying. "I'd never forgive myself if I took you away from the giraffes and leopards."

Shane grinned. "They are awesome. The other morning, we were in the second Jeep on the road approaching the waterhole…"

I listened with half an ear to Shane's excitement, pleased that he seemed happy, and signed off with another promise to let him know if anything changed.

Sticking the phone into my pocket, I pinched the bridge of my nose. My eyes watered as the fluorescent lights strobed in my peripheral vision. Sometimes things were better with my eyes closed, so I did that, groping behind me for the back of a breakroom chair.

"Here."

Neil's voice made me jump, but I kept my eyes shut as he guided me down to the seat. "Thanks."

"Headache? Vertigo? Nausea?" He sounded matter-of-fact. *Thank God for Neil.*

"Yes," I muttered.

His huff of breath wasn't quite a laugh. "Damn. You want to just sit here?"

"Can you get me some water?" I had ibuprofen in my

pocket, but I'd never learned to dry-swallow. Choking as my headache kicked in would probably kill me.

"Sure thing." A moment later he bumped a bottle against my fingers.

"Thanks." I squinted enough to see what I was doing as I opened the cap, took a sip, and tossed back four little tablets of relief. Hopefully. The door to the back of the shelter opened, and the cacophony of barking dogs made me flinch.

"You know what?" Neil said. "Go home and get horizontal."

"The crappy part doesn't last long," I told him, although the downside to fewer episodes was that they'd started hanging on longer. When I told the doc on Friday, she'd mentioned vestibular migraines, and I was determined not to develop those, like I could hold them off by force of will.

"Sharon's leaving in ten minutes. She can give you a ride."

"I don't need a ride."

"Arthur." Neil squeezed my shoulder and when I opened my eyes, he bent to look at me. "You worked all week. Give your body a break. Let the nice volunteer give you a ride home."

I tried to wave him off, but a flash of pain behind my eyes made me grunt and squeeze them shut again.

Neil didn't say, *I told you so.* He just said, "I'll let Sharon know you're riding with her."

This bout seemed to be more headache than the vertigo that could put me on my ass, so I made it out to Sharon's car without making a fool of myself. She drove carefully and didn't make chit-chat, which meant she was my current favorite person.

When we got to Brooklyn's house, she asked if I

needed a hand but I waved her off. "Thanks so much. Remind me to double your salary."

She—being a free volunteer—laughed, as intended, and drove off.

When I used the key Brooklyn had given me to open the front door, I wasn't greeted by any of the dogs. The reason why was probably explained by the happy barks I heard from the backyard.

Xandra sat in the hallway, blue eyes staring at me, then headed toward my room with a flick of her plumy tail. Bed was her favorite thing. Mine too, right now.

As I toed off my shoes, Brooklyn appeared. "Hey, Arthur, you're back—" At my squint and wave, he dropped his voice to a whisper. "—early. Headache?"

I nodded very carefully. "Going to lie down."

"Anything I can do?"

"Nope. Thanks."

I made it into my room. Xandra lay on my pillow, but I shut the door against the dogs. They had Brooklyn, lucky pups, and while Xandra could be quiet, Twain and Eb didn't know the meaning of the word. A little isolation would be perfect right now.

I lay down inch by inch, not jarring myself. Through the throbbing in my head, I noted that my leg really did feel a little better. Maybe trading the crutch for a cane at tomorrow's appointment wasn't a pipe dream. I let Xandra keep my pillow and took the spare, laying my head down beside her. She purred for a moment, loud enough that I almost regretted not shooing her out, but then she quieted, and the murmur of her contentment soothed me. I kept my eyes closed and tried to relax every muscle in my body, as soft distant sounds told me my other fur-babies were well entertained.

Sleeping had seemed unlikely, but at some point, the

meds must've kicked in, because I woke to low afternoon sunlight filtering around the curtains. My headache still lingered, and I flinched at the loud crashing sounds from the living room that'd roused me.

I struggled to my feet and headed out to see what was happening, almost tripping over Twain in the hallway.

Brooklyn and I arrived at the same time, to find Cheyenne sitting on the couch, Eb up on the furniture with his head in her lap, and a movie with some kind of shooting and explosions on the TV.

I flinched and grabbed for the wall as a building blew up in technicolor brightness and sound.

Brooklyn hurried in. "Turn that off!" He snatched the remote from Cheyenne and snapped off the screen.

"Hey! I was watching that." She grabbed the device back and turned it back on, just in time for another rattle of gunfire.

I might've whimpered because Brooklyn looked my way.

"Stop it right now." Brooklyn grabbed Cheyenne's wrist to get the remote, and she shoved him hard.

"Don't you touch me."

"Sorry!" He let go, raising his hands apologetically. "But it's too loud. Arthur has a headache. Turn it off."

"Oh." She glanced my way, then hit the button. "You could've said so."

"I wouldn't have had to if you'd listened to me."

The siblings glared at each other, frowns eerily alike.

I murmured, "Hey. It's okay. Thank you."

Cheyenne pushed up off the couch, displacing Eb's head.

When he didn't get off with her, I pointed at him. "Down. You know the rules. You have lots of soft dog beds." His fondness for digging with his nails before lying down had ruined two couches before I'd reluctantly decided I needed to make that a rule. I definitely didn't want him to destroy Brooklyn's stuff. "Get down. Don't think it's okay just because you can con Cheyenne. I don't want you learning bad habits."

"Sorry," Brooklyn said. "I did tell her, but I guess she forgot."

"*She* might've been too busy cooking dinner to listen." Cheyenne flounced off, at least as much as a teenager could flounce while wearing blue jeans, throwing over her shoulder, "I worked on dinner for an hour. Are you coming to the table?"

I really wasn't sure if my stomach could handle food, but I didn't want to make her think her effort wasn't appreciated. When Brooklyn tilted his head in enquiry at me, I muttered, "Sure."

"I fed the dogs," he added, waiting for me to pass before following close at my side.

"Thank you."

"Couldn't find Xandra."

"She was in with me. I'll get her food later." She needed her med with her dinner, but waiting half an hour wouldn't kill her, even if she'd guilt trip me.

In the kitchen, Cheyenne had set the table for three. She bent over the oven, potholders in her hands. As we approached, she pulled a casserole dish out. "It's tuna-noodle casserole. I made—"

The smell of cooked fish hit me like a punch to the stomach. I gagged, pivoted, and staggered down the hall to the bathroom.

I had no time to close the door, so I could hear Brooklyn say, "That was the last can of the cat's tuna, for her medication."

"Well, how would I know that?" Cheyenne's voice rose.

"And now my cooking makes Arthur puke. I swear, I tried, okay? I just wanted to be helpful." She reached a full-voiced shout. "You have to tell me shit!"

"Don't say *shit*."

"You're not my mother!"

"Keep your voice down, Chey!"

"I'm not *Chey*, and screw you too. If you don't want me here, just say so. I can hitch somewhere else." Stomping footsteps down the hall were followed by the slam of her door.

I winced and clung to the toilet, but having rebelled once, my stomach seemed more settled. I straightened and cupped water in the sink to splash on my face. I hated hearing them fight. Especially since it was all my fault. Without me, they could've been watching a movie and planning to share a nice dinner. Now they were screaming at each other, and Cheyenne was talking about risking her safety again.

Behind me, Brooklyn said, "Sorry about that. She didn't mean to make you feel bad."

"Of course not." I rinsed my mouth too, and added, "Probably a good thing I'm moving out, though."

"You're what?"

"Moving out. This was only temporary. I mean, I really appreciated it, more than I can say. But I talked to Shane today, and he asked me to stay at his place. To, um, look after his plants. I promised I would, now my leg's healing. Theo knows a cab driver who'll give me a deal on rides to the shelter in the mornings." I was lying through my teeth by now.

"But I don't mind."

"No, seriously, this is good timing. You and Cheyenne need some space without a stranger around, to get to know each other again and figure out her issues."

"You're not a stranger."

"I am to her." To Brooklyn too, really. It'd only been what, ten days? It might've felt like we'd known each other forever, but that wasn't objective reality. "I meant to pack earlier, but my headache slowed me down."

"You didn't say anything." In the mirror, Brooklyn's face over my shoulder looked sad. Even hurt.

"Sorry about that. You've been wonderful. Awesome. The best, really." I cleared my throat to quit throwing out ridiculous adjectives. "The dogs have loved it. But you have a business to run and you need your space. And Cheyenne's a kid. She needs her brother. It's time for me to get out of your hair so you can focus on what's important."

"You're important too."

I waved that off. He had to say it, of course. Brooklyn was such a kind man, he'd never let me think badly of myself. "Sure. But priorities, right? I have a ride coming later to get me to Shane and Theo's." Another lie, but I would, as soon as I figured out who to call. "I just need to pack."

"Are you sure? You look—" He hesitated and I bet he was censoring the words, *like crap*. "—tired. Wouldn't you rather sleep here and think about it in the morning?"

I was tempted, but then something thudded in Cheyenne's room, like she'd thrown something against the wall, and I knew what I had to do. "No, I'm good. Just give me an hour. You need to figure out what you're going to say to Cheyenne. After you let her calm down, because my experience with sisters says do *not* push her right now unless she tries to head out the door."

Brooklyn glanced down the hall. "You're probably right."

I straightened, settled my crutch under my arm, and

turned, plastering a smile on my face. "I wish I had other words of wisdom, but I don't. Good luck."

"Uh, thanks."

Brooklyn trailed after me as I went to my room. I didn't want him to watch me, didn't want him to see whatever expressions my face was going to have as I got ready to leave this little haven, so I said, "I'm going to change clothes," and shut the door in his face. Gently, slowly, but unmistakably.

Once I heard his steps recede down the hall, I got out my phone. *James?* No, he and Colin would be in the middle of feeding the kids dinner. *Neil?* He'd already worked a full day, part of it making up for me slacking off. In the end, I called Joe, Kevin's dad.

"Hey," he said. "What's up?"

"I need a huge favor," I told him. "I need a ride for me and the dogs and Xandra over to Shane's place in about an hour."

"I thought you were staying with that guy from the shooting. Did something go wrong?"

"No, no." I tried to sound casual. "Just, his little sister turned up and she really needs the room. And I have Shane's place as a permanent invitation. So I'm going to move out of Brooklyn's house and give his sister my space." More half-truths, but I think I sold it.

Joe said, "Sure. I'll bring the big SUV, if we're moving all the dogs. Do you want extra hands to carry things? Alec could come."

"No." One person witnessing my pathetic retreat was enough. I hadn't brought much stuff over, because Brooklyn already had all the dog beds and toys and bowls my little family needed, and I'd gotten by with a few changes of clothes. "We should be good."

"Okay. Text me the address. I'll be there in an hour."

"Thanks. I really appreciate it."

"Hey, friends and family, right? We do what we have to. I'm sure Brooklyn appreciates it."

Family. We do what we have to. Not my family, and apparently not most of Brooklyn's but at least he and his sister would have a second chance to forge those bonds. "Right. Thanks."

An hour later, I stood on Brooklyn's front step with Eb and Twain on leashes. A grumpy Xandra and even more grumpy Chili were already in their travelling crates in the back of Joe's SUV with my bag. I wanted to just go, get out of there, lick my wounds and figure out how to move on in private.

But I owed Brooklyn more than that. He leaned against the doorframe, one arm braced on the wood, the pose seeming artificial like a fake "handsome man at ease in the sunset glow" photo. The late sun picked out blond highlights in his hair and scruff, and shadowed the hollow of his throat. *I know what his skin tastes like there.*

Not a helpful thought. I said, "I really appreciate everything. You practically saved my life. I hope things go well with Cheyenne."

"Me too," he muttered, glancing over his shoulder. She still hadn't emerged from her room, even to assuage curiosity about me thumping around. "How's your head? And stomach?"

"Better," I reassured him, which was true. "I'm not going to puke in Joe's car, I promise."

"I'm glad." He hesitated. "You'll let me know if I can help? With the shelter, I mean."

"Or if I can help you," I said. "With your sister or anything."

"Sure."

"Yeah." My headache might've eased, but the pain in

my chest was making up for it. Couldn't blame that on the trauma, though. I held out my hand, as if to a stranger.

Brooklyn closed his long fingers around mine and squeezed.

I want to see you again. You should come visit Chili. Call me sometime. I'm going to miss you. I couldn't get the words out of my tight throat.

I gave that kind, sweet, gorgeous, frowning man a nod, and crutched off down his driveway to settle the dogs in the back seat for the ride to Shane's.

Joe was blessedly quiet for most of the drive, but as we turned down Shane's street, he asked, "You sure you know what you're doing? He didn't look like a guy who wanted you to go."

Maybe not. Trading easy hook-up sex for a difficult sister probably isn't on Brooklyn's favorite things list either. But he's not a man to dodge his responsibilities, and all I can do to help is clear the way. "Yeah," I said. "I know what I'm doing."

CHAPTER 12

BROOKLYN

"HE DIDN'T HAVE TO GO." CHEYENNE EYED ME AS WE SAT at the dinner table. She'd eaten about half the tuna casserole on her plate.

I'd managed to push mine around a lot but, despite having spent the entire day with six dogs, I wasn't hungry. "He did have to go." I sighed and put my fork at the five o'clock position. "You…" *Made it impossible to stay? Were horrible? Gave him no choice?* I didn't finish the sentence.

"You didn't tell me that he had a headache. Or that the last tuna was for his cat. If you don't *talk* to me, then how am I supposed to know things?" She pouted.

"Cheyenne…" At least I remembered to use her full name. Breaking myself of the habit of using the nickname I gave her when she was little was proving tougher than I thought.

"Brooklyn…" She arched an eyebrow. Then relented by wincing. "I'm cockblocking you, aren't I?"

"Where did you learn that word?"

"Oh God. Just because I lived with Mom and Dad

doesn't mean I never went to school. Or encountered books."

"Books in the library?" Because the Piperston library commission had, at least when I'd been there, been run by some Baptists who took exception to every book that wasn't about the resurrection, Armageddon, or maybe cookbooks, woodcraft, similar shit. No fiction that wasn't squeaky fluffy, no real history, definitely no current affairs. Not all the families were religious—but none of them wanted their kids contaminated by woke global world views.

Once I'd been booted and had moved into the outside world, I'd discovered how very warped my family's perspective had been. I might've been curious as a teen, but perhaps a bit wary, before I'd encountered real life outside the community. After? I knew I'd never go back. Never espouse those views again.

She rolled her eyes. "No, you dumb fuck. Not in the library."

I glared. "Look, I get that you've never been allowed to swear before—"

"And yet, I did anyway."

"—but you're not welcome to come into my house and drop curse words whenever you feel like it. Especially when we've got company."

"Arthur."

"Or anyone else. Classy is important—"

"You swear."

I ground my teeth. Because she was right, of course. She was usually more right than wrong. "Whether I do or not isn't the point. This is my house. These are my rules. I never swear around clients, for example. Or anyone I don't know."

She harumphed.

Breathe. She's been through a horrible—

My phone buzzed with an incoming call. *Arthur? Maybe he wants to let me know that he's settled and is doing okay. That he wants to alleviate my fears. Because he's kind and considerate like that.*

I checked the screen.

New York. Unknown number.

That meant it was more likely spam than a business call, but I couldn't neglect a potential customer. "Brooklyn's Doggie Daycare," I answered. "Can I help you?"

I was braced for a sales pitch about insurance or new windows, but there was just silence on the other end, followed by dead air as they ended the call.

"Wrong number I guess." I hoped. I couldn't rule out someone from back home, trying to find me, but surely then they'd have asked about Cheyenne. Must've been coincidence. "Where was I?"

"Telling me how the dinner I cooked was so amazing that you couldn't eat any." She started to rise.

"Cheyenne!"

She plopped back down on her butt.

"I've let it go so far, but we need to talk."

She pretended to check a wristwatch that she didn't have. "It's been less than twelve hours since our last heart-to-heart."

Shit. "That's true. But I still don't have a grasp on why you're here. What was so urgent that you couldn't wait. I need more."

"You said we could talk about it with Arthur."

I barked out a laugh. "First you drive him away with your antics, and now you want—"

"What antics?"

"You slammed your door, threw a shoe at the wall and made a dent, Cheyenne."

She crossed her arms in clear defiance.

"You're not four anymore. You've got your words, and I'd appreciate if you would use them. So, if you could just—"

"I'm supposed to marry Harvey Jefferson. On my eighteenth birthday."

My jaw dropped. "What the fuck?"

"Yeah, exactly. So, like, that wasn't going to happen. But they weren't giving up."

"So you ran?"

"Well, I was planning to, if I could get away. But then Mom tried to bribe me with a fancy wedding dress, not just something Mary-Sue would sew. She was heading to New York to pick up some radiation-counter thing Dad wanted, because he said it was too fragile to ship. So, she offered to take me along, and we'd go round the consignment stores and find a real dress. While we were in New York City, I gave her the slip and...you know the rest."

I blinked. "Harvey? Isn't he already married?" The town didn't endorse bigamy—that I knew of, anyway.

"Nancy died last month while losing their third child. Like, super tragic. But that's not enough reason for me to marry a thirty-year-old."

She said *thirty* like the word was dirty or something.

I wasn't going to point out I was thirty. Or that I'd gone to school with Harvey. To someone seventeen, I'm sure we both looked old.

He'd been a nasty bully back then. I'd been surprised, when I'd been home, to hear he'd married Nancy—a sweet-tempered young woman in our sister Nevada's class. Cheyenne had brought me up to speed on the insular community and everything that'd happened in the twelve years I'd been gone, while I had nothing to do but lie around and heal. In some ways, the list had been long. On the other hand, since just about everything was predictable, she managed the recitation in less than an hour.

None of them mattered to me, and Harvey less than any, as long as that cruel bastard was out of my life. "You can't marry him."

She rolled her eyes, the *duh* unspoken. Still, she hunched her shoulders. "You know I wouldn't have had a choice."

Even knowing how serious our parents were about the community, it was hard to believe they'd hold her there by force. I'd gotten out. Except she was a girl, expected to obey, and in fact, I hadn't escaped. I'd been expelled. Therein lay the difference. If Cheyenne thought they'd force her, she was quite possibly right. I drew a deep breath. "You really don't want to marry him, right?"

Her eyes widened, as if she questioned my sanity. "Hard no."

"I'm relieved to hear that. But I needed you to say it. Because if we're going to fight to keep you here, you'll need to be crystal clear with everyone you speak to about this. If you waver—"

"I won't."

No, I didn't figure she would. With her intuitive nature, she'd likely figured out early on that Harvey wasn't a man to be crossed. Just…bad news. He was being groomed to be a leader and had some of the sharpest prepper skills— good with electronics, methodical about rotating his supplies, the most fortified homestead, and a top-notch sharpshooter. Plus, whatever other resources he'd accumulated that I hadn't figured out while I'd been home recovering. "Okay. We need to see a lawyer."

"Why? Can't I just stay here? They'll never find me."

"Cheyenne, *you* found me. Even if I take my photo off the website, you're right that my name isn't all that common. I've never tried to hide, and I'm not going to now. To keep you safe, we need to seek some kind of court order that allows you to stay, but in my custody."

"I want to be an emancipated minor." She jutted her chin.

"If you were younger, then maybe. Although I'd still try to convince you to let me be responsible for you." *As much as anyone can be.* "I'd guess that by the time we get permission for you to be emancipated, you'll be eighteen anyway. I think you need a job and stuff first." Or at least that was what I assumed. Once we'd cleaned up from dinner, I was going to pull out my laptop and do a bunch of research. "Look, one of my clients, Phillip..." I rolled my eyes upward. "He was worried about custody of his dog if anything happened to him. He was super stressed about it. He said this great local lawyer, Wynn Cavannah, arranged documentation to ensure Wally would go to Phillip's boyfriend, Jeremy. I mean, I sure as shit hope nothing happens to Phillip, but life's unpredictable like that. And, together, they rescued Flora—"

"Brooklyn?"

"Hmm?"

"You're rambling. I don't need to know about Phillip, Wally, Jeremy, and Flora."

I squinted. "Yeah, probably not. But I'm saying we need a lawyer to make an application to the court for me to be granted custody. Your birthday's in less than two months, but that's long enough for Mom and Dad to demand you back."

"I'm aware." She rolled her eyes.

If she was half this difficult with our parents, I had an

inkling why they wanted to marry her off. Although irritating didn't mean I was put off by her defiance. That spark was part of who my little sister was. Our parents with their demands for complete submission to the head of the household? Yeah, I could see my dad and sister clashing. Something told me she wasn't meek and mild at home either, no matter how well she'd faked it when I was back there before.

We need a plan. "Let me do some research, and I'll call Mr. Cavannah first thing in the morning."

"You've got dogs coming first thing in the morning. Is Arthur bringing his dogs back? Are they part of your crew? It's super cool that you get to work with dogs all day. Can I work for you? That could be my emancipation job, right?"

"Yes, it's cool. No, I don't normally care for Arthur's dogs. Maybe we should stick to the topic at hand."

She rose, grabbing my plate as well as hers.

"I can help." I stood as well.

She shot me *that* look. "You go do whatever research you have to do. I'll clean up the kitchen."

Tidying up was my least favorite task, but if someone else cooked, I always pitched in to help. "But—"

"We agreed I could stay here if I cook and clean. I cooked and now I'm cleaning. I'm also going to run the vacuum through the place." She turned and headed to the kitchen.

I let out a long exhalation. We hadn't actually resolved anything. Or had we? At least I knew why she ran. I was going to research…

I headed to my little alcove where I had my desk, filing cabinet, and an uncomfortable chair. All in a little crammed space without a window. An incentive to do all my paperwork quickly, and move back into the light. Still, I flipped on the lamp and booted up my computer.

At the last minute, I remembered to select incognito. Not a guarantee I couldn't be traced, but an added layer of protection.

I started with researching California custody arrangements and, as I'd suspected, I needed a lawyer. I located Mr. Cavannah's office phone number and left a long, rambling message. Somehow, that felt like a huge accomplishment.

Next, I ran a search for Cheyenne.

Nothing.

I was surprised. Not that I couldn't find anything from her ordinary life—our town barely interacted with the outside world and we were paranoid as hell, so things like social media footprints were nonexistent. If Cheyenne had any sort of online account—and I couldn't conceive of how she'd be able to create, let alone maintain one—how could she access it? Doing anything under the eagle eye of the librarians would be risky. Our family had a computer, but the laptop was completely under my father's control. She might've been allowed to type a term paper, but that would've been it. And if she had an account under an alias, I didn't stand a chance of locating it.

No, what I found really interesting was I couldn't find a missing-person bulletin. The quickest way to locate someone these days was to post it on the internet. That shit went viral all the time. Beautiful young woman like her? Missing for nine days? Catnip.

Yet I couldn't find a single mention of her anywhere.

My phone buzzed.

I almost ignored it.

Wynn Cavannah.

Shit, almost missed him.

I swiped to accept. "Hello?"

"Brooklyn West?"

"Yes, sir. I'm Brooklyn."

"I hope you don't mind me calling. I saw your message and figured you'd probably still be awake."

Given I'd sent the message about twenty minutes ago, that'd been a good bet. "I didn't mean to disturb you."

"You're not. My husband's out tonight, and I've been wandering around the lighthouse. My phone notified me of a message on my business line, and I wondered if it might be important. Sounds like you're in a bit of a difficult situation."

Since I'd word-vomited Cheyenne's predicament to his voicemail, he was aware of just about everything. I cleared my throat. "Can you help us?"

"Yes, I believe I can. You said something about an in-home doggie daycare business?"

Had I?

Word vomit.

"Uh, yeah."

"Would it be okay if I came to your house tomorrow? I like to get out of the office sometimes, and I have to say I like dogs. If it's okay for me to be there, of course."

George, Hiro, Poppy, and Jett. No one shy with strangers. No Maisie and none of Arthur's dogs, unless he changed his mind. For a moment, I hoped and crossed my fingers—*don't think about Arthur. Focus.* "I'd really appreciate if you could come here. Cheyenne and I will be home all day."

"Text me your address. I'll come first thing, say nine a.m.? Then we can get a petition going with the courts. I think you've got a strong case, but I have a lengthy list of questions to ask both of you."

"I—" I swallowed hard. "I'm worried about her."

"You have the right to be. Legally, you should be calling your parents and letting them know that she's safe and with you—but I understand why you haven't. If you can establish it's for her safety, that protects you. That's why I want to put a priority on gathering information and then get an emergency request in to the court tomorrow."

After a moment, the tightness in my chest eased a bit. "Yes. Thank you." I had no idea how I'd pay him, but it didn't matter—whatever it took to keep my sister safe.

"Nine o'clock all right?"

"Yes. Perfect. Thank you."

"Good night, Brooklyn."

"Good night, Mr. Cavannah."

"Just Wynn. We're going to be working pretty closely together, so Wynn's fine."

My heart lightened a little more. "Yes, thank you."

He cut the line.

I texted him my address, and then I stared at my phone. My first instinct was to call Arthur. To share this news with him. To get his perspective on things. But he'd chosen to leave and disentangle himself from this mess. I didn't blame him. The West family could be a disaster at times.

Still, I popped off a quick text asking if he was settled and how his menagerie was doing.

When I went to bed an hour later, he still hadn't responded.

CHAPTER 13
ARTHUR

"You're right," I told Twain, thudding my shoulder into the wall to avoid whacking him with my cane on my way to Shane's front door. The bell rang again, and I winced. "It's my own stupid fault my head hurts." He whined and hovered at my heels.

I'd come back to Shane's after my doctors' appointments and lazed around all afternoon, instead of going to the shelter. The surgeon had said my thigh was healing well. No more bandages and I could shower again if I wanted to. Which, heck yes! First thing I did when I got back. And she let me trade the crutch for a cane, which felt a bit ambitious right now as I tripped over my damned dog for the second time.

The less said about the neurologist the better. I'd lied through my teeth about how tolerable my symptoms were, which was ridiculous—I knew that—but I didn't want to be a burden or an object of pity. But lying also meant I didn't have any new medications for the next time pain and vertigo hit. Today was tolerable, but I'd been kicking myself for the past three hours.

"Coming!" I yelled, at a longer buzz of Shane's doorbell.

When I reached the foyer, I looked out the tiny window, since I didn't have the link to the doorbell cam, and then cracked the door open. "James. What are you doing here?"

"Mama sent me." He squinted in the late afternoon sun and hefted two bags of groceries. "Are you gonna let me in?"

"Of course. Just got to corral the pups." I caught Twain's collar with one hand and dropped my cane to hold Eb's with the other. Chili hated strangers, so she wouldn't come to the sound of the door, and Xandra was basking in the back window ledge. "Come inside quick."

James ducked around the door and shut it. He had a dog too, so he knew the drill. Eb gave a happy bark and pulled toward the bags, sniffing noisily. James raised the sacks high. "Not for you, greedy guts."

"Wait," I said, as James headed for the kitchen with the bags raised above Eb's nose level. "How does your mama even know where I am? I haven't told her yet. And why send you?" I bent, fished my cane off the floor, and followed him.

"Mama knows everything." James flashed me a bright grin as he set the bags on the counter. "In this case, Joe told Kevin that he drove you and the menagerie to Shane's, and Kevin told Danny when they met while out on a morning dog walk. Don't ask me why the topic came up, but small town, you know. Danny told Mama, and she got hold of me to ask if you'd likely have food in the house, since Shane expected to be gone a month."

"Uh." I pulled my phone out.

James and Danny's mama had blown up my phone the first couple of days after my accident, making sure I was doing okay, and she'd texted daily since. Even offered to come down that second day, or to send one of the extended family to help out, till I'd convinced her I was fine. I was just one of James's many friends, but Mama treated me like family. Even though she had a whole lot of real family who needed her more than I did. "She didn't ask me."

"Of course not." James began putting milk and eggs and cheese in the fridge. "Mama's no fool. She knows if she asked you, you'd say you were fine, great, don't bother. So she just skipped the middleman and sent me."

"Oh." I sat down with a thump on a kitchen chair. Eb came over to lick my wrist before focusing back on the tall Black dude with all the food. Eb had his priorities.

James glanced over his shoulder. "Looks like she was right. You have next to nothing in here. Some condiments. And cat food."

"I didn't have time to shop yet." Or energy. "I had appointments."

"With the doctors? How'd that go?"

"I'm healing. I get to ditch the crutch, but still not drive for three more weeks, which sucks."

"You know Colin and I are home most days, right? Happy to give you a ride wherever."

James worked his computer-security business from home. Colin, while mostly recovered from his liver transplant surgery, had enough money to be a stay-at-home foster dad. Which didn't mean they weren't busy with those kids and that business, especially first thing in the morning. "Thanks."

"Thanks, he says," James muttered to the carton of yogurt in his hand. "But will he call? No, he will not."

"I would if I needed to."

"Exhibit A." James swept his hand up and down the

mostly empty fridge, put the yogurt away, and closed the door.

"I could've gone shopping. It's not that late."

"Hey, you're lucky I dissuaded Mama from coming down here and cooking for you."

I'd never turn down Mama's awesome cooking, but she had her heart problems and her family. I wouldn't want her to stress herself. "Thank you. Anyhow, I could go out to eat."

"Tell me that scowl on your face isn't because your leg's killing you." He pulled out a chair and straddled it backward, arms crossed on the back, gaze fixed on me. "So. Why are you here instead of at Brooklyn's? Because I heard the way you talked about him. You liked him."

I looked down at Twain, ruffling his silky ears. "Yeah, but his teenage sister arrived. It's all a big thing. She needed his time and space, and there wasn't room for me."

"And when he settles up with his sister, you'll go back?"

"I'll be healed up enough to go back to my own place by then."

"Aaargh! You'll at least call him and ask him out? Date the guy?"

I shrugged. "Maybe." If he called me, if he wanted to. I wouldn't hold my breath.

I spent way too much of my time asking people to do things for me—adopt this needy dog, donate this money, mention the shelter in that story or blog or website. As much as I *adored* having the shelter and space to help so many more pets, and as much as Neil took a lot of the begging duties off me, it still felt stifling. The dogs and cats and rabbits and iguana and all were innocent and important. I could ask for them. Asking for myself was one step too far.

Anyhow, Brooklyn was new in town. He hadn't met

many people yet. Gaynor Beach was full of hot gay men. Also kind gay men, and funny, smart, going-places gay men. All sorts of guys who were closer to his age, and didn't come with a pack of rescue dogs and a job that ate their every waking moment. He could do better.

James was shaking his head. "Arthur, we've been friends for what, four years now? I bet I know what's going on in your mind."

"Hah." I straightened. "Did you guess I was debating what I should make for dinner?"

"Sure you were. Have you talked to Brooklyn today, or texted him?"

"We texted last night." Or at least, he had. I'd left it on read, because I'd been tired, headachy, and emotional, and likely to say things I didn't mean to, if I'd gotten started. And then in the morning, it was embarrassing that I hadn't at least said thank you. So I put it aside to think about later, and the longer I waited, the more embarrassing it got.

"Aren't you curious how things went with that teen sister?"

"I guess." Yeah, I was. I liked Cheyenne, despite how clearly she didn't want me around. She had spunk, and from what little Brooklyn had told me about his parents, I had mad respect for her, keeping that independent spirit despite them.

"Give me your phone." James held out a big hand.

"Why?"

He waved at me. "Trust me."

"Okay." I touched the lock and passed my phone over.

"I won't look at the messages before, I promise."

"You can." There was nothing questionable down in words.

"Really? That's disappointing. Okay, how about this?" He recited aloud as he typed. "'Hey there, sorry I left you on read last night—'" He aimed a narrowed frown at me. "'I was really tired. Had errands this morning but I wanted to know how—'" He paused typing. "What's the sister's name?"

"Cheyenne."

"Really? And he's Brooklyn? Their parents had a theme." He went back to typing. "'—how Cheyenne is doing. And how you're doing. Let me know if there's anything I can do to help.'" He eyed me. "Is that okay?"

It was what I should've sent if I didn't have my head a long way up my ass. The click of small nails in the hall made me say, "Add, 'Chili misses you.'"

"She does? That little four-legged viper doesn't miss anyone."

"She's not that bad. And she really likes Brooklyn."

"Wow, he must be a saint. Done." James typed, hit send, and passed the phone back to me.

Brooklyn's not a saint, but he is a good man. I missed him a lot in that moment. Missed his dimpled smile across the table and the sound of his voice and his hand under my elbow when I overbalanced.

Before I could put my phone away, it chimed. The name at the top said *Brooklyn*.

> **Brooklyn**
> We're making progress. Had a decent chat, talked to a lawyer. How are you doing? Did you have your doctor's appointment? What did they say?

James caught my wrist and tipped the phone toward him so he could read the screen. "That doesn't look like a guy who's not interested."

"I guess."

He stood, pushed the chair in, and pointed a finger at

me. "Text him back or call him, whatever. And eat. Or I'll sic Mama on you."

"Oh no! Threats!" I managed a smile.

"Believe it." He hesitated. "You know we're doing this because we care about you, yeah?"

"I know." Meeting James, back when we'd both struggled to finish that 5K charity run, was one of the best things that'd ever happened to me.

"Okay. I'll let myself out. You touch base with your guy."

He's not my guy. Even if I wished he was. Eb and Twain followed James to the door, but I trusted him to let himself out safely and make sure the door was latched with my pups on the correct side.

My phone pinged again. Brooklyn hadn't waited for my answer.

> How's Chili taking the change of venue?

James was right. I couldn't pretend Brooklyn was just being polite.

I replied,

> She's fine. Misses you. She sniffed around the place and whined at the front door last night. Is Cheyenne okay?

> Will be, I think. My parents don't deserve to get her back. Hopefully my lawyer can make that happen

I did a quick check of my contacts, then offered,

If he can't, there was a lawyer, Wynn Cavannah, who helped us with the shelter. He seemed really smart

Small world. That's who I hired. Or small town, I guess

I smiled.

Yeah. Small town

Which made me think of Shane, James, Mama, Joe and Kevin, Danny, plus Neil and all the volunteers, helping me out. There were good sides to that small-town feel.

We kept on texting, ordinary stuff. I told him I'd swapped the crutch for a cane, and he sent me a champagne bottle gif, which I told him was premature. He sent me a brief video of Poppy romping with Jett, while a new little dog lurked in the corner of the yard.

I asked,

Who's the new baby?

Sadie. It's her first time here. She's very shy with people, but the other dogs seem to perk her up

I peered closer at the screen.

What kind of dog is she? A terrier mix of some kind?

Brooklyn called me on video chat and after a second of hesitation, I switched over. "Not sure," he said, aiming his camera at the little dog to give me a better look.

She had wiry beige-and-white hair, half-flopped ears, and a long, pointed nose. From the little I could see, she seemed thin, perhaps ten pounds in weight. When the other two romped past, they dwarfed her.

Brooklyn guessed, "Maybe some Maltese? The woman who brought her just said 'a little mutt.'"

I flinched. "That's not very kind." Even if it was descriptive.

"Yeah, I didn't like the owner much. She didn't even say goodbye to Sadie like most people do, but she signed off on the fee schedule."

"How long do you have Sadie?"

"Technically, she was supposed to go home an hour ago. The owner's late."

I frowned down at the screen.

Brooklyn aimed the camera at where Sadie wagged her moth-eaten tail when Jett paused his backyard-world domination zoomies to sniff noses with her. At least she looked happier. But then as Brooklyn approached with his phone, her ears went down and she backed off a couple of steps.

I said, "Yeah, nervous baby."

"I'm going to try some more treats. I want her owner to see her having fun so she can come back and romp with the herd."

Chili suddenly barked down the hall, bolted into the kitchen, and charged toward me, her little feet scrabbling on the tiles. When she reached me, she bounced up and down and whined loudly.

"Is that Chili?" Brooklyn asked.

At the sound of Brooklyn's voice, Chili began barking louder. I flinched. "Hush, baby." That worked about as well as expected. "You need to see Brooklyn?" I tilted the phone. "Here, dude, tell this dog everything's fine and you

155

haven't forgotten her."

Brooklyn laughed and began crooning to my dog. The view on the screen switched to his front camera and there he was. I hadn't forgotten what he looked like in twenty hours, but something about seeing him there in his familiar yard in the October sunshine hit me under the ribs. I *wanted* him.

Wanted his soft voice as he teased both Chili and Sadie, murmuring to the little white terrier that if she learned to be a drama queen like Chili, she could have all the treats and attention.

Wanted his silky, straight hair that flopped over his forehead, a texture my fingertips vividly remembered.

I wanted to kiss those dimples and that mouth, and to feel the scritch of his stubble on my skin. Wanted to give him beard-burn in all the right places.

Sitting there in Shane's kitchen, I longed to be in that backyard with an intensity that took my breath away. My dick went hard and my hands shook. I was about to say something—don't ask me what—when, off camera, Cheyenne called, "Hey, that lawyer guy is back at the door. Do you want me to let him in, or what?"

Her voice dumped a bucket of cold water on me. Of course, I wasn't going to run over there and kiss Brooklyn. Of course, he had other important things to do. I hadn't really forgotten, just set it out of my mind for a moment.

"I'll let you go," I said.

"Sorry." He stood, taking the phone with him so I got a swooping look at the kennels behind him. "I have to see what he says. Chat later, maybe?"

"Sure," I told him. I wouldn't hold my breath, or expect too much, but if he did message, or call? "You know where to find me." I tapped the red button.

CHAPTER 14

BROOKLYN

I STARED AT WYNN ACROSS MY DINING ROOM TABLE. FOR A moment, when he'd showed up at my door that morning, I'd been intimidated by the big, bald-headed lawyer who looked more like a biker than an intellectual. But his steady gaze and kind eyes had won me over. He'd gathered a lot of information and headed out to "see what he could put into motion."

Now, seated across from him again, I didn't like what he had to say. "What do you mean she can't just tell the courts that she wants to stay with me and that she isn't safe with our parents?" I hated referring to them as *our* since I'd long ago given up ownership of them. As they'd given up ownership of me—unless money was involved, of course.

"First, you're supposed to have been residents of California for six months to petition California courts." Wynn's eyes shone with compassion. The man had a sturdiness about him that I respected—but that didn't, in this moment, ease my nerves.

"Uh…" I wracked my brain. "We're in October. I

arrived early March…" My panicked brain couldn't do math.

"That's more than six months. But you'll need proof."

I leapt from the chair at the dining room table. "I have my short-term lease from the first place I rented…" I shouted that as I headed for my alcove. Thank Christ I kept everything organized, because thirty seconds later, I had the document in my hand and was heading back to the table.

"Do you think I should feed Sadie?" Cheyenne glanced toward the family room.

I can't forget about the dog. I turned to Wynn. "Do you mind if I try calling her owner? She was due almost two hours ago." I tried not to nag owners, but I was getting worried.

He waved me to do so. "You have a right to be concerned. I hope nothing's happened to her."

"Food?" My sister gazed imploringly at me.

"I'll ask when I get hold of the owner. We have more tuna, right?"

"You bought a six-pack of tuna tins when we did the grocery order."

"Maybe find one but don't open it yet. The owner said she didn't have allergies, so she should be fine." I didn't like to disrupt feeding routines, but the dog might be truly hungry by now. "And don't feed her without me there. You getting bitten is not going to earn me brownie points with the courts, either." The little dog was fine with other dogs, but her nippiness toward humans worried me.

Wynn glanced up from the laptop he was busy working on, where tabs were open to a mountain of paperwork. "You'd be correct with that assertion." He was about to resume typing when he cocked his head. "Do you think the dog's been abandoned?"

158

I shook my head. "No. I mean, I doubt it? Cases like that are damn rare." I belonged to an online group of other daycare owners. Only two had mentioned this ever happening. Both times, the dogs had been older and in need of advanced medical care. Although, *my bad*, both daycare operators warned new people starting in the business to always check the ID of the owner at first drop off and confirm all their pertinent details. Which, in my dealing with Cheyenne's crisis this morning, I hadn't remembered to do. "I'll call."

After snagging the intake form for Sadie, I stepped into the kitchen and yanked my phone from my back pocket. In retrospect, the woman hadn't put much on the form that was helpful—no second contacts at all, no email. Again, she'd been in a rush and I'd been distracted. *Have to do better in the future. She was likely delayed or in a car accident or something...* I entered the number into my phone and dialed.

"We're sorry, the number you have dialed is not in service. Please hang up and try again."

I stared at the phone.

The message began to repeat, so I disconnected the line and checked the phone number.

Dialed it again, putting in each digit carefully.

Got the same automated message.

Four times.

Although much of the writing on the form was chicken scratch—legible but barely—the phone number was clear enough. No chance of an incorrect digit.

Fuck. "Uh, I just need to check something on my computer." Like googling the woman and finding her ASAP.

Cheyenne appeared. "Sadie needs food. So do we. Do you want me to whip up some chicken salad sandwiches?"

"God, that would be amazing." Grilled cheese at lunch was a long-distant memory. "And see if Wynn wants some?" The urge to say Mr. Cavannah overwhelmed me, but I managed to follow the lawyer's directive.

"You're worried. Did the owner not answer?"

"I'm sure she just reversed some digits. And she's been detained. By a car accident or a health crisis, or even just job overtime."

Cheyenne arched an eyebrow.

Fuck. "I need to run a quick search."

"Okay." She headed toward the fridge and retrieved the rotisserie chicken we'd bought with the grocery order.

I headed to my alcove. Instead of sitting, though, I snagged the fully charged laptop and brought it back to my large dining room table. I'd thought the tabletop too big when I bought it—because when was I going to entertain ten people? Now, as Wynn spread everything out and Cheyenne was bringing food plus my stuff? Not so enormous.

After fifteen minutes, I sighed. "I think the name she gave was fake. Or she's got a zero digital footprint. I suppose that's possible. I mean, Cheyenne doesn't have one…"

Wynn met my gaze. "I don't imagine the police would bother to investigate, but that intake form might have actual fingerprints."

"Yeah." I snorted at the idea of the cops taking the time to fingerprint my doggie paperwork. "Not the crime of the century, even if Sadie was stolen. I'm going to check the missing dog posts."

"You think she was stolen?" Cheyenne entered carrying one plate piled high with sandwiches, another with cut vegetables and three little containers of salad dressing. She put them on the table. "Hold that thought." She exited the room and was back fifteen seconds later with three plates. "Grab a container of dressing, your veggies, and then sandwiches." She nodded to me. "Wynn said he's fine with this."

"Grateful, in fact." Wynn took some veggies.

"I doubt she was stolen," I said. "She's not some fancy purebred. Unless it was a family revenge thing, like getting back at an ex. I still think the owner's just late, but it's weird that the phone number's not in service, the address seems to link to a different name, and there's nothing about her online."

Wynn nodded. "Starts to feel more than coincidence. You didn't see ID?"

"No." I groaned. "I should've. I know that. But I was busy, and people love their pets, you know? A bounced payment sometimes happens, but I don't usually have to worry they're not the real owner or won't come back."

"What do we do now?" Cheyenne scurried to the kitchen and came back with a glass of chocolate milk for herself. A treat she never got at home, so I'd happily bought her some. I could worry about how much junk food she was consuming later.

"You're right of course." I took a sip of my water and kind of wished it was whisky—even though I rarely drank. And certainly wouldn't as long as Cheyenne's situation was up in the air. "Well, for now, we'll just wait. After we've eaten, we'll need to feed Sadie. And the owner might still show up, the number might be a mistake." *I can hope.*

"Let me know if you have problems with the owner and need legal advice." Wynn snagged a sandwich. "Thank you so much." He inclined his head to Cheyenne.

She beamed. "My pleasure. You're going to help me stay out of my parent's clutches." She nudged the serving plate toward me and started pulling the crust off her sandwich.

I grabbed a sandwich and selected carrot slices, celery, and pieces of red pepper from the neatly arranged veggies. My favorites. Cheyenne was pulling out all the stops to seem helpful. I offered my sister the best smile I could muster.

We ate in silence—likely each contemplating what would come next. In the next room, Sadie whined a few times, then went back to her silence. Poor pup probably was getting hungry.

Wynn finished first. He wiped his mouth and fingers with a napkin and moved over to his laptop. "Okay. So Cheyenne hasn't been in the state of California for six months yet—"

"I could *say* I have. It'd by their word against mine." Cheyenne gave an unconvincing grin. "I could say I was hanging out on the streets in LA."

I kept a sigh to myself. "The entire town of Piperston could attest to you being there two weeks ago. As well as school records."

"Those could all be falsified." She jutted her chin.

Wynn shook his head. "Do not begin by lying to the courts. School records could easily be entered into the record, and their veracity is likely to outweigh yours—"

"Fine then." Cheyenne huffed and crossed her arms.

I shot her a *watch yourself* glare.

Her hazel eyes flashed defiance.

God, I may be in trouble. And yet, I didn't question the decision to want her here with me.

Wynn continued, "We really should apply via the court system in New York. The location closest to where Cheyenne lived for the last six months would be the appropriate venue. Where's the nearest family court?"

"Next town over." Cheyenne continued to glare at me. "But then we're screwed."

"The judge is our uncle, my father's brother." I sighed. "And even if he wasn't, any local judge might side with my parents, at least in terms of sending a runaway home. They'd risk losing the next election—as well as their standing in the community—if they didn't do what the townsfolk expect of them. The locals don't overlook violent crime, but teens are expected to owe obedience and loyalty to the head of the house." Physically disciplining kids was considered a normal part of life unless bones were broken. "I once heard the sheriff say, 'If kids are acting up, sometimes you have to pop them one.' Direct quote."

"Well, that complicates things. Let me do a bit more research."

"It's appreciated." I could only imagine what this legal bill would be. Maybe I could refinance my mortgage and take some cash against the equity? I also had a bit squirreled away for a rainy day.

Today it was fucking pouring.

Focus on the things you can fix. "Why don't we feed Sadie?" The dog had been quiet in her pen since those few whines, but I imagined her smelling the chicken as we ate and felt bad. "Then we need to figure out what to do with her."

Wynn scrolled on his computer. "Hm. You're responsible for her for the next fourteen days. If the owner turns up before then, you're entitled to charge a reasonable amount for the care of the dog. If the owner does not turn up, you're required to spend ten days searching for a new home. Does she have a microchip?"

I blinked. "That never occurred to me." I checked my watch. Seven-fifteen. The vet clinic would be closed by now. "I'll take her to the vet tomorrow. Dr. Louisa can check her over and see if there's a chip." Except I had two dogs coming early tomorrow, whom I was responsible for.

This is getting out of hand.

"If the owner doesn't show up by morning, see whether there's a chip and go from there." Wynn eyed me. "No sense borrowing trouble. Right now, I'll get started on your California guardianship petition. The worst the court can do is reject it. We can't apply for an emergency measure till we have a case number." He patted the stack of my papers, with Cheyenne's driver's license on the top. "I'll let you know if I need info that isn't in here. I'm surprised, from what you say, that your parents let a teen have a license."

"Nah," Cheyenne drawled. "Driving's a useful skill. We're all expected to get it the day we turn sixteen. Lots of us have been driving tractors and other equipment long before then."

"Ah, of course." Sadie whined and Wynn flapped his hand at me. "Feed that poor dog. Let me type and then we'll go through things."

Cheyenne rose. "I'm helping with Sadie."

I was too tired to argue.

"Can I use this?" Cheyenne held up a can of tuna.

"Sure. Mix in a little leftover rice so it's not too rich." I cleared the plates as Cheyenne prepared a bowl of tuna-mash for Sadie. "We'll need to buy her some proper canned food tomorrow. All I have in client leftovers is some big-dog kibble that I don't think she can chew." What I'd seen of her teeth was not pretty.

"Is there a good pet store in town?" Cheyenne eyed the food she'd prepared, then added shredded chicken on top.

I nodded. "There's B&B. Bales & Bowls. They're amazing." I'd acquired so many toys from them that they gave me a professional discount. "I can ask them if they'll take some of my new brochures while we're there." I was impressed that I'd thought of my business, with everything going on. "Okay, let's feed the pooch."

We headed for the family room.

I held up a hand to stop Cheyenne. "I'll take the bowl and go in."

"I'm coming." She clutched the bowl tight to her chest.

"The dog's unpredictable. We don't want you to be injured under my supervision. That's a quick way to land you in someone else's care."

"I'm coming."

God save me. Please. "At least stay back." Because life was too short to stand and argue.

"Yep."

Sadie had been pressing her nose to the mesh of the big crate I'd enticed her into as we approached the family room, but when I opened the gate, she backed into the far corner, her eyes tracking our every move. We stepped inside the room, and once the latch was secured, I held out my hand for the bowl.

"I'll offer this to her. Go sit in your chair. With your legs up."

"You're going overboard. She's a lovely dog."

Said dog growled.

I tensed.

Cheyenne crooned, "Poor baby," and told me, "She's hungry—you've got food. I'd be growling too."

"Fine. Chair."

Amazingly, she did as bade—sitting crosslegged in the chair I now thought of as hers.

I placed the bowl of tuna on the floor just in front of Sadie's crate, then I opened the door and stood aside.

The dog, with her ears back, glanced from Cheyenne to me and back to Cheyenne. Finally, she stepped out and made her way to her food. The first bite was more of a nibble as she tested the food. Almost like she thought we might be poisoning her. Slowly, though, she started eating bigger bites.

I let out the breath I'd been holding as she finished the entire bowl and then licked it. *Okay, next challenge.* I snagged a slip leash and gently reached toward her. She dodged back with a lifted lip.

For a moment, I wished Arthur was there. I imagined how he'd coax her with that deep low voice that made dogs want to trust him. *And not just dogs.* I imagined him using Chili—well, maybe not Chili, but Eb or Twain—to keep this scared little dog company and make her feel at home. *He should be here.* My house felt empty, even with Wynn and Cheyenne and Sadie there…

I gave myself a mental shake. I'd known Arthur all of ten days. He wasn't an essential part of my household. No matter how I felt. *Focus on the job staring up at you with little brown eyes.*

"You need to go peepee," I pointed out. "So we'll go outside now. Cheyenne will refill your water bowl and if you're really good, I might have a treat for you."

Sadie's ears perked.

"Treat?" I dug in my pocket for the bites of soft beef treats I kept there and tossed her a tiny one.

Watching me with extreme caution, she extended her neck and lipped it up.

"Good girl. Treat?" I held out the next one on my palm, barely breathing. After a moment, she took two steps forward and ate it. Then backed up, but only one step.

"Treat?" After three more bites, when she'd stopped jumping back, I brought the leash out again. "Walkies?"

She tilted her head, one ear cocked higher than the other, but didn't growl. I eased the loop around her neck and dropped a treat for her before she could panic. When she ate it and didn't freak out, I straightened and used my happiest voice. "Good girl! Walkies! Go pee!"

She allowed me to guide her to the patio door.

I would've just let her loose to do her business, but if I couldn't catch her, we'd have been in big trouble. Still, I did my best to keep as far away from her as I could, following with the leash loose as she wandered.

Sadie sniffed for a long time before doing her business.

I snagged a poop bag from my pocket—because I always had several handy—and scooped, then coaxed her step by step to where I could put it in the bin.

The dog gazed up at me, then stared off into the distance. A low whine came from her tiny throat. Another whine.

"I'm so sorry. I don't know why she did this. But I'll take care of you, I promise. Okay?"

She blinked. Then headed back to the house.

When I coaxed her into her crate, though, she started whimpering.

I gave her a chew toy with bits of treat in it but she ignored it.

"Why can't she come and sit with us in the dining room?" Cheyenne stood near the gate, watching. "Or you could let her roam free in here. She doesn't seem the destructive sort."

The room was pretty well dog-proofed, but separation anxiety could make dogs do dangerous and destructive things. "We don't know her well enough, yet. So, for now, she stays in the crate where she's safe."

Wynn appeared in the doorway. "I've come up with an idea."

"Great." I gave Sadie one final look before heading out of the family room, shutting the gate tightly.

Sadie whined again. More like crying.

She sounded like a human infant—which tugged at my heartstrings. That gut-deep instinct to soothe. "Sorry, girl." I whispered, hoping she'd settle when we were out of sight.

Cheyenne glared.

I sighed. "We can only do what we can do. Let's see what Wynn has up his sleeve, okay?"

After a moment, she nodded.

We retook our seats in the dining room, eagerly awaiting Wynn's idea.

Well, eagerly might've overstated things. I was filled with dread as I tried not to think of all the ways taking my parents to court could go horribly wrong. *Maybe we can just not tell them and pretend I don't know where Cheyenne is.* But I wasn't a child, to indulge in magical thinking. I knew better. "What's the thought?" I asked.

Wynn shot his gaze between Cheyenne and me. "I think we need to get your parents on the record with the wedding threat." He scratched his chin. "I know a judge here in Gaynor Beach who is very focused on human trafficking—children in particular. If we give her proof that Cheyenne is being trafficked to her future husband, we might be able to circumvent the laws about jurisdiction and recording."

I cocked my head. "What?"

"California's a two-party recording state. Normally, we'd have to ask permission from your parents to tape the conversation, and then they'd never say anything incriminating."

I opened my mouth.

He held up his hand. "Yes, preppers hate the government—so they wouldn't give us authorization to begin with. However—" He checked his computer. "Basically, the exception is if there are threats of violence and therefore, by recording, we are possibly proactively preventing felony violence against a person, then we don't need consent. That violence can include human trafficking."

"Really?" Cheyenne's eyes widened. "So if they say they're going to force me to marry Harvey, then I won't have to go back?"

"Well…" Wynn glanced my way.

I gestured for him to speak freely. Cheyenne deserved to know what she was up against.

"Hopefully. We'll have to see what you can get them to say."

"Okay." She leaned forward. "Let's do this. Except, I don't have a phone."

"We'll use Brooklyn's. Your name would come up on caller ID, right?"

I nodded. "My number's listed because of the business, and my name's right in the title. I don't differentiate between work and personal—no point paying for two phones if I don't need them."

"Oh no!" Cheyenne stared at Wynn. "I don't want them to know where I am."

His tone gentled as he said, "If we go ahead with this petition, they'll find out tomorrow. The parents have to be notified, by law."

"Then maybe we shouldn't." She turned to me. "Just wait till I'm eighteen."

"You could do that," Wynn agreed. "It would mean not registering for school. Not being insured to drive. The biggest risk would be no health coverage and no treatment permission. And if your parents find out anyway and want to, they could prosecute Brooklyn for harboring a runaway. They could ask the local police to send you back."

"Do you have to tell the law about me? Because of your job?"

Wynn shook his head. "Brooklyn's paying me as his lawyer, so this meeting is confidential. If you were an endangered minor, I'd be required to report it, but you're not." He watched us calmly.

I told Cheyenne, "This is your call. I can't imagine Dad's going to drive out here and shoot us if he finds out where you are, but there's risks both ways."

Cheyenne frowned. "I suppose they'll probably guess where I went. I said a few times I was going to run off and live with you, when I got mad at them." She took a deep breath. "Fuck them. I want to do this legally. I want to see their faces when a judge tells them I'm not their property anymore."

"You do know it won't happen quite like that," Wynn told her.

"Whatever. I don't want to spend two months wondering if Dad will have the cops haul me home." She nodded. "I want people to hear what he's like."

"We could still do it with a burner phone," I suggested.

"Possibly," Wynn agreed. "Would your father answer an unknown number?"

Cheyenne scoffed. "No way. He hates spammers. And he doesn't do texts, never looks at them, so I can't text 'This is Cheyenne.' Everyone in the community uses Signal for messaging, for security. If the phone rings with an unknown number he'll just ignore it." She raised her chin and straightened her shoulders. "Use Brooklyn's."

Wynn waited a moment for her to change her mind, then turned to me. "May I see your phone?"

I yanked it out of my back pocket.

No texts from Arthur. That would've been a comfort in this moment. *He's probably busy.*

I unlocked the phone and handed it to Wynn.

"Okay, great. This is the latest model. There's recording software I'm going to get you to download. You'll be able to record right on your phone. I'll keep mine next to it and record as well so we'll have two copies." He turned his attention to Cheyenne. "You're going to be on speaker phone. If they question it…" He considered.

I suggested, "Just say you stole my phone. And that you don't know what the buttons are for and you can't get it off speaker." See? I could bullshit through just about anything.

She nodded.

Wynn handed me the phone and told me the name of the app I needed to download. Within moments, I had it, and Wynn turned his attention back to Cheyenne. "Let's role-play this a bit. We need two things from them. First, that there's a threat of force or economic coercion. If they don't make any direct threats, you'll need to say something like 'What if I don't?' and get them to threaten to hit you or hold you against your will. 'You'll regret it' isn't enough. We need, 'We'll hit you' or 'You're not leaving the house till you agree.' Concrete threats."

"Okay." I was impressed that her voice didn't waver.

"Second, that they insist on you marrying Harvey. Not just that they want you home, or are mad that you ran away, or belong with your family, but that your safety hinges on you marrying the man they have selected. That's the trafficking part."

Again, she nodded. "I can do this."

The steely look of determination in her eyes had me believing her.

"Right." Wynn glanced at me. "You know your parents better, Brooklyn, and what kind of things they would say. Cheyenne, you pretend to make the call. Brooklyn will pretend to be your mom and dad. I'll chip in and let you know what statements are useful, or with hints about how to coax more out of Brooklyn."

"Got it." Cheyenne held her hand to her ear, thumb and pinky extended in a fake phone. "Briiiing, briiing. Hi? Dad?" Her voice wavered now, but her fierce scowl suggested it was intentional.

And, *fuck my life,* I got to pretend to be my parents and berate and threaten my sister.

We practiced for fifteen minutes, then took a water break and for me, a mental break. I stared out the kitchen window as I sipped from my glass. This was bringing back all kinds of bad memories, although to help Cheyenne? I could do it all day long.

It was hard, though, putting my father's words in my mouth, watching Cheyenne flinch, even in make-believe. I stared at the dark side yard, half-hidden now by reflections, and imagined Arthur standing behind me, setting a hand on my shoulder. If I called, I bet he'd come back. He'd support me.

But I was a grown man and he was probably nursing that headache and surely didn't need more of mine. This was probably harder on Cheyenne than me.

"Okay?" Wynn's voice came softly. "I think we're ready, but we could put it off till tomorrow."

"No!" Cheyenne said sharply. "I'd forget stuff. I'm ready now."

"It's three hours later there," Wynn pointed out. "We'll probably be waking them. Is that likely to be good or bad?"

"I think it's good," Cheyenne said. "They'll be mad and not thinking about what they're saying. Brooklyn?" I saw her hands shaking, but she crossed her arms and raised her chin. "I'm ready."

I wanted to hug her and tell her to forget it, I'd protect

her, I'd find a way. But her steely-eyed courage made me say, "Then let's do this." I nodded to Wynn who set up his phone to record. I hit start on the app and once it indicated it was recording, I entered our parents' phone number and hit send. Quickly, I slid the phone over to Cheyenne.

After three rings, my mother's voice came through the speaker. "Brooklyn Whalen West, is that you? It's the middle of the night! Why are you calling? Do you know where your sister is?" Her demanding tone had me wondering if Dad was nearby, because she was usually quite meek when he was within earshot. Maybe waking her had shaken her calm. Or they were just that angry.

"It's me, Mama." Cheyenne spoke softly. "How are you?"

"Child, we've been worried sick."

The harsh edge to her voice had my hackles rising. She wasn't worried—she was angry.

"Sorry, Mama. I just—" She blinked. "—I didn't want to marry Harvey, so I came to Brooklyn's. But I don't like the town here. Everyone's so…queer." She rolled her eyes at me.

"Are you surprised, your brother being that way? Time to get back where you belong. You're in California?"

"Yes." Again, very quiet. "I stole Brooklyn's phone so I could call you."

"Oh, here's your father. You listen to him, Cheyenne. You do what you're told."

Another eye roll.

"Cheyenne? Where are you?" Dad's low volume held the menace of an arctic chill.

"Gaynor Beach, California." Her hand trembled as she inched the phone closer to her. "But I want to come home."

"We'll have one of your brothers drive out to get you."

"Can't you send me money for a bus ticket? I have ID."

"You stay put and don't move an inch. We're not giving you a penny to run off with. Denver will leave first thing. You're going to owe your brother bigtime."

Despite trembling hands, she still managed to smirk and shake her head. "Okay, but if I come home, you have to promise you won't make me marry Harvey. That's not going to happen."

"Cheyenne Abigail West." Again with the frigid tone. Hell, I was intimidated by him—and I'd been out from under his thumb for twelve years. When I'd stayed with them, the lure and promise of money had kept them civil to me. Today? He was ready to lose his shit.

"Yes, Father?"

"You will stay in a motel until someone comes to retrieve you. You will not leave that room under any circumstances. Then you will come home and you *will* marry Harvey. We'd do it right now, but the damned state took away our freedom to decide when our children are ready for marriage. So you'll live in our house till the day you turn eighteen, and then you'll be his."

"I want to come home...but I'm not marrying Harvey."

"Cheyenne. You. Will. Do. As. You. Are. *Told.*" The volume on the last word crackled over the phone.

This time, I rolled my eyes. My heart pounded and a metallic taste tinged my dry mouth—a part of me was terrified—and yet I had enough distance to realize our father really did have the ability to go over the top.

Dad's voice suddenly changed. "Wait. What are you up to? Do you have me on speaker?"

"Uh, I don't know. I've never used this kind of cell phone. It came up this way, but I'm hiding in a closet. I don't think Brooklyn can hear me." She met, and held, my gaze.

"Very well. I am the head of this household. You are the child of my flesh. I have raised you, housed you, and clothed you for seventeen years. I have seen to your education. I have been far more lenient with you than with my other children."

I hadn't seen any proof of that, but I hadn't been around.

"I appreciate that, Father—" With just the right amount of tremble. "—but I can't do it. Not Harvey. Don't make me."

"There will be a marriage, Cheyenne, or there will be serious and lasting consequences."

"What consequences? Dad, don't." Her eyes flickered panic.

I grabbed her left hand and pressed our clammy palms together. *Look into my eyes. Believe I'll keep you safe. Whatever he's threatening will never come true so long as there's breath in my body.*

Dad growled, "Cross me and find out. Remember the time you brought home that useless puppy of Mr. Gordon's, the sickly one, and stole our food to give it?"

Tension radiated through Cheyenne. "Y-yes."

"You remember I tanned your hide till you couldn't sit for a week, and the mutt still died? That's what happens when you defy me. Everyone in this family pulls their weight, everything has a purpose. And Harvey and I have a purpose for you, girl. You get your ass back here, you do as I say, and you won't have to sleep on your stomach for a month."

"Harvey's mean. He'll…hurt me."

"Harvey's a decent man. Nancy gave him two living kids and had no complaints, and you're going to do the same. You'll marry that man as soon as it can be arranged, and take care of his kids, and do your wifely duty. Or you won't have to wonder about those *consequences*."

Cheyenne gasped, pressing a hand to her mouth.

Never, in my entire life, had I been so angry. I wanted to reach into the phone and kill my father myself.

Finally, through tears, Cheyenne spoke. "What if I don't come h-home?" She gulped a sob on the last word.

"You're seventeen, underage, a runaway. I'll set the cops on Brooklyn, throw him in jail where perverts like that belong. They'll drag you back here in handcuffs. Don't you *imagine* you can get away from me again." He let that hang for a moment. "Now you go out and find a motel. A cheap one, you hear? Do you have money for a cab?"

"A few dollars," she lied. She'd spent the thirty-six she had on food to survive her trip to me, but I'd given her a hundred to keep tucked away in case she needed it for something. We'd both felt safer if she wasn't broke, should the need arise.

"When you find a place, have them call me and I'll put your room on my card. And *damn* you girl, for making me use it. I have half a mind to have the cops haul you to jail after all, save the money, but the last thing I want is Left Coast cops all up in my business. Don't make me change my mind."

"I w-won't."

"Find that motel and stay put. Gonna take three, four days, but you don't budge. You barely breathe. While you're alone, you can contemplate your marriage to Harvey. He has two young children in need of guidance and…love." He said the word with such contempt that I winced.

"Yes, Father."

"Behave." With that, he cut the line.

Cheyenne shoved the phone toward me. I located the

app and stopped the recording. I listened to the first few seconds to confirm we had it. The app asked me if I wanted to store a copy to the cloud. I figured two were better than one, and I saved the recording.

Wynn had been doing something with his phone as well. Finally, he nodded toward Cheyenne. "You did great."

"He's an a-asshole." Her voice shook.

"Yeah, he is." I offered what reassurance I could. I wanted to hug her, but there was a brittle quality to her tone, and the way she wrapped her arms around herself said she wouldn't welcome my touch.

"We got what we needed." Wynn's approval came though warm and strong in his voice. "Physical threats and a focus on the marriage against your will. Well done. I know folks two decades older who wouldn't have kept their cool as well."

Cheyenne's pale face took on a bit more color. "Thanks."

Sadie whined, loud enough to make me jump.

I chuckled hoarsely. "Okay, that was good timing. Would've been difficult to explain the dog to Dad."

Cheyenne nodded. "Yeah. Can I...go sit with her?"

"Chey...enne." Damn, I'd nearly used my nickname for her. "Don't get attached to Sadie. The owner might show up at any time."

"You know she won't, Brooklyn. You *know* that. If she were my dog, nothing would've kept me from coming back here to get her." She blinked. "I certainly would never allow someone to leave her to die—" She gasped again, tears filling her eyes.

I didn't know about the puppy or what happened, but clearly it was a painful memory for Cheyenne. Yet another cruelty of my father's I'd never forgive. "Yeah, go and maybe talk to her. Do not, under any circumstances, open the crate or stick your fingers through to touch her."

She nodded.

Even in her current state of distress, I believed her.

"I think I should sleep on the couch in there—to keep her company." She turned to Wynn. "If this doesn't work out—if I have to go back—I'll run away again. Only no one will ever be able to find me."

Slowly, Wynn nodded. "I understand. To be clear, though. Do not, under any circumstances, say that to the judge. She'll think you don't plan to obey her court orders, and that can have consequences. You can legitimately say you fear for your safety. I heard the conversation and can attest to it." He smiled. "You get some rest. Brooklyn and I have the review of paperwork to do and then I can get things filed in the morning. Rest well, okay? Know I'm doing everything I can."

She rose slowly and then, to my surprise, put a hand on his forearm. "I believe you. Believe in you. That you can save me." With that, she headed toward her bedroom. Likely to put on her pajamas that we'd bought for her today. Maybe she'd brush her teeth, and then I had no doubt she'd grab a blanket and pillow and head for the family room.

Maybe that was best for all of us.

I checked my phone. I'd said, "Chat later," to Arthur and I desperately wanted to hear his voice. But there was no text from him, and it was getting late, and maybe he was in bed. I could wait till tomorrow.

I sighed, then turned my attention back to Wynn. "What's next?"

CHAPTER 15

ARTHUR

I stayed up too late, waiting for Brooklyn to get back to me, but he never did. On the plus side, by the time I gave up, my head and stomach were better enough for me to scramble some eggs on toast for a midnight snack and enjoy them. I focused on that instead of the hollow feeling of wondering if something important had come up, or I just wasn't a priority.

Next morning, I'd fed and exercised the dogs in the yard, taken joy in a real shower, dressed, and was about to call for a cab to the shelter, when my phone chimed a text.

> **Brooklyn.**
> Any chance you'd have a little free time this morning?

My immediate reaction was, *for you? Absolutely.* I didn't want to be corny, though.

> Sure. What...

What can I do for you? What do you need me for?

Want me to come over and kiss your... I shoved down my newly active libido and went with,

> What's up?

And was glad I hadn't gone sexy or personal when he replied,

> It's this dog, Sadie. The owner never came back. I need to get her to the vet to see if she has a chip and make sure she's healthy. Plus maybe Dr. Louisa will recognize her

I had a chip reader at the shelter, but couldn't offer the other two things.

> Sure. You want me to take her?

> Would you? That'd be a lifesaver. Cheyenne wants to go, but she's not 18, to start an official record, and I have two meathead daycare pups I can't leave alone with her either

> Glad to

I answered, then realized,

> except my car's at the shelter

James had driven it there after my accident and I hadn't used it since. And I wasn't cleared to drive.

> Cheyenne can come get you in my SUV. She just can't do paperwork. Where are you staying?

> Shane's place

I texted him the address.

After a pause, my phone rang for a voice call. Brooklyn again.

I answered, "Yeah? Problem?"

"No, God, I'm so sorry. I didn't even ask if you were okay or how your head is doing or if you have to work or anything. I just leaned on you."

The sound of his flustered tones made me feel warm inside. "Seems like I leaned on you a lot last week. I don't mind. Happy to help. My head's okay and as long as Cheyenne's driving, in case the vertigo hits, I don't mind seeing Dr. Louisa one bit." The vet was one of my favorite people. She'd often cut me a break with rescue pets and still gave the shelter a big discount.

"Good. Great. Thank you." He blew out a long breath. "It's been a *long* day and a half, I tell you."

"What's wrong?"

"Other than the dog? Well, not *wrong* so much as stressful. More for Cheyenne than me, so I'm glad Sadie's keeping her distracted. But life's making me a bit nuts."

"Want to talk about it?"

"So much." His tone warmed. "You have no idea. But we need to get moving on Sadie."

"Afterward," I offered. "I can come by your place and we can chat."

"Do you have time? That'd be…You know, that would be *awesome*."

The idea that he wanted me there, that the thought of talking to me made him sound so happy, filled an empty space inside me. "Absolutely. Count on it. See you later."

I realized after I hung up that I didn't know how fast Cheyenne would show up, but I was dressed for work so that was fine. I called the shelter and let Neil know I'd be taking a personal day. I apologized again, but he assured me they'd be fine. He'd cover the front desk, which had been my main job while my leg healed. He laughed at my apologies and told me I had vacation time coming, which wasn't true, because I set my own schedule. Plus even if I did, the month Shane was away would be the wrong time to take it. But he was trying to make me feel better for ditching my work again, so I thanked him.

When Brooklyn's old SUV pulled up out front, I said a final goodbye to the pups, and to Xandra who turned her back on me and gazed out the window.

Cheyenne looked somehow older when I eased into the passenger seat and glanced her way. The expression on her face, maybe, some strain in her eyes I didn't remember. Not that I'd spent a lot of time looking at her. But I had to ask, "Are you okay?"

She flicked a glance my way. "Brooklyn made me put Sadie in a crate in the second row. I wanted her beside me. She doesn't like the crate."

"It's safer, though," I told her. "Ask Dr. Louisa about the dogs she sees thrown through the windshield or hit by an airbag."

"Oh." She backed out of the driveway. "I guess."

I didn't add that a dog standing in the driver's lap could end up dead and smooshed into her chest by the airbag. I was maybe a bit obsessed with car safety, but I didn't have to gross out the teenager. I turned to look over my shoulder and murmured to Sadie, "Hey, girl. Doing okay?"

"Her owner never came last night. She didn't want her. It's not fair she still has fourteen days to take Sadie back." Cheyenne glowered harder.

"It's the law," I said mildly. "But Brooklyn could charge her a thousand dollars a night for unscheduled boarding fees. Good bet the owner would rather sign her over than pay."

"Really?" A slow smile crept over Cheyenne's face. "Yeah. I like that. You're okay."

"You didn't think so yesterday." I wanted to bite my tongue when her smile vanished, but she sighed.

"Sorry. I was kind of a bitch. Things are weird and scar—strange right now."

"That's okay. I can't imagine hitching all the way across the country at seventeen. Finally getting to a safe haven and then finding your brother busy with someone else."

She shot me a fast glance. "Yeah. Something like that." The GPS directed her through a left turn.

"Are you going to be able to stay with Brooklyn? I know he hopes you will." I figured knowing that she was wanted would be important right now.

"God, I hope so. Dad was scary mad about me being here."

"Your father? He knows where you are?"

"Yeah. We had to call him. The lawyer said so. But Dad said he'd send my brother after me, and I wasn't going to escape again and all that bullshit." She flicked me another look, like I might comment on her language.

I figured she was entitled. "For what it's worth, Brooklyn will never let them take you away."

"Brooklyn's the smallest of my brothers. Well, least strong, anyway. Tall like a beanpole, but the others are fighters."

"Well, I won't let them either. Is your brother bigger than me?" I hoped I could make her feel safer.

She looked me over at the stoplight. "No, I don't think so. About your size."

"So Brooklyn and I together can take him, right?"

The crinkle of her nose said she was doubtful, which

was fair enough because honestly, I'd never been a fighter even without a bad leg.

I added, "Chili and Sadie can trip him, Ebony will sit on him, Xandra will use him for a scratching post, and Twain will blind him with face-licking."

That got a tiny giggle from her. "Okay." Then she sighed. "At least he's driving. That means we have a couple of days before Denver can possibly get here even if he drives straight through. I looked the distance up in the library back home."

"Denver's his name?"

"Next oldest brother after Brooklyn. Denver, Austin, and our sister's Nevada, then me."

"Wow, your parents really had a thing, huh?"

"All-American." Her lips twisted.

I hurried to add, "Although Cheyenne's a great name."

"I don't mind it. I wouldn't want to be Nevada. Or be like her." Her hands tightened on the steering wheel, her knuckles whitening. "I'm not going back. Just not."

"I promise," I said recklessly. "Brooklyn's pretty new in town, but he has me, and I have friends, people I can call on." I maybe hadn't realized until this whole episode how many friends I had. "Worst comes to worst, we'll sic James's mama on him. She's a force of nature." I gestured. "There's the clinic."

We parked and Cheyenne got the carrier out of the back. I let her carry the dog inside, since I was still ungainly with the cane. We stopped at the front desk, and I told the receptionist, "We have a dog abandonment situation. We need to get her scanned for a chip, and figure out if she's been missed by anyone."

"Aw, Arthur. That's too bad." Christa had worked the front desk a lot of years and knew me well. "I'll let Dr. Louisa know you're here." She called to the back.

A few minutes later, the head technician, Oscar, came to meet us. "Hey, let's get you into an exam room. We can scan for a chip and weigh her in there, if she's small enough to fit in that carrier."

When we coaxed the dog out on the floor, Oscar eyed her. "I'd swear that's Sadie."

"Yes. That was her name. She was left at my friend Brooklyn's doggie daycare and never picked up."

"Let me verify." Oscar waved a circular wand over Sadie's shoulders, then went to a computer terminal in the corner and entered her chip number. "Yes, same Sadie. They just left her?"

"Unless they were in an accident and are in a coma. But the phone number came up as out of service."

"Those creeps!" Oscar paused as the little dog jumped at the anger in his tone. He murmured, "No, not you baby. Here, have a treat. Have three treats." He tossed her some tiny bites, and went on quietly, "Sadie belonged to Mrs. Robertson, an elderly client who passed away a few weeks ago. Her son and daughter-in-law called asking about putting Sadie to sleep, but we said we wouldn't do it. She's only seven, and basically healthy. She has some anxiety, and takes time to warm up to people, but she's not aggressive, just afraid. Dr. Louisa sent them all kinds of behavior references and the shelter info."

"I guess they decided abandoning her was cheaper than paying our shelter drop-off fee," I grumbled. We waived the fee for folks who really couldn't afford it and for strays, but for voluntary surrenders we did charge a modest amount. "Cheapskate creeps."

"Well, she'll be better with you than people like that." Oscar tossed Sadie another small bite. "We can send you her medical record. Just pretend we didn't until the fourteen days for surrender are up. Will you put her up for adoption?"

"No!" Cheyenne burst out before I could say anything. "I'm keeping her. I mean, Brooklyn and I will. She's already been abandoned too often. It's horrible when people treat you like garbage!"

Oscar and I exchanged glances over the vehemence in her tone, and I gave a tiny nod to say, *yes, there's trauma there and we're aware of it.* He nodded back, then said, "Clearly, she's never going to have to worry about that again."

"Right." Cheyenne nodded firmly. "Never."

Oscar walked us through Sadie's chart, confirming she was up to date on shots, had a recent exam, needed a dental soon, and then sussed out which food she ate. They had it in the clinic, so I grabbed four cans. Oscar gave me Mrs. Robertson's contact info, for whatever that was worth. The phone number was the same out-of-service one.

We coaxed Sadie back into the carrier with only one little grumble. When we reached the SUV, I paused to buckle the carrier in securely. Cheyenne stood back, eyeing me. "Those vet people know you."

"I did rescue for a lot of years and now I run an animal shelter, so yeah."

"A shelter? For homeless cats and dogs?" Her eyes lit up.

"Yes. When we get the chance, you can come by and I'll show you around."

"Cool." We got in and she started driving back to Brooklyn's, but she seemed to be thinking about something. Halfway there, she asked, "*Are* you and Brooklyn boyfriends?"

"Would it bother you if we were?"

"No. Although—" She smirked. "—you could do better than my brother."

"No, I couldn't. Believe me, I've been around the block a few times." Mostly in my youth, but same difference. "Brooklyn's the best guy I've met. Look at how he's taking care of Sadie, and you. He was so kind when I was injured."

"I guess. So are you boyfriends?"

I scratched my beard. "I'm not sure. We were heading that way when you arrived."

"Okay. So if you wanted to stay? You and Eb and Twain and Chili and Xandra? I wouldn't mind."

"Stay at Brooklyn's, you mean?"

"Yeah. There's room. He even has two bathrooms. We only had one for all our family. And your dogs could make Sadie less scared, and there'd be more people around."

More people in case her brother or father showed up. I couldn't imagine how scared she must be down inside.

"And it would make Brooklyn happy." She flicked a glance my way. "He was sad when you left."

Part of me was thrilled, in a twisted way, to hear that. "Brooklyn and I should talk. People don't usually move in together this early in a relationship."

"But you were living there when I arrived."

"Because I was hurt."

"I still think it would be cool. And I could help walk the dogs till your leg gets better."

"We'll talk about it. With Brooklyn."

When we got to Brooklyn's and brought Sadie inside, happy barks greeted us from the back room. We headed there, and Cheyenne set down Sadie's carrier. The little dog had her nose smooshed to the front and her tail wagged as she watched a pair of young vizslas chase each other around the room.

"They love everyone," Brooklyn said. "Release the kraken."

I opened Sadie's crate and she romped out to meet the dogs, who paused for a moment to sniff butts, then resumed their play. She followed them, seeming happy just to watch.

Brooklyn came over to us. I'd texted him the info while we were in the car, so he said, "Hey, Arthur. I guess we're keeping her, huh?"

"Yes!" Cheyenne said. "For sure."

His lips curved but he didn't take those gorgeous hazel eyes off mine.

I said, "Hey. Good to see you."

"Yeah. Thanks for helping out."

"Any time." I wanted to hug him or maybe go for a kiss, but instead I managed an awkward smile.

Cheyenne said, "Good talk, guys. I'm going to, um, go for a long walk around the block. Several blocks."

Brooklyn said, "Not yet. Not till we get you a phone. But I appreciate the offer. Maybe you can take the crazy twins into the backyard?"

"And Sadie?"

"If she follows them. Don't try to touch her."

"Okay. But the vet said she's just scared."

"Scared dogs bite. The other two are marshmallows. Take some treats with you."

When Cheyenne had followed Sadie and the vizslas into the yard and closed the sliding door, Brooklyn turned back to me. "You don't have to work today?"

"I took the day off."

He frowned. "Is your head bad? You should sit down. I'm sorry—"

I waved him off. "I'm okay today, just took vacation time. Although I won't turn down a seat." I hobbled to the couch, dropped down with a grunt, and patted the cushion beside me. "Join me?"

Brooklyn approached, looking tentative, and perched on the edge of the couch beside me. We stared at each other in silence.

I'd never been brave, but someone had to go first. "I missed you last night."

"God, yes. I wished you were here." Brooklyn slumped.

It felt natural to wrap my arm around him so he could lean against me. "Did you see the lawyer? What happened?"

Brooklyn described the lawyer's advice and recording their parents making awful threats.

I hugged him against me. "It's amazing you and Cheyenne are the kind people you are, with parents like that."

"They weren't mean all the time, just really strict, especially if we disobeyed Dad. Lots of kids had it worse. Mom would bake cookies sometimes, and Dad taught me to ride a bike and a horse."

I was glad if he had some good memories. "Do you think it's risky, them knowing where Cheyenne is? Couldn't you have used, like, a burner phone?"

"They wouldn't have answered a burner, and the lawyer said it wouldn't matter. Part of the petition for guardianship is a required notification to the parents. Wynn was doing the filing today, so they'd have found out anyhow, just one day later."

"Will that petition change things, if they find out you're asking to keep her and she's not willing to come home?"

Brooklyn rubbed his eyes. "I don't know. The optimist in me says once the courts are involved, they'll wash their hands of her. But Dad sure hates to be told what to do, and he was furious last night. He might tell Denver to bring her back anyway."

"I think Cheyenne's pretty scared, although she's hiding it well."

"Me too," Brooklyn said. "I mean, I think she's scared too. Not that I am."

"Uh-huh." I let a little skepticism into my voice.

After a moment, he said, "Okay. I'm worried too. I don't think Denver would, like, forcibly kidnap her, but he's a chip off Dad's block. He's likely to yell and threaten."

"Do you think you should live somewhere else for a while? Shane and Theo aren't back for a week. You could both come there. Or I have other friends. We can find somewhere."

"I can't. I have multiple dogs booked in every day next week."

"Cancel?"

"It's my livelihood, and I'm just getting started. If I cancel on people, I'll lose their business." He pressed his lips in a thin line and leaned his head against my shoulder. "I'd ask you to come back and stay here, but I don't want you to think I only want you around to be protection against my brother."

"Not *only*," I told him. "But if you want me around for other reasons, *and* want me to help protect Cheyenne? I'm in."

"Really?" He rolled his head so he could look up at me. "You'd do that for me?"

I had to kiss him. No other choice. Our lips met for one wonderful moment, his mouth soft against mine, his hand finding my cheek.

I told him, "I'd do just about anything for you. Live in a comfortable house, with extra dog toys and people to walk them, and someone who can cook? Not a hardship."

"It comes with a teenager who's pretending to not watch us through the patio door."

"We can work around her."

"God, I want to." Brooklyn arched his neck to kiss me again, then snuggled back against me. "I feel like I'm taking advantage."

"You're not, believe me."

"There might be danger."

"But probably not, and if there is? You think I want to be somewhere else if you and Cheyenne are in trouble?"

"Oh," he breathed, as if that was a revelation.

"Tell you what," I suggested, because having him close was giving my dick all kinds of ideas, and there was a teenager around. "When those two boarders go home, do you think you could let Cheyenne watch Sadie for half an hour and you drive me back to my place? I need to walk and feed, and then pack my stuff."

"Sure." Brooklyn said it so casually I knew he wasn't imagining what I was.

"Or maybe a whole hour. There will be things in the bedroom I want to pack."

A slow smile spread over his face. "Oh. Of course. Packing the bedroom."

"If you're up for it."

"That's a yes, absolutely. Although I need to stop thinking about it or I won't be able to get off this couch."

"Same." I lifted my arm off his shoulders and shifted around so the hardening of my dick would be less obvious. "So what do we do until then?"

"Lunch," Brooklyn suggested. "And then in the afternoon, you can help me train those vizslas on some obedience commands and pick over the yard. Till they head out at four. Unless their mom's early. Sometimes she is."

"Fingers crossed," I said. "But if not, I'm a patient man. I can wait a few hours."

"I'm not." Brooklyn grinned. "But I can fake it till four o'clock."

I held his head between my palms and leaned in for a deep kiss—

"Hey, guys. Bruno rolled in something icky. Oops." Cheyenne put a hand over her eyes but she was laughing. "Sorry."

"We're just kissing," Brooklyn said. "And you don't look sorry."

She swiped her hand over her mouth and chin, wiping away the grin. "Should I go try to clean up Bruno?"

"He'll knock you over. I'll get him." Brooklyn pushed to his feet. He turned to me, and this time there was nothing awkward and everything hot about the meeting of our eyes. "I'll see what I can find for you to do before we head out at four."

"But he's coming back." Cheyenne leaned toward us. "Right? With the dogs."

Sibling rules said one of us should tease her, but she'd been through a lot lately. I said, "With the dogs and cat, definitely. It'll just take a bit of time to pack."

Brooklyn added, "I'll count on you to hold down the fort with Sadie here. We won't be gone long." I tried to catch his attention, and he flushed, avoiding my gaze. "Well, not very long."

I breathed, "That's what you think," as softly as I could near his ear.

He glanced at me then, and his smile was bright. "We'll head out after Arthur cleans up all the poop out in the yard."

If Brooklyn was trying to give me second thoughts, he needed something better than that.

"On it," I told him. "And looking forward to having you help me pick up, with my bad leg and all." I winked.

"Yes. That will be good. We'll get it done faster. I mean, after four, most likely, when the terrible twins are gone." He breathed fast, eyeing my face.

"Holy cow, guys." Cheyenne flounced past toward her bedroom. "Get a room."

And while we meant to do so, soon, in all seriousness, for a moment we stood there laughing and hanging onto each other. Until hanging became kissing, breathing optional. Until it took Cheyenne muttering as she brushed past the other way, to make us, reluctantly, let go.

Four o'clock couldn't come soon enough.

CHAPTER 16

BROOKLYN

THEO AND SHANE'S HOUSE WAS...BIG.

And yet understated. Well-loved, with landscaping that looked low-maintenance and desert-friendly, neat but not...formal, and a backyard fence meant more for dogs than for curb appeal.

Arthur unlocked the door, entered the security code, and hustled in—to be greeted like the long-lost conquering hunter. Returning to bring food to the starving masses.

Eb and Twain fawned over him, while Chili greeted me like a friend she hadn't seen in, oh, two days, and Xandra regarded us from her perch.

Pretty much what I expected.

I clapped my hands. "How can I help?"

"If you could feed the gang and give Xandra her med, that would be amazing. I can head to my bedroom and start packing things. Third door on the left." He waved down the hall.

As I oriented myself, looking for the kitchen, he hobbled away. A reminder he wasn't fully healed. He'd said something about showers and bandages on the drive over, but I'd been too obsessed with getting inside his pants again to listen. Now we were here, though, I hesitated. *What if he's not healed enough? What if I'm too in my head about Cheyenne? What—*

Chili nudged my leg. I bent to smile at her. "Oh, you heard him say I was the food dispensing machine, huh?"

Three sets of ears perked.

I grinned. "Which way to the kitchen?"

Eb loped off with Twain hard on his heels.

Chili gazed up at me.

"Pets as soon as you're done eating." Nothing better than petting a dog for stress relief, except I hoped to be stroking a certain ginger hunk before too long. So yeah, actually, something even better.

We made our way to the kitchen and, quickly, three dogs had their food. Xandra appeared for her canned diet and I was happy to provide her with a small plate, her pill delivered in a teaspoon of tuna first. She purred loudly enough to put a smile on my face.

I eyed the patio door and counted hours backward from when Cheyenne had picked up Arthur. "Let's run outside, shall we?"

Twain wiggled his butt as Eb licked his bowl to ensure no crumbs remained.

Grateful the yard was fenced, I let the dogs out.

Eb and Twain quickly found trees to water. Chili sniffed and, keeping close to me, squatted, then bounced off to sniff at some ornamental grass. The garden was peaceful, the dogs cute, and the air fresh, but a beat of arousal in me wanted to cut this idyll as short as possible. The thought of Arthur and a bed and his meaningful stare made it hard to stand there casually and call encouragement and smile at their antics. The shortness of my breath had nothing to do with Eb tugging on Twain's ear.

I was willing to keep them out longer but, as if they sensed my urgency, they all returned, and we headed inside. I eyed them. "You've got to give me privacy—I don't have much time."

After a moment, Eb and Twain headed for their beds in the family room and an array of chew toys.

Xandra had returned to her window ledge, watching something outside with a flick of her plumy tail.

Chili eyed me.

"I promise I'll be back, okay?" I wanted to make the ridiculous promise that I'd never leave her again—but I didn't have the right. Arthur was coming back to my place as much to protect Cheyenne as to be with me. Had our situations been reversed, and he had a sister in need of protection, I'd have been by his side as well.

But him returning couldn't mean as much as I wanted it to mean. We barely knew each other. Basically, we'd bonded over gunshots, dogs, and head trauma. Not exactly the promising makings of something permanent. *Too soon* my head told me. *Exactly right* my heart rejoined.

After a long moment, I gestured to Chili's bed.

She eyed me, obviously making certain I meant it.

I nodded.

Finally, she headed toward the bed and flopped.

Taking that for the win it was, I hurried down the hall and found the third door on the left. I stood at the doorway of the large room and whistled. "Wow, nice place you have here."

Arthur, who had his suitcase on the settee and was filling it, chuckled. "Yeah, and this is just the guest bedroom. Biggest of the bunch, but—"

"I can't even imagine the primary bedroom."

"Well, it's spectacular. I'd offer to give you a tour..." His voice trailed off.

I grinned. "We have better things to do."

Slowly, I entered the room. Then, telegraphing my movements, I made my intentions clear as I closed the door. "So we don't get any four-legged visitors."

He eyed me. "Before we begin, I should probably point out I don't have condoms. I mean, I know I'm negative... tested after, well, and it's been a while..."

"I'm negative as well. Also tested recently. But I hooked up with a guy last month for a hot minute. We used protection, but I'd still prefer to get a retest before...you know..." *We go bareback. Jesus, are we already having this discussion, even though we haven't had sex?*

"Thanks."

I yanked my wallet out of my back pocket and dropped two condoms on the bed. "From my private stash in my bathroom. Unless I'm reading this wrong—"

"Oh, you're not. Hell, even Cheyenne knows how much I want you. Want this—" He gestured to the bed.

"Damn girl sees too much. Knows too much. She's so intuitive—so sensitive. Keeping my feelings from her is difficult."

"Do you have to?"

I blinked. "Do I have to what?"

"Keep this from her. I don't let people into my private life easily, but I'd never ask you not to be honest with her."

"There are some things she doesn't need to know."

He reached over to finger a condom wrapper. "Well, you do have an expressive face."

"And she gave us her blessing. But we need to, uh, move things along. I don't like leaving her alone."

"We could go back—"

I strode over to him. Likely cutting off his words with

my speed and clear vehemence. I grasped his bearded cheeks in my hands, lowered my mouth, and kissed him like I'd been wanting to do for two fucking, insane, overly-long days. Our tongues clashed as we pushed for dominance.

The kiss drugged me, intoxicated me, and yet was wildly intimate—all at the same time.

He grasped my biceps, urging me closer. Even as he did, though, he swayed.

I pulled back. "What's wrong? Leg or head?" No matter how much I wanted him, I'd never want him in pain for me.

"I've been standing too long without my cane. My doc would read me the riot act."

"Maybe we shouldn't—"

This time, he put his index finger against my lips. "Oh, we are so doing this. I'm healing. My head isn't hurting. I don't have vertigo. And, anyway…" He glanced slyly at the bed. "We have a horizontal option right here."

"Then let's get you naked and in whatever position you can be comfortable in. On your side, with pressure off your leg?"

He shook his head. "I want to be able to see your face." His cheeks reddened. "We can arrange my leg so it doesn't hurt."

I had the feeling he would've said *doesn't hurt too much* if he hadn't been pretending he was fine to move things along. I'd be careful for him. "Lube?"

He pointed at a full bottle on the bedside stand. "Borrowed a spare from Shane's stash—because I live on optimism."

Funny. I'd never seen him that way. Pragmatist? Yes. Realist? Absolutely. Optimist? I considered… Yeah, okay…maybe. The way he plunged into animal rescue that could be full of heartbreak, and still was so warm and hopeful. Around me he'd been both honest and passionate. Those were traits I admired greatly. "Let's get you undressed and laid down." I grinned. "As quickly as possible."

"Yes. That." He reached for the buttons on his plaid shirt.

"No, let me. You hold onto me for balance. That'll get my engine revving." *Yeah, like your cock needs any urging—you're ready to go as soon as you can.*

He did as I'd asked, gripping my arms as I undid his shirt and slid it from the waist of his sweats.

I took a moment to admire the pale skin with the heavy pelt of red hair furring his chest and arrowing downward. "Let me slip this off you."

He nodded.

I slid the shirt down his arms, as he let go one hand at a time, and tossed it over the open suitcase. I wanted to kiss, lick, and nibble, but I was aware he needed to be horizontal first. I snagged his sweatpants and slid them past his hips.

His cock strained against his boxers.

I brushed my knuckle over it lightly as I knelt to ease his pants off. "Hands on my shoulders."

"Wait!"

I paused with his waistband just under his ass. "What?"

"My thigh. I don't need the bandages anymore, but it's not pretty. We could—"

I cut him off by running my hand over his bulging boxers. "I'm not some prissy twink in a bar. I don't need pretty, and you don't have to hide your honorable scars."

He hummed at my touch, then scoffed. "Honorable. A man shooting to protect his chickens."

I kissed his thigh through the fleece fabric, the

lightest brush of my lips. "A wound taken to protect a scared dog and a teen boy. I said honorable and I meant it."

"Oh." He looked down at me, his eyes intense and his fingers tightened on my shoulders. "Okay. Thanks."

I tented the elastic wide as I eased the band past his right thigh. He was right, it wasn't pretty, but it also wasn't that bad. There was a big ring of bruising, purple, green and yellow, and a center hole the size of my fingertip that was thickly scabbed over and healing. The exit wound on the back was bigger, rougher and spread out, but similar. I slid the waistband to his knees, then leaned in and kissed his furry thigh six inches above the wound. "I'm so glad it wasn't worse."

"Me too," he murmured. "Yay for small caliber and bad aim. Although he wasn't really aiming at me. I don't think."

"Is he still in jail?"

"Unless he made bail. Last I heard, he was trying to get the money. They just charged him with misdemeanor negligence and criminal endangerment, and firing a gun within city limits, so it's not too much."

"He could've killed you." I suddenly felt dizzy, looking at that wound and imagining what it might have done if he'd hit Arthur in the chest or the head. I forced my eyes away. "Attempted murder. He should be locked up forever."

Arthur let go of one shoulder to cup my cheek in his wide palm. "I love how fierce you are for me, but it was an accident, mostly." He added, "I asked the cops if they were feeding his chickens, but they'd dumped the duty on Pam at the rescue. As if she needs more work."

"Pam?"

"She runs the local in-home fostering program. I used

to do that, but when I got the chance to start the shelter and save more pets, I jumped on it."

I bet you did. Arthur was a protector through and through.

"She still does vital work. The shelter helps, but there are always more pets and some who don't do well in a crate. And chickens." He actually chuckled. "I got a huffy text string from Kevin complaining that the sheriff wouldn't let him volunteer to feed Frank's chickens. Conflict of interest. Kevin insisted helping Frank's birds should show he was unbiased, so not a conflict but proof of goodwill. He was peeved they forbade it. But I'm glad if the cops are keeping the kid away from a man like that, even while he's in jail."

I scowled. "I hope the bastard serves a bunch of time. He hurt you."

"My sexy defender." Arthur rubbed his thumb across my lip, then put his hand back on my shoulder as his eyes darkened. "Get me naked."

He'd worn socks in the house so I slipped off one, baring his knobby, pale foot, and then the other. I helped him ease his ankles from the sweats and boxers until he stood naked before me. "You okay?"

"If we slow down or stop every time you ask that, we'll never actually make it to bed. Let me lean on you and I'll get in."

I guided him, yanked the covers down, and eased him onto the bed. He really did look much better, at least to me, than he had in a while. The furrow in his brow had smoothed out, telling me that must've been a sign of pain. His color was good, cheeks flushed, not pale, and the creases by his eyes were smile wrinkles. He ran a hand down his broad chest, his eyes on mine.

God, I want him. Within a few moments my shoes, socks,

jeans, boxer briefs, and henley were a distant memory. I ran a finger over my abdomen. "You're not the only one with scars." I didn't want to explain it now, but the surgery had left its mark, only now beginning to fade.

"Saw that last time. Don't care." Arthur smiled. "You take my breath away."

That felt a little fanciful, but given what he'd endured in the past two weeks, I could understand. Our meeting had begun with a bang, and it'd been dramatically up and down ever since. And to be honest, my breathing wasn't all that steady right now either.

He held out a condom.

I grinned and took it.

He appeared relieved.

I scooted over to grab the bottle of lube, and then headed back to the man waiting with his arms open. He'd eased his injured leg to the side, flat on the bed, and raised the other leg. The pain wrinkle hadn't returned as he lightly stroked his erect cock. I scooted between his thighs. Then sighed. "I wanted this to be all romantic and stuff. Go super slow, kiss every inch. Last time—" *You were injured.* "And this time—" *I want to take my time…*

"You have a sister waiting. It's okay. We'll find a moment, when everything's calmed down, to go slow." He squeezed his shaft. "I'm pretty desperate here—so I'm good with fast even if your younger sister wasn't home alone."

"I'm going to not think about sisters." For a few minutes, anyway. I held the bottle of lube. "Do you mind if I prep you? I kind of like—"

"I don't mind lying back and letting you do the work. At all." He held my gaze. "It's been a little while."

"Oh." The local gay men were blind, not to see what they had in their midst. At the same time, I could imagine he was so busy he didn't take time for himself. Between the shelter and his wonderful menagerie, he'd barely been able to slow down after having been shot. "Let me know if I go too fast."

In the interest of moving things along, I opened the condom packet and rolled the rubber on my very perky cock. My touch and the sight of Arthur waiting, open for me, turned perky to rock hard. Truly, Arthur was lovely— all strong muscles under the soft padding, ginger hair, and pale skin. Even the bullet wound didn't mar his unique perfection.

I coated my fingers with lube.

He grinned.

I leaned forward and ran my fingers around his rim.

He nodded.

Slowly, I slid one finger in, his ass giving way easily, and enjoyed the heat and his soft groan. I loved prepping partners with whom I had a connection—but there hadn't been many. Hookups were mostly one and done. I savored the intimacy that this act brought with it when deeper feelings were involved. *Like now, with this man.* After I gauged Arthur was fine, I added a second finger.

He held my gaze with an intensity that nearly robbed me of breath. "I'm okay."

I chuckled. "And I didn't even have to ask." I scissored my fingers, opening him up a little. Then I twisted my wrist in just that perfect way and brushed his prostate.

He gasped. "Yep. That's it."

A drop of precum dripped from his tip onto his belly.

I leaned forward to lick it, reveling in the salty taste. I wanted to do everything at once—give him a blow job, fuck him until he came hard...make gentle love to him so I could prove how much I treasured him. How much he meant to me. Because I had the distinct impression Arthur didn't always feel he was worth the effort. Well, to me, he absolutely was.

Still, I slowly withdrew my hands. I coated my cock with lube as he grinned. Perhaps a little nervous, but a smile nonetheless.

I bent and kissed his soft stomach. "I'll take care of you."

"I know you will." His words were quiet and sure.

I eased his good leg up over my hip, angling away from the bad one, and positioned myself over him so my cock nudged his entrance.

Again, he nodded—giving me the permission I sought.

I pressed in, reveling in the pleasure as his tight body accepted me. When my crown breached him, he blinked and then offered that shy smile I loved so much. Once inside him, I started to move, slowly, inch by self-torturing inch. I'd withdraw a bit, then push in. Pull back, thrust forward. Over and over, driving farther inside. Connecting us in a way that expanded in my chest.

"I'm good." He said the words as I seated myself deep.

"I'll—" I sought the right word. "—take care."

"You can be vigorous. I'm not going to break."

No, he wouldn't. Because I'd never go too rough. Never do anything that might hurt him. He hadn't shown a single sign of his head being a problem, and even though I didn't entirely trust him to be honest, I also had to believe he trusted me enough to speak up if he needed a break— or even to stop.

I pulled out and thrust back in.

He grunted. In a good way.

Over and over, I drove deep inside Arthur, pleasuring him, pleasuring myself, our gasps and grunts melding. Increasing the force as I took him higher and higher. Chasing my own orgasm. "Can you jack yourself?" At the moment, I focused on not jostling his leg too much. Or pushing his head against the headboard. Or any of the other things I might do to hurt him, as spiraling need made it hard to focus.

He grasped his cock and jerked to the punishing rhythm I set. I chased my orgasm, even as I clung to the fact I wanted him to come first. My partners coming first didn't always happen—but I rejoiced when it did. For Arthur, I was damned well going to make it happen.

Come on. Come on, Arthur. I watched a flush creep up his neck and his eyes darken.

"I'm coming." He gasped the warning two strokes before his cock erupted. Slick spunk spilled over his hand and a jet hit my chest. He groaned, deep and low, and shuddered again.

"Thank fuck," I muttered, hanging on to the edge of my own release by the skin of my teeth. "Yeah. Fuck, yeah." As his channel squeezed me hard, my own orgasm overtook me. Release sent me flying right off the cliff and over the ocean. Threw me into the vastness, and the rolling thunder of the waves.

I shut my eyes, release sparking over every nerve. This was every pleasure I'd ever known, every moment when I felt as big as the universe. I suddenly wanted to go to the sea with Arthur. To sit on the sand, at night, and gaze at the moon. Count the stars. Share this incredible feeling.

I'd never seen the ocean before leaving my family's home. Now, I walked on the boardwalk whenever I could, and the power and peace of it spoke to me. From now on, the crash of the waves and that feeling of flying free would remind me of Arthur. All this fanciful shit that had nothing and everything to do with this moment of connection. I blinked.

Our gazes locked.

That had been—bar none—the most intense climax of my life. A sign Arthur Bjornsson was coming to mean even more to me than I was willing to admit. Because even if we'd just sat on the sofa and cuddled tonight, I realized the intensity of my feelings would've been the same. Intimacy was what I craved.

Having a seventeen-year-old sister as a chaperone would make that difficult going forward. Still, I had to try.

But thinking of Cheyenne and the situation she was in dumped cold water on my bliss. We had to get back. I needed to protect her. She had to come first.

I realized I'd stiffened and looked away, when Arthur said, "Cheyenne."

That he brought up her name meant he understood my dilemma. My problem. My worry.

"Yeah." Slowly, I withdrew. "You okay?"

"I'm beyond okay." He crunched up to grab the back of my head and kissed me. "And Brooklyn?"

"Yeah?"

"We'll take it slow, and we'll take care of Cheyenne. But I don't want this to be the last time you drill me through the mattress."

"No," I admitted, meeting those incredible blue eyes. "Me neither."

Thirty minutes later, after quick showers, quicker packing of the suitcase, and loading the menagerie into my SUV, we headed home.

CHAPTER 17
ARTHUR

My little furry pack descended on Brooklyn's place like it was home. Of course, most of it was basically a dog paradise, with plenty of cat perches even if they weren't designed that way. I'd worried about Sadie's reaction to invasion of her space, from how Brooklyn described her, but she attached herself to Eb like he was her big brother. When Eb flopped down next to Cheyenne on the family room floor to be loved on, Sadie lay down calmly too, although out of touching range.

Cheyenne scratched Eb's chest and eyed me. "So, you and my brother?"

"Yeah." I shifted on the couch, trying to stretch my leg out a bit. I would never regret asking Brooklyn to top me, but my stupid muscles were complaining now that the haze of orgasm was gone.

"'Yeah' isn't an answer."

"'So' isn't a question," I noted.

"Are you boyfriends now? Like, for real?"

As I hesitated, unsure how to answer, Brooklyn called

from the kitchen, "Cheyenne, quit harassing my boyfriend."

I barked a laugh that had Sadie cocking her head, eyeing me. "I guess you have your answer."

"Does that mean you're going to live here?"

Brooklyn came in, drying his hands on a towel. "That comes under harassing. We haven't made real plans yet, thanks to *someone* who knocked on the door in the middle of the night and has bigger problems than we do."

"I could go somewhere else." She crossed her arms, looking fierce, but I thought I saw fear in her eyes.

I said, "Nope. No way. You're stuck with two big brothers for the foreseeable future, or at least till you turn eighteen."

She mumbled, "Coulda had that at home," but she flushed and looked pleased.

Eb nudged her to keep going with the petting.

"Speaking of your big brothers," I said. "I want to see pictures, especially of Denver. I need to recognize them if they show up."

Brooklyn came and sat beside me. "Turn sideways." He gestured with his finger and when I rotated, he lifted my foot to his lap. Having my leg straight and elevated made me sigh with relief. He rubbed my calf gently. "You overdid it, huh?"

"In a good cause." I smiled at him. He met my gaze and echoed the smile with something a little wicked in the curve of his lips. I took a short breath.

"Ugh. I'm going to the kitchen for something." Cheyenne got up and headed through the gate, leaving it open.

Eb followed her and I called, "Wait," as he reached the gate. He looked back over his shoulder.

"He can go through," Brooklyn said. "The gate's for boarders, not residents."

"Okay," I told Eb, who trotted off toward the kitchen, his big tail thudding on the wall as he wagged. Twain scampered after him. I called to Cheyenne, "But no food. We fed them at Shane's place."

"Got it," she called back.

I leaned more comfortably into the pillows and decided I could get used to a hot guy massaging my foot. "Mmmm. But I still want to know what your brothers look like."

"I'm not sure there are pictures out there. We had a few around the house, but I didn't take any with me when I left."

"Yearbook?" I suggested, although people changed from high school.

"We don't have a real yearbook at our school," Cheyenne said, coming back in with an ice pack in her hand. "Do you, um, want this?"

I made grabby fingers. "You're a goddess of a borrowed sister. Give it here." When she passed it over, I laid the ice over the burning muscles of my thigh and sighed. "Yeah. That's good. What do you mean, no yearbook?"

"You have to understand the mindset," Brooklyn said. "Photos mean being traceable and identifiable, especially with facial recognition software these days. The adults in our community try to keep our digital footprint to a minimum. No social media for fun, although they monitor it for information. No posting pictures. No smartphones for anyone except male heads of households."

"Seriously? No internet?"

"Minimal. Back when I was a junior, the local high school decided to put their yearbooks online, but my dad and his group took over the school board and nixed the funding to scan in back issues. And they persuaded the school that the yearbook should be a voluntary end-of-year celebration only, which means the half of the kids who live in town did pictures, and those of us out in the boonies didn't, and there's not a formal class list that's so easy to find."

"Wow, that's pretty hardcore." I was surprised. "Yearbooks are as American as apple pie."

Cheyenne sat down where Eb had flopped on a big rubber mat and rubbed his belly. In a voice that sounded like a quote, she said, "Sacrifices must be made." Then in her own voice, "Not that I care about a yearbook."

"Would be handy now," I pointed out. Plus, I'd been hoping for a look at Brooklyn at eighteen. I bet he'd been cute.

"Denver looks a lot like Brooklyn," Cheyenne said. "He's three years younger and his hair is darker and he wears a lot more beard, but if you see someone that reminds you a lot of Brooklyn, that's probably him. Or Dad, if the guy's hair is receding in front and going gray. All of us take after Dad, except Nevada, who looks like Mom."

"Okay, that helps," I said. "What about Harvey?"

Cheyenne looked up sharply. "Harvey? Does it matter? He's home watching his two little kids. I hope."

"It just occurred to me that if your brother wasn't eager to drive all this way, he might tell the guy you're supposed to marry to go get you instead."

Cheyenne shivered. "God, I hope not. Denver's a creep and he wants to be Dad's mini-me, but Harvey's scary."

Brooklyn said, "Showing him to Arthur would be a good precaution, though. I'm not sure where we'd find a photo."

"Workplace?" I suggested.

Cheyenne shook her head slowly. "He works at the lumberyard, but it's run by one of Dad's friends. I doubt they post work photos online. WildApple Building Supply, if you want to check."

I dug my phone out of my pocket and searched, but the listing was pretty basic. No staff info or photos. "Nope. What about his wedding? He was married, right?"

"Yeah, but Nancy was local so I bet they kept the photos off the internet."

"Big wedding?" I asked. "Small? Any guests from the outside? What was Nancy's maiden name?"

"Medium-sized," Cheyenne said. "Her name was Kleeberg."

"That's not too common," I noted. "Worth a look." I put the name into an online search with no luck. "Maybe the Book of Face," I quipped. There were no profiles with that name, but when I checked for photos, two came up. And looky there, wedding pictures. "What about these?" I turned the phone and Cheyenne came over to look.

"Oh fuck, yeah."

"Cheyenne," Brooklyn chided. "Language."

"That might be a titch hypocritical," I suggested, nudging his crotch with my heel. I remembered a few f-bombs recently.

He glared at me, then sighed. "Okay yeah, sorry, Cheyenne. I promise to stop nagging about your language."

"*Thank* you."

"Is one of those men Harvey?" I asked.

"That guy." She pointed a finger at the dark-haired, bearded, hulking man on the left of the photo. "That's him." Her finger shook and she snatched her hand back.

I tried to zoom in on the photo but it lost resolution pretty quickly. "Maybe on a laptop."

"I'll get mine." Brooklyn stood and set my foot on the couch. He brought the laptop over and squatted by me, opening it on his knees and logging in. Cheyenne knelt beside him to see better. He found the page and photo, then zoomed.

On Brooklyn's bigger screen, I could make out a hawk-like nose and heavy brows on Harvey's face above a bush of beard that could've hidden any kind of chin. He held his bride's upper arm and his grip looked more like restraint than affection. He looked older than twenty-five in those photos which were dated five years back. I could totally understand why one glance made Cheyenne shiver.

"I think I'd know him," I said after another long scan. "But download that in case we need to put our friends on the lookout."

"It won't matter, though, right?" Cheyenne appealed to Brooklyn. "Once you have legal custody, there's nothing he can do?"

"Right." Brooklyn squeezed her shoulder. "Even without my custody, he has *zero* rights. Unlike our dad. They can't force you to marry him and without a marriage, he's just a mean stranger, no authority."

"Yep. I know." But she swallowed hard.

"And Harvey does have little kids and no wife. Not likely he can be away for a week. Dad said he'd send Denver. He expects to be obeyed."

Cheyenne nodded.

I used my phone to pull up more information. "Okay, doing some math. The trip from Piperston, New York to Gaynor Beach is forty-two hours of drive time. Last night, you talked to your father when? Seven o'clock?"

"More like nine, by the time we had everything ready," Brooklyn said.

"So if Denver jumped in his car midnight their time,

and drove without stopping more than to pee, the soonest he could be here would be…" I did some mental math. "Three p.m. tomorrow."

"I doubt Denver would kill himself to get here that fast." Brooklyn straightened and set the laptop up out of dog-reach. "He won't challenge our father, but I bet he'll resent being sent off like an errand boy to fetch his sister. If he didn't leave till morning, and took at least one full night's sleep, he won't get here till late Thursday at the earliest. Probably three days with driving fourteen hours a day, which would push it off till Friday."

"Right." I sat up a bit. "So we're completely in the clear until tomorrow afternoon, and on yellow alert through till Friday, and then red alert. When will you hear from Wynn?"

Cheyenne said, "He was filing the paperwork this morning. He said there'd be notice if it was accepted or rejected within twenty-four hours, and then a court date within ten days for the emergency injunction."

What will you do if it's rejected? I didn't ask, because I was afraid her answer would be to run, and I didn't want to put that thought into her head. I'd brainstorm with Brooklyn later.

"I *hate* this." Cheyenne leaped to her feet and paced back and forth. "Why can't our family be normal? Why did they have to be freaks? If my friend Emma hadn't let me use her smart phone all through school, I'd probably think that's just the way life is. I'd be like Nevada, marrying some bastard like Harvey and having his babies and cooking and mending and canning, and waiting for the UN to invade America."

"I know." Brooklyn went to stand near her as she paused, her head tipped back, her hands clenched in her long, straight hair. "Hey, I do know. When I got kicked out,

I was so damned lost. I'd never even been to the city, and there I was, like a total hick, wondering how I'd survive. I got luckier than I deserved, meeting another gay man at the bus station and going home with him."

"You went home with a stranger?" Cheyenne stared at him. "You could've been, like, murdered."

"I got lucky, like I said." Brooklyn flashed me a look that suggested not everything had been rosy, but I figured we'd have lots of time to get to know each other's sore spots without a vulnerable teen listening. "And now you have me."

"And me," I added, because yeah, I hadn't known Cheyenne long, but anyone Brooklyn cared about was under my protection too. "We'll get you through this crisis and you'll be complaining about homework and zits again soon."

"Instead of marrying Harvey. Shit, I'm looking forward to that." She hiccupped a laugh, then sobbed. When Brooklyn reached out toward her, she fell into his hug. He looked at me over her shaking shoulders and I gave him a thumbs-up. There were times in my teens I'd have killed for a hug. Brooklyn was a great brother.

"Maybe you guys could take Eb and Twain for a walk," I suggested. "It'd probably be good for Cheyenne to get out of the house while we know the coast is clear."

"Can we?" Cheyenne straightened and wiped her eyes with the heels of her hands.

"Sure." Brooklyn rubbed her back and stepped away. "Some exercise would do me good, too."

"Can we take Sadie?"

"She didn't seem to like the leash last night," Brooklyn said. "Let's give her some time to settle in."

"Okay. But I get to walk Ebony."

Damn, I did like that girl's sass. Luckily, I had Eb

trained to wear a head collar that would give her some leverage if the big Lab saw a squirrel. "Sure. You wash up. I'll get their leashes on them."

When she'd vanished down the hall, Brooklyn came over and sat on the arm of the couch by me. "Do you want to come along?"

"I want to cuddle up to my nice ice pack."

"I'm replaced already."

I tugged him down for a kiss. "They recommend hot packing after cold packing. You could regain most-favored status."

He met my lips eagerly, sliding his fingers into my hair, but we heard Cheyenne's door open. "Hold that thought." Brooklyn got to his feet and pointed at me. "You stay put and rest. We'll get the dogs out. Do you think Chili wants to go?"

I looked over to where she lay, one eye open, belly-up in one of the biggest beds. "Nope. She's all about self-care. Have fun."

When I had Eb fitted into his head collar, Brooklyn and Cheyenne leashed him and Twain. As they headed out of the room, Sadie retreated to a mat in the corner. I eyed her, hearing the front door open, then close. "Relax, honey. I'm not moving from this couch. You're safe."

And so was I. Even with a nasty argument with Cheyenne's brother coming up, I felt at ease in a way I hadn't for a long time. I wasn't alone. The supportive shoulder Brooklyn had given Cheyenne would be offered to me the moment that sweet man thought I needed it. The comforting awareness settled deep in my belly. I closed my eyes and let the ice pack numb my thigh.

Later that evening, after the chores were done and Cheyenne had gone to her room with Eb and Twain in attendance, I was lying in my bed chasing sleep when the door clicked open, then shut. Brooklyn tiptoed in and came over. "This okay?" he whispered.

I tented up the covers. "Get in. I thought we were being discreet for your sister."

"We're being *quiet*," he said, slipping in beside me, still in his sleep pants. "Last thing I want is for her to hear us having sex. But she knows we're together, and I need you tonight."

I put an arm around him and hugged him close. "Been a heck of a few days, huh?"

"You could say that." He laughed, a sound that came across more rough than amused. "I hate Harvey. He made my teen years less than fun. He's *not* touching Cheyenne."

I stayed silent, leaving room for him to tell me more, but he shook himself, like setting the topic aside. "You know what would be more fun? Keeping each other quiet while we come."

"Uh. Yeah. Can do that. Kissing or blow jobs?" My dick, which had been soft, got optimistic at the thought.

"I like a man with plans. Start with one, move on to the other?"

I cupped the back of his head and kissed him. He slid his hand down past my waistband and, heck, yeah, this was a great way to end my day. I had to press my palm over my mouth to stay silent by the time his talented lips and tongue got to work on my cock. Then I returned the favor, and his groan as he knelt over me, spilling into my mouth, was loud enough that Sadie barked from the family room.

"Oops." Brooklyn stared down at me, his chest flushed and heaving, his eyes bright.

I swallowed and licked my lips as he slid free. "With luck, Cheyenne will never know what woke the dog. Could've been a rabbit. Or an anaconda."

Brooklyn snorted. "You did not just go there."

"No, *you* just came here."

We got the giggles, which I totally blame on stress relief. By the time he was done falling over and smothering his laughter against my neck, and we'd each had a sip of water from my bedside tumbler, sleep came easy. I dropped off between one breath and the next, with Brooklyn safe in my arms.

CHAPTER 18

BROOKLYN

W<small>E WERE IN THE EYE OF THE HURRICANE RIGHT NOW, AS</small> I sat at the dining room table with my laptop, trying to work. The kerfuffle with our family had died down over the last two days, with no further word from our parents. I'd expected Dad to blow up my phone once the petition for emergency custody was accepted for processing yesterday —*Thank God for Wynn*—but Dad didn't call or text. I wasn't sure if I was relieved or worried.

Given Cheyenne had never checked into the hotel either, I knew that meant things would be even nastier when Denver showed up. By now, they'd know she was with me. He'd have to come here, instead of just pulling up to some motel and demanding a chastened Cheyenne slide into the passenger seat of his pickup.

At least the petition being in the pipeline meant one less thing to worry about—my sister had the right to be with me legally, for now.

The court date for the emergency hearing was set for the end of next week. That meant eight days of waiting.

Likely Denver would show up long before then,

determined to drag her home, so chaos was certain to ensue.

Hence thinking of this as the moment of calm before the next half of the storm hit. And wasn't the backside of a hurricane always worse?

I had other things to do, but my fingers clicked on the picture of Harvey that I'd saved to my hard drive. We'd printed out multiple copies, along with a general description of Denver and circulated them to our friends and neighbors. We were into yellow alert now—the "only if he's crazy" drive time. By tomorrow morning, we'd be full on red "he can make it, no sweat" timing. Someone was coming, and not knowing who and when was making my stomach hurt.

I'd cancelled Poppy and Jett for tomorrow, out of an abundance of caution. But I couldn't put my life and work on hold forever. If we were still in the clear on Monday, I'd need to allow the dogs back.

Having Arthur's three here really helped. Helped all of us, maybe Cheyenne most, but even for me, the calm furry energy kept me from being as tied up in knots.

Eb flopped in the family room, gently snoozing.

Chili lay resplendently across my feet—her new favorite spot.

Arthur and Cheyenne were out walking with Sadie and Twain. Now that Sadie was settling in, Arthur had decided she could use leash training, and Twain was good doggie company.

Sadie did best with another dog to model calm behavior.

At odd moments, I saw signs the little white dog was growing attached to Cheyenne—almost like she understood my sister was her savior—but Sadie was still skittish and nippy when suddenly approached.

But in the backyard with Arthur's three pooches? Doggie heaven.

I worried about Cheyenne taking on too much, or getting bitten, but Arthur was guiding her step by step, and I saw how it steadied Cheyenne to be strong for someone else, even a small dog. I couldn't imagine how my sister must feel, waiting for her life to be decided by older people she didn't trust. God, I was proud of her, though. No whining, no hiding in her room, just chin up and shoulders back and keeping on going.

Along with training Sadie, Cheyenne was doing a lot of housework.

A lot.

My house had never sparkled this much—at least since I'd begun the daycare.

Meals were pretty sweet as well. Her cooking even meant more stolen moments for me with Arthur. Between his work at the shelter and the daycare for me, and mentoring Cheyenne, we didn't have a ton of extra time. I treasured that last hour after Cheyenne went to bed, when I could duck into Arthur's room and be his boyfriend and nothing else, and let the world run without us for a little while—

Wham! Wham!

Pounding on the door came so loud Chili leapt up.

The racket jolted me out of my reverie.

Shit.

Eb came skittering into the dining room.

Double shit.

I grabbed my cell phone and, out of an abundance of caution, sent Arthur a text.

> Don't come home until I text it's safe.

As the pounding continued, I forced a grin at the dogs. "Let's go to Arthur's room, kids!"

My fake joviality had Chili trotting along, but Eb appeared skeptical.

"No, really, everything's fine."

Still more pounding.

Finally, Eb followed me as well.

And, of course, I slammed the door in their faces, closing them in. As much as I would appreciate Eb's company and support, I wasn't going to risk Arthur's dogs. I'd seen Denver kick a baby calf once. Not letting Chili near his boots.

The pounding was unrelenting. The noise set my teeth on edge and I was sweating. I'd forgotten how much I *hated* my brothers.

Call the cops or—

A shout. "Cheyenne, get the fuck out here!"

Is that Denver's voice? It sounded like him. I didn't want to confront my brother in front of the neighborhood, but I wasn't certain I wanted the cops showing up either. And letting him escalate would not endear me to anyone. So much for being a boring neighbor.

Mentally apologizing to everyone in the vicinity, I opened the front door. "Denver, she's not—"

Shit.

Not for the first time in my life, I'd badly miscalculated. I attempted to slam the door, but a big, booted foot prevented me closing it. Steel-toed, of course. *He always wore steel-toed boots.*

Harvey grabbed me by the shirt-front and hauled me out onto my front porch. He held on tight as he shook me like a rag doll. "Where the fuck is Cheyenne?"

You're not eight. You can fight back. Except I didn't want to. I was a strong believer in nonviolence. Every bone in my body rebelled against the idea of raising a finger against anyone, even this guy. But Harvey had never listened to words.

This is for Cheyenne. I planted my feet on the ground and glared at the vicious asshole. "Cheyenne's not here. I have no idea where she is. She stole my phone and took off." *Please believe me.* I was never a competent liar—or good at praying—but I'd do both if it kept my sister safe.

His grip tightened. "I don't believe you. Denver says she never checked into any motel like your daddy told her. He says she's still here."

Fucking Denver. Just had to be chummy with the biggest bully in Piperston. Big fucking surprise—like seeks like. Denver's bullying tendencies hadn't been nearly as strong as Harvey's, but I'd caught him harassing some of the weaker boys in his class at school. When I tried to intervene, Dad said those sissies needed *toughening up.* One reason I'd never gone to him about Harvey.

"I swear she's not here. I don't know where she is." *Hopefully far away from here. Hopefully Arthur's keeping her—*

"Let go of him, Harvey!" Cheyenne jogged toward us, Sadie skittering around on her leash at my sister's side. Behind her, Arthur was hobbling as fast as his cane would let him.

Shit.

Fucking hell.

My nemesis slammed me against the doorjamb, knocking the wind from my lungs and whacking my head on the door. Then he whirled and stalked down my front walk. "Get in the goddamn truck, Cheyenne, or I swear, you'll be sorry. You won't like what I can do to them."

I blinked. *Who are them? Me? Arthur? The dogs?* I tried to shake my head, still off-balance from the impact.

Harvey stomped to the sidewalk where Arthur and Cheyenne stood.

Arthur, silly man, was trying to put himself between Harvey and my sister. He'd handed her the leashes and was sort of brandishing his cane.

I adored him, but even as he tried to convey strength, his leg was clearly giving him problems. *Probably ran here when they heard the bellowing. So much for heeding my warning.*

Yeah, but if Arthur was in trouble, would you stay away?

To protect Cheyenne? Maybe.

"Harvey, you're not wanted here." I injected as much determination into my voice as I could. "I'll thank you to get in your pickup, and get the hell out of here before I call the cops."

He pivoted back to glare at me and my stomach dropped.

I knew that look. Had seen it many times. Had endured what usually came next.

Arthur raising the cane appeared to give my nemesis pause.

I didn't know if my boyfriend could do any real damage with the cane—although blunt instruments rarely required precision—but I worried about the risk to himself if he tried.

"What are you doing here?" Cheyenne had stopped out of Harvey's reach, peering around Arthur. She stuck her chin in the air.

I heard the quaver.

Likely Harvey did too. Men like him got off on having others tremble and cower.

I said, "Harvey's just leaving." Slowly, I strode the few steps off my porch and down toward the street, trying to sound confident, trying to seem imposing. Hiding the way my own belly quivered like Cheyenne's voice.

Again, Harvey glared. "I'll take my future wife and be on my way."

Cheyenne barked a laugh. "No fucking way am I marrying you."

Great, Cheyenne, poke the beast. Back where we came from, women didn't swear and they didn't answer back. That just wasn't a thing. Not if they knew what was *good for them*.

Harvey's nostrils flared as he glowered at me. "You let her get away with such filthy language?"

"She can say whatever she wants." Arthur's voice was dead calm. "It's a free country. Listen to Brooklyn and get out of here before we call the cops. We have a court order giving him custody of Cheyenne. Heck, she *can't* leave since she's under his protection."

I wasn't sure if that was exactly right, but who cared? *At least he's making it clear she's here with us legally.*

"Your California order doesn't mean jackshit back in New York." He said *California* as *cali-forn-eye-eh.* Basically, spelling out the last two letters and showing his absolute ignorance. Or purposeful disdain. Could go either way. He laughed in my face. "You always were a pussy. You think you can stop me now?" Then focused on Cheyenne. "Get into the truck, girl, or there will be consequences."

She shook her head. "Three against one, Harvey. You can't bully us." Again, just a touch of quaver. As if she wasn't certain we three could take the massive man.

Hell, I wasn't convinced.

If Arthur was healthy and Cheyenne didn't have two leashes? Possibly, but even then, not without getting hurt. The men of Piperston learned to fight, and Harvey had relished the training, while I'd always dodged as much as I could get away with.

The rage at my own impotence angered me. *Should've spent the past twelve years bulking up and training, preparing for this confrontation.* Except that notion was ludicrous. No way could I have predicted Cheyenne showing up and needing my protection from my old nemesis.

"Get lost, Harvey." Arthur's blue eyes glinted steel as he dug in his pocket. "I'm dialing 9-1-1 right now."

A decent threat, given my former community's desire to stay off the radar of the law. Well, the law they didn't control. The Piperstown sheriff was one of the community, but Harvey's cop friends back home wouldn't be able to protect him out here.

"Cheyenne!" He bellowed her name, lunging toward her.

My sister yelped and flinched back.

I fought the urge to punch him with my bare knuckles, not sure if I'd make things worse.

But it was Sadie who snarled like a miniature wolf, jerked her leash out of Cheyenne's grasp, and leaped at Harvey. What the damn dog thought she'd do was beyond me, but clearly she was freaked out by this entire shitshow.

Harvey scooped her up by the scruff.

She yelped in pain.

Cheyenne gasped and reached for the dog. "Let go! You're hurting her!"

Arthur, forced to lean on his cane and barely balancing, tried to step in front of her while growling, "You hurt that dog and I'll bash your head in."

Harvey bared his teeth. "If you want this stupid dog to live, Cheyenne, you'll get in the fucking truck. Hell, I might even let you keep the scrawny piece of shit."

Never. Not in a million years will he let her keep the dog. Just as likely, he'd throw Sadie out of the window on the interstate and cackle when she got run over.

Little Sadie, apparently highly unimpressed with this

turn of events, twisted in his grip and sank her teeth deep into Harvey's arm.

He howled in pain, and tossed her. Hard.

She hit the ground with another yelp and took off down the street, the leash trailing behind her.

"Sadie!" Cheyenne appeared ready to chase after her, but didn't dare bolt past Harvey.

"I'm going to kill that fucking dog." Harvey glared at me. "Then you. Slowly." He turned his attention to Arthur. "You as well, you crippled turd. Think you can fuck my future wife and get away with it?"

What the hell is he talking—

"You! Get away! I've called the police!" Mrs. Bollinger stepped onto her porch, brandishing her cell phone in her bony little hand. The pint-sized woman barely reached my chest, but she knew how to bellow. Often yelled at noisy kids on the street.

Up until this moment, I'd considered her an interfering woman with nothing better to do than complain. Right now, though, I wanted to kiss her.

"Yes, officer," she added loudly into the phone. "Making threats and abusing animals. Hurry!"

Harvey clamped his left hand over his bleeding right wrist and took a step toward Arthur and Cheyenne, but jerked his head up as the sound of a siren carried across the previously still night. "This isn't over." He glared at all of us, including Mrs. Bollinger. With most families tucked into their homes for the night, we'd been mercifully alone. No small children coming out to witness this clusterfuck. No one else for Harvey to threaten.

He strode to his pickup, swung in, and slammed the door. With a loud squeal of tires, he pulled away and rounded a corner before the approaching cop car came into sight.

"Brooklyn?" Arthur's voice was urgent as he hobbled up to me. "Did he hurt you?"

Cheyenne was wailing. "I have to find Sadie! She might be hurt!"

The sirens were approaching.

Mrs. Bollinger was bellowing after Harvey.

The cacophony of noise rang inside my skull.

There'd be statements, and Sadie had vanished, and my pounding heart was stuck in my tight, airless throat.

"I…" My gaze met Arthur's as my pulse raced and a feeling of helplessness flooded me.

"You're okay. I've got this." His gaze implored me to trust him.

And I did.

CHAPTER 19

ARTHUR

I WAS GOING TO HAVE NIGHTMARES ABOUT THE MOMENT Cheyenne and I rounded the corner and saw the hulking shape of Harvey pinning Brooklyn against the doorframe. Nightmares in which my damned leg was shackled to a cement block and I couldn't run, couldn't get there to help him, which was what it'd felt like. But we'd survived, and it was Harvey who'd had to run.

Brooklyn gazed up at me, his hazel-green eyes so dilated they looked black, his face so pale that a few unnoticed freckles stood out. "I've got this," I told him, hoping I was right.

The way he relaxed and a little color came back into his cheeks made me feel ten feet tall.

I grabbed Cheyenne's arm as she looked ready to sprint after Sadie. "Wait, give me Twain. You go inside, get Eb. She's more likely to come to him than to any of us. Grab a bunch more treats too and a couple of slip leads, in case. And flashlights since it'll be dusk soon. Hurry!"

She nodded and rushed toward the house. That young woman had a ton of courage. Facing down a six-foot tall hulking creep trying to drag her away with him, sassing him back, and barely a moment later, she was focused on her dog.

No one was hurting Cheyenne on my watch, *ever*.

I told Brooklyn, "You deal with the cops. You have the guardianship petition in progress. And you own the house."

"Okay. But Sadie…" He glanced down the street as a cop car came into view, lights flashing, siren echoing.

"If Cheyenne and I can't catch her before you're done, we'll be grateful for your help. Fingers crossed, though." I ached at the panic lingering in his eyes and wished I could put my arms around him, but the cop pulled up at the curb and got out, looking our way.

"Good luck." Brooklyn stepped toward the street and my moment to offer any kind of comfort was gone.

Later. I'll hug the hell out of him later.

Cheyenne sprinted back out the door with Eb bounding happily beside her at the unexpected walkies. At least one of us would get a bonus out of this mess.

"Here." She passed me some treats, a flashlight, and one of the slip leads. "Now what?"

"Now we see if this is going to be easy or hard. I'll keep Twain, you keep Eb. We'll head the way Sadie went. Come on." Normally, I'd swap for the bigger dog, but my leg was on fire after the mad dash to get to Brooklyn. Cheyenne would probably do better than I could.

I hobbled down the sidewalk, looking around. Twain heeled obediently, even though he no doubt wanted to sniff everything in sight, and I spoke to him in my happy training voice. "Good boy. Heel! *Clk, clk.*" I clicked my tongue in approval, a sound Sadie might already recognize. "Treat!" I passed him a bite.

Following my lead, Cheyenne did the same for Ebony.

"*Clk, clk.* Treat." I passed Twain another bite. "Speak!" He bayed his surprisingly deep beagle bark and I rewarded him.

"I don't see her," Cheyenne murmured sadly. "She could be anywhere."

"Easy, now. Happy voices." I made my tone manically cheerful, in contrast to my words. "She was scared, so she's going to run a bit before she stops."

"Do you think she's hurt?" Cheyenne was less successful at faking cheer, but she was trying. "Harvey *threw* her, the motherfucker. I wanted to claw his eyes out."

"She wasn't limping. Hopefully she's fine. And she got him good with those little grubby fangs."

"He was *bleeding*," Cheyenne noted with relish. "I want to, like, buy Sadie steak for the rest of her natural life."

"You hear that?" I called to the bushes and front steps we were passing. "Come on, Sadie. Steak for life, baby. Treats, girl. Expensive treats." I clicked and rewarded Twain again.

Near the end of the long block, Twain suddenly paused in trotting beside me and peered off to the right, his beagle nose twitching. Could be a rabbit, or a piece of paper, but...

I asked Cheyenne, "Can you crouch down? Look under that hedge? If I try, I'm not going to get up again without a forklift."

"Sure." She squatted, fending off Eb who took that as an invitation to lick her face. "I don't see—no, wait, yes. There she is!"

"Okay," I said. "I'm going to let Twain go meet her, real slow." I knotted the slip leash to his regular leash to make it longer and tossed a treat toward where Sadie was hiding. "Get it, Twain." He happily trotted three steps and snarfed it. I tossed the next one farther. "Get it." Then tossed one deep under the bushes. "Get it, Sadie."

"She's just looking at it," Cheyenne reported. "Not coming out."

"She's scared, poor baby," I said with the cheer of a used-car salesman unloading a lemon. "Such a good girl. Okay, get it, Twain." He had no problem going to the end of his double leash and under the edge of the bush. I tossed some more treats that way, and Twain snorfled happily.

Eb whined, a line of drool dropping from his lip.

"Give Eb a bite," I told Cheyenne. "Good boy. Treats! All the treats! Then toss some more her way."

She did as I suggested, peering under the screening foliage. "She's not moving. Wait, she just took the closest one. Good girl! Good Sadie!"

Bite by bite, aided by Twain's enthusiasm and Eb's loud chomping, we drew Sadie out of her hiding spot. When she and Twain were done eating side by side, I called Twain to come. He obeyed, tail up and wagging, and Sadie clung to his side. Her ears and tail were down, but she stuck to her canine buddy.

"I'm going to walk Twain toward home," I said. "Let Eb follow if he likes. Let Sadie get well past you, then reach down and snag the end of the leash she's pulling."

It took a couple of false starts, but we got the two smaller dogs headed past Cheyenne, with Eb sniffing and pacing alongside Sadie. Cheyenne stood back as they moved away from her. One step, two, three...Cheyenne bent and snatched up the end of Sadie's leash.

"Yes!" She grinned at me, eyes bright, the leash tight in her fist.

The world wobbled around me and I braced my cane, then sat down, right there on the sidewalk. The hard thump on my butt went almost unnoticed in my head-rush of relief. *No loose dogs getting hit by cars. Thank God!*

"Are you okay? Should I call Brooklyn?" Cheyenne bent over me.

Eb decided it was my turn for a facewash.

"I'm fine." I nudged Eb off me, took a couple of breaths, and used his sturdy shoulder along with the cane to help myself to my feet. The vertigo was still there, but mild enough I stayed upright. "A little dizzy. It happens." Sadie was hanging back, ears down. "Give baby girl more treats, huh? Sorry I scared you."

"Me or Sadie?" Cheyenne tossed some sausage bites. "Because yeah, don't do that again."

"It's not half as bad as when I first hit my head a couple of weeks ago." I realized with everything else going on, I hadn't focused on my symptoms, but they *were* better. I hadn't had a spin-till-you-puke episode in days, and this one didn't feel that severe. "I'm just glad it didn't happen in front of Harvey."

"Ugh. Yeah. I was glad you were standing there swinging the cane and looking fierce."

"Fierce, that's me," I said, not meaning it one bit. Although I would've hit him if I could've, for Sadie and Cheyenne.

"Do you need help?"

"Nah. Give me a few minutes." The episodes of vertigo were shorter again, too, which hopefully meant they weren't going to turn into vestibular migraines. I'd read up on those, and they sounded horrible. I leaned on my cane and breathed.

Cheyenne stood beside me, crooning to the dogs and tossing treats, while swaths of glorious sunset colors flooded the Gaynor Beach sky in the west.

"How are you doing?" I asked Cheyenne after a bit. "That must've been rough for you."

"I don't want to think about it." She shifted her weight foot to foot. "Now we've caught Sadie, I can say I'm not sorry she ran off, except for how scared she was." She glared down the block to where three cop cars sat at Brooklyn's curb, lights flashing although the sirens were now off. "She got me out of there. I don't want to talk to the cops."

"I understand that, hon, but I think it's inevitable. Harvey tried to—" At the last minute, in the hope of keeping nightmares down, hers and mine, I changed *kidnap* to "—make you go with him. The cops need to know about that. Best-case scenario, they pick him up and we never have to see him again, except in handcuffs."

"God, Dad's going to be *furious* with me if I get Harvey arrested."

I braced against another swoop of vertigo. Eb leaned on my thigh and his solid bulk helped ground me. "You do realize that's pretty messed up? That your father would be less mad at Harvey for dragging you across the country against your will, than at you for stopping him."

Cheyenne gave a wet laugh. "Honestly, if I had to stop him, Dad would rather I whack him on the head with your cane than bring the cops into it."

"Too bad, so sad. This is California, not some redneck town in upstate New York. Harvey wants to come here and act like a thug? He'll get treated like one, under the law."

"But what if..." Cheyenne's voice dropped to a shaky whisper. "What if the judge doesn't agree? What if they send me back to Dad next week? Mr. Cavannah said the biggest risk is that judges don't like to break up families without a strong reason."

"Your recording is a strong reason. Harvey showing up

and being a vicious asshole, instead of sending your brother Denver, is a strong reason." I closed my eyes, which didn't help the whirling feeling, so I opened them.

Cheyenne was shaking her head, like she wasn't convinced.

And I couldn't deny, expecting judges to always do the right thing was optimistic, even for me. I couldn't promise her a win in court. All I could do was say, "Hey, if it comes to that? If they say you have to go back? Brooklyn and I won't give up." I took a breath and promised recklessly, "If they ship you home, we'll show up there and get you loose. One way or another. Law or no law."

"You can't say that. And you're the one saying we have to talk to the cops."

"Because it's your best shot. And we obey the law, almost always. Except when our conscience says no." I took a breath. "Can you keep a secret?"

"Sure?" She took her eyes off the whirling emergency lights to look my way.

"A few years back, there was this local guy who had two Dobermans he kept on his business property as guard dogs. He used to abuse them to make them mean. People nearby knew it, and one of the neighbors recorded some stuff and called in the cops for animal cruelty."

"Good!" Cheyenne said fiercely.

"Yeah. Except when it went to court, the recording was ineligible as evidence and the neighbor changed his story. I think the bastard threatened him. So he got the dogs back. No consequences."

"This isn't making me feel better."

"You're too tough to let Harvey intimidate you and all three of us were there," I reassured her. "But the moral of the story is that those two Dobermans vanished from the property a week later. The guy never found a trace of them. He raged and blustered but no one knew anything. So he put in cameras and bought an expensive pair of so-called-trained Presa Canarios. And guess what?"

"What?"

"Those Presa Canarios somehow dug under the fence and escaped and were never seen again. And now he just has his cameras and a lot of old Beware of Dog signs."

"All right!" She eyed me. "Did you have something to do with that?"

"Me?" I set a hand on my chest and smirked. "If I happen to know someone down in San Diego who rehabilitated a pair of abused Dobermans, and I have a friend who knows camera angles and I'm also good at digging? Pure coincidence."

"Sure it is."

"The Presas took some work to place safely," I admitted. "I'd have preferred to get more evidence and use the courts, but every day he had those dogs was a day they became more traumatized, and they were scary big. A hundred and thirty pounds apiece." The crimson and gold grew brighter overhead and the world was settling down a bit. I tried a tentative step and didn't fall over. "Come on. Let's head back."

"Don't wanna," she muttered but she walked at my side as I hobbled toward home, my leg on fire but the dizziness easing.

Twain and Eb kept Sadie between them, and she seemed to be doing okay, sticking close to her buddies.

"Should we take Sadie to the vet now?" Cheyenne asked. "That might be urgent, right? If Harvey hurt her."

"Looking for more escapes?" I shook my head. "She's walking okay, breathing okay, she's alert, she took treats. I'll check her over later, but right now what she needs is less handling, less trauma." *Same as you,* I thought, but I

KAJE HARPER & GABBI GREY

couldn't protect the girl in the same way. "We'll go in the side gate and leave the dogs in the yard for now." I could give her one more minute to prepare.

We coded through the outer gate lock and then opened the inner gate. I set Twain loose, and bent to unhook Sadie's leash. She eyed me but didn't snap as I unclipped her, just scampered after the beagle across the grass. Eb galumphed behind them.

"We'll give them some decompression time," I told Cheyenne. "Come on."

When we slid the patio door open, a bunch of people turned to us. Brooklyn, four cops, and to my surprise, Wynn Cavannah.

Brooklyn leaped to his feet. "Did you find Sadie?"

"Safe in the backyard," I told him.

"Oh, thank God."

His eyes met mine, and I really wanted to cross the room and fold him into a hug. Maybe get a hug too, because I was not in great shape. This wasn't the time, though. We had to focus on Cheyenne. "Cheyenne caught her. She was brilliant," I said, because every bit of praise had to help.

"Cheyenne West?" the female deputy said. "I need to take a statement from you. Is there somewhere private you feel safe?"

"My room?" Cheyenne glanced at us. "Can Brooklyn and Arthur come?"

"Sorry. We need your independent statement."

"I, however, will come along as her attorney," Wynn said. "That's why Mr. West sent for me. If that's all right with you, Cheyenne?"

"Yes. Thank you." She hadn't moved from her spot a foot inside the door.

I stuck my head back out and called, "Ebony, come!"

When the big dog trotted over I brought him inside, closing the door on the other two. "Here, Cheyenne, take Eb with you too. He'll lick the mouth of anyone who's mean to you."

That got me a twitch of a smile, but she took his collar in a tight grip.

"Just don't let him on the bed," I added. "Lead on." I waved toward the hallway. Best for her to get this over with.

Cheyenne raised her chin and coaxed Eb with her toward her room, while the female deputy and Wynn followed her.

The oldest male cop said, "She'll be okay. Deputy Rampersad is great."

"Thank you." I took one careful step after another, leaning on my cane, until I could ease down onto the sofa. The groan I let out as I took my weight off my leg was nearly orgasmic, and I saw Brooklyn's lips twitch before he hurried over.

"Did you hurt yourself? Is it bleeding?" He knelt by my feet.

"I don't think so. I'm fine, just a bit more exercise than my doctor recommended."

"I texted you to stay away, you and Cheyenne." Brooklyn's tone took on a bit of bite.

"You did?" I rolled my ass to one side to dig out my phone. The screen was blank, free of notifications, even after I touched my way in. "I don't see—" As I spoke, the phone pinged. *"1 new message."* The time said, *"1 min."* I opened it and sure enough, —*Don't come home…*—

I laughed helplessly and turned it for Brooklyn to see. "The risk of counting on technology. Although, Brooklyn?" I met his eyes. "I'd never make you face Harvey alone, and I'd bet Cheyenne wouldn't either."

"I wanted you to keep her safe."

"He had you pinned up against the door. You deserve to be safe too."

The oldest cop said, "And on that note, we need to take your statement too, Mr. Bjornsson. If there's a space we can use?"

Brooklyn pushed to his feet and set a hand on my shoulder. "Don't move, Arthur." He frowned at the cop. "You can take his statement right here. I'll go to the kitchen and, um, fetch him an ice pack. Because he was shot, in case you don't remember, and he's still healing."

The cop sat in the armchair and looked at me. "I do remember. Two violent incidents in less than a month, Mr. Bjornsson? Is there a pattern there?" He sounded curious, not accusing, but still, *Aaaaargh. No. Pure coincidence.*

I took a breath, preparing my answer, and Brooklyn sucked air through clenched teeth before stomping off to the kitchen to fetch me some sweet relief.

CHAPTER 20

BROOKLYN

"She's settled?" Arthur offered me a small smile. He looked damn good in my bed.

After what happened tonight, we weren't sleeping apart.

That said, I'd offered to stay with Cheyenne. Camping on her floor like we had when she was three and got sick.

She'd rolled her eyes. With way more bravado than she felt, though.

I'd seen the worry behind the cool front.

But she'd pointed to my room and made it clear she expected me to hunker down with *my man*.

After we'd tucked Sadie and Chili into crates side by side, Twain and Eb had happily settled in Cheyenne's room. With the dogs, her new cell phone by her bed, and all the house alarms set, she swore she felt safe.

I'd keep my door cracked just in case.

No hanky panky tonight. And, judging by the pain etched on Arthur's face, he wasn't up for anything either.

"She's down and soon to be out. She's exhausted,

Arthur. As are you." I grabbed my sleep pants and an old T-shirt as I headed into my bathroom. I would've loved to give my boyfriend a striptease, but now wasn't the time.

No. Not the time.

I had the quickest shower on record—to wash away the gross, stinky sweat of the night—dried myself off fast, donned my sleep clothes, and headed into the bedroom.

Part of me hoped Arthur might already be asleep. I'd read the questions in his eyes earlier, as I tried to keep my cool in the aftermath of Harvey. He knew. He *knew* I hadn't told him everything before and he was curious. I didn't read hurt…just curious.

He was propped against the headboard in his sleep clothes. He'd turned down the bed, and he patted the space next to him.

I stalled. "How's the leg? Do you need another ice pack?"

He shook his head.

"Heat, maybe? Oh, I should've brought the heating pad in here. I can go—"

"Brooklyn." Quiet and sure.

I ran a hand through my hair. "Yeah?"

"I'm okay. Well, this evening's chaos aside, I'm okay."

"You don't look okay." I felt bad saying it, but I needed to be honest with him. "Have you taken your painkillers?"

"Yes. I had some with milk and a couple of cookies while you were taking care of Cheyenne."

I cocked my head. "You ate my cookies?" I tried for mock outrage. "The ones Cheyenne baked just for *me?*"

As I hoped, he smiled. "I happen to know she made them for both of us. Well, peanut butter for you and chocolate chip for me. You'll be relieved to know I didn't venture into your container. I won't say I wasn't tempted. They looked delicious."

"They are." Slowly, I eased onto the bed. "And you can have as many as you want."

He took my hand. "I know."

Our gazes met.

He smiled. Then he squeezed my hand. "We need to talk."

We don't need *to talk. We can just kiss and cuddle and fall asleep and pretend the past four hours didn't happen. Why can't we do that?*

Because I was a fucking adult and acting like a five-year-old wasn't the way to impress my adult boyfriend.

Right?

Worth a shot…?

Nope. I'd be an adult. I blew out a breath. "Harvey."

"Yeah, Harvey." He waited.

"I said we were in the same class at school."

"I remember."

"Well—" I scratched my chin. "Cheyenne didn't know about the bullying. The unrelenting and unceasing bullying. No, that's wrong." I closed my eyes, not wanting to be back in that schoolyard in New York, but finding myself there anyway. "He taunted and tormented me and was horrible. Then, other times, he'd act all friendly and make me think things would be okay. Then, for no reason, he'd come at me again."

"Cycles of abuse." Said quietly.

"Yeah. I later came to understand the psychological torture he was inflicting on me. Like some spouses of abusers experience. When they think they can't take anymore and are about to run, the abuser seems to change their ways and gaslight them. He'd tell me I'd earned the right to hang out with him, and I'd question whether my memories exaggerated how bad his violence had been." Even now, I teetered on the edge of memory and illusion

—trying to piece together what had been real and what had only been alluded to, threats of worse whispered in my ears.

"Violence?"

"He hit me a lot. God, I sound..." I bit my lower lip. "Mostly where people couldn't see. Not teachers or parents. My mom saw the marks a couple of times, but I told her I fell out of trees, or some shit like that. Either she was clueless, or maybe she suspected and didn't care, or she figured my father'd beat me and I'd deserved it."

"Oh." Arthur continued to hold my hand. "I'm so sorry, that's wrong."

"Yep." I pursed my lips. "But my dad could lay into me something fierce as well. And some of the teachers used corporal punishment. Spare the rod and all that bullshit. Child Protective Services were never called. The outside world's rules didn't apply. Hell, I didn't even know such rules existed until I got out."

A silence descended.

Much as I wanted to sink into it, I couldn't. Now I'd started, I needed to get it all out. "I put up with the bullying. Had no choice. Harvey was taller for most of our lives, beefier, and stronger always. I fought when ordered to by a coach, but that was it. I don't think anyone was surprised when I came out as bisexual. *All queers are sissies.*" I gazed at Arthur. "Now we both know that's not true."

He offered a small smile back.

"I came out at eighteen. Normally men in our community wait until they're a bit older to marry—so they can provide properly for their families. I thought—" I swallowed. "I figured I had time. For what, I have no idea. Time to figure shit out? I was just out of high school and at the same time arrogant and naïve. I knew the lay of the land where I lived. The outside world...I didn't understand it. We'd been made to fear it. So I figured I was better staying put."

I pulled my hand from Arthur's and wiped it on the sheet.

He kept his hand steady.

After a long moment, I put mine back in his. "Then one day Daddy came home and said I was marrying Rachel Monroe. Just like that. Rachel was fifteen, for God's sake. But her parents were willing to sign the papers, and my uncle the judge was going to sign off on it, which made it legal back then. She must've been willing. In retrospect, I wonder if she wasn't hoping to get away from something worse. Worse—" I cleared my throat. "—there was always worse."

"Yeah." Again, quietly.

I kept going. "I think something was going on with Rachel. Maybe that she was pregnant? Our daddies decided they could fix their two problem children at the same time. I tried to explain that I was too young *and* I was queer. Bisexual." I huffed out a humorless laugh. "Dad said bisexual meant I could marry a girl and that, for God's sake, I was going to. That I either did what was good for the community or that I could leave. I'd hoped if I said I was bi, then they'd back off." I rubbed my forehead.

"I'm guessing not." Quiet. Encouraging.

"Nope. The minister was called and, in a family conference, I was ordered to do my duty with Rachel or to leave town and be disowned." Dread welled within me— much as it had that day. "I knew marrying her would be the biggest mistake of our lives. That I would be condemning us both to misery. And, frankly, I was terrified of Dad and of the trap I'd be walking into."

"What happened?" He asked the question gently—like he was coaxing Sadie to come for a treat.

"I packed a bag. The minister drove me to the bus station in Syracuse. He bought me a ticket to the *City of Sinners and Globalists*. Known as New York City to the rest of the world. Truthfully, I'm surprised Mom took Cheyenne there. Well, except that she needed that fragile part for something or other of Dad's."

Arthur cocked his head.

"The UN, the symbol of all they hate, is in Manhattan. Communism had fallen, so they had a new enemy. The New World Order, the secret cabal working to replace American independence with international oppression." I rolled my eyes. "Washington would've been just as disdained, if not more so. Embassies, democratic power. Obama, no less. Man, that didn't go over well with my family."

"Right. I hadn't put that logic together."

"There is no logic." I repeated the words. "There *is* no logic." I sighed. "But I was an eighteen-year-old kid in the Port Authority bus terminal in New York City with a bag and fifteen dollars in his wallet."

"That's...rough."

"Right?" I sighed. "And this guy walked over to me and asked if I was okay. I mean, I must've looked really fucked up for someone to notice." I rubbed my forehead again. "That was Tom. He'd just dropped his buddy Lance at the bus station and he was about to head home when he saw me. He later said he recognized pain. I..." I blew out a breath. "Only later did I realize how lucky I was. He took me home. He fed me and he coaxed the story out of me. I'll be honest—he recognized the danger of what I'd left behind far more than I had, with the secrecy and the guns and all. He convinced me to not tell anyone about where I came from, just be glad I was out and move on. Then he got me a job cleaning fry machines at a local burger joint.

Not glamorous, but I was able to pay him rent and, for the first time in my life, see what the outside world was all about."

"Sounds like he saved you."

My gaze shot to Arthur's. "He did. And he didn't ask for anything in return. Then he introduced me to his friend Marty. Marty had a spare room, so I moved there. He trained dogs for stage and screen, and that's how I got interested in animal behavior. He gave me tons of lessons and I sort of thought he'd bring me in as a partner in his business. But then he met Lynette and they decided to move to the country. Suddenly, he didn't have room for me. He took his business with him."

"That must've been tough."

"Well, I was older by then. Able to strike out on my own—but not with enough experience to pass myself off as a professional trainer. I'd been studying psych behavior classes at night to use while dog training." Impotence welled within me. "But when Marty left, I lost my cheap room as well. By the time I found somewhere I could afford, attending school became really hard. I took a few more classes, but after six years, I barely had two years' worth of schooling. You need at least a master's degree in psych to do anything worthwhile. So, I quit school, quit the dead-end job I'd been working, and I found a good sales job. I was starting to make some decent commissions when life kicked me in the balls again."

"I really am afraid to ask." Arthur's blue eyes radiated compassion.

Do I really need to keep going? Why not just say "and that's how I got to Gaynor Beach" and leave him to fill in the blanks?

Because he deserved more. Hell, if I was honest, so did I.

From a practical standpoint, Cheyenne knew a lot

about what had happened next. I didn't want Arthur to know less about my life than my sister did.

"I got appendicitis. Being a manly man, though, I just figured it was indigestion. My girlfriend at the time, Becca, tried to talk me into going to the doctor. But I had a work shift and a ridiculously high deductible with my crappy health insurance and…I took some antacids and went to work."

"Uh, that doesn't sound good."

"Nope. I wound up on the floor, incapable of moving. Paramedics had to come and rush me to the hospital. I told them I was allergic to penicillin and it was written in my chart, but someone missed the note so, after surgery, they were pumping me full of antibiotics to deal with the ruptured appendix and they gave me Zosyn IV. Which is a penicillin."

"Oh shit."

For Arthur to swear, he had to know how big of a deal that had been.

"Anaphylactic shock. Throat swelled up, got dizzy, vomited. I couldn't breathe, went into circulatory collapse." My heartrate kicked up a notch as I remembered the sheer panic. I'd flailed despite the searing pain in my gut, my air choked off, my body weakening until I couldn't fight. I hadn't understood why I couldn't breathe, but I'd understood I was dying. Hell, by the time I passed out, I'd thought that was it. In my mind, I said *goodbye* to Cheyenne and figured that was the end of my life. Funny…Becca, Marty, and the rest of my family hadn't factored into any of those final frantic thoughts.

Just Cheyenne, the little sister who'd idolized me, whom I didn't get to see grow up.

"They got me breathing again, but things were dicey and I wound up in intensive care for three days. I was so sick—nauseous and hurting, delirious with a high fever, infection, and kidney damage. Becca bailed on day three. Nice woman. Very sweet. Not into drama in the least."

"Having your boyfriend critically ill was *drama*?"

I shrugged with a nonchalance I didn't feel. "It was abundantly clear she wasn't invested in our relationship." I took a deep breath. "Frankly, I wasn't all that invested either. I didn't love her, not enough. I didn't mourn losing her as much as not having someone at my side while I faced the mess I was in." *Between the weakness, the pain, and the nightmares of being choked to death.*

"Still, to ditch someone when they're in intensive care…" He winced.

"Yep. But as she walked out the door, in waltzed my parents."

Arthur's eyes widened.

"All was forgiven and they were there to take care of me." I rubbed my forehead for the millionth time. "And in that moment, I bought it. Wanted their help, even. In truth, I didn't have the next month's rent, the job had been good but fighting for commissions was brutal, and I was so sick I could barely sit up. New York's an at-will employment state. I couldn't expect them to hold my job for me through recovery. The idea of someone taking care of me—even people as fucked-up as my parents—sounded good. And they brought Cheyenne, so grown I almost didn't recognize her but still my little sister. They knew how to manipulate me…and it worked."

"They were manipulating you? Why?"

"One of their prepper friends was a nurse at the hospital—a source of drugs and health supplies for when Armageddon comes. She told them they could make a bunch of money off me. I had no idea at the time. I actually thought they might still see me as family." I took in a sharp breath, forcing myself to face the memories. "So I went home. Spent two weeks in my old bed with Cheyenne taking care of me. I had time with her I never thought to have. I got to know her as an almost-adult. She'd just turned seventeen. A spitfire. I cautioned her to get her high school degree and then, if she wanted, that I'd come and get her. Hell, I didn't have any right to make that promise, but I did."

"Well, she's here now." Arthur eyed me. "I don't understand why your parents really thought you were worth bringing home."

"You mean aside from Becca making me look straight? Well, that nurse said the hospital lawyers were preparing to offer me a big settlement. No question them administering that drug was malpractice and caused significant harm." I grinned without humor. "My folks saw a huge payout in the future, one they'd control if they controlled me."

Arthur winced. "Were you considering suing the hospital?"

"Hiring a lawyer and shit?" I sighed. "That might've taken years. The final kidney damage wasn't too bad, I was still alive, and I had my strength back. But I could have, and they knew it. They offered to cover my medical care plus a decent payout. Which was when I discovered my parents were planning to take the settlement."

He chuckled. A grating sound because it was scorn and not amusement. "Of course they were."

"Right? So, once I was healed, I bailed the hell out of Piperston. I stayed with a New York friend on his couch until the money came through. Then I sent five hundred to my parents for their hassle, gave my friend as much as he would let me, and bought a used SUV. I chucked my very few belongings in the back, picked Gaynor Beach, as far away as I could get, and left New York in the rearview mirror."

"That was brave."

"Brave...stupid...a little nuts...all of the above? Yeah. I rented an apartment, and a local real estate agent eventually found me this place. I had enough for a down payment and to cover the renovations to make a safe doggie daycare. But I still need to find more regular clients to keep from going under, and this mess won't help. Having the cops at my door doesn't exactly engender trust in my ability to keep dogs safe."

Slowly, Arthur nodded. "I'm sure, once truthful word gets out, that everything will be okay. All our friends know what's going on. Gaynor Beach is a small town—if bad news travels fast, surely good news will as well?"

I blinked. "What good news?"

"Well, they're going to catch Harvey. He has New York license plates, even if none of us remembered the number. Every cop in town will be looking for him." Arthur offered the smallest of smiles. "He doesn't seem like the shiniest penny in the jar."

"No, he's not. It's just...I'm not feeling optimistic right now, Arthur. When I left New York, I swore I'd never look back. I swore I'd be someone who embraced life and only saw the good. Harvey, Denver, and the rest of my fucking family are dragging me back to that dark place." I took a ragged breath.

"Remember Cheyenne."

My gaze snapped to his.

"She's part of that past. She's also your future, Brooklyn. You'll figure out how be positive because you need to take care of her. That's your mission, now. I know you. You'll do whatever it takes, and if that means confronting your past once and for all, then that's what you'll do. But here's the great part." He smiled.

There is no great part. There's only shit piled on more shit—

"You're not alone anymore."

And with those simple words, my heart lifted. I blinked.

He gripped my hand even tighter. "We're together, Brooklyn. For whatever that's worth—"

"That's worth everything." How could I express how much this meant to me? It'd barely been two weeks, and yet I knew I'd found the person I was meant to be with. The man who might give me the strength to save myself. I blinked rapidly.

He caressed my cheek. "Why don't we lie down? I want to cuddle you tonight, okay?"

I threw a glance at the door, still wound up tight, and somehow, Arthur understood me.

He thumbed my lip, then lowered his hand and squeezed my fingers gently. "You go check on Cheyenne first if you need to, and I'll get under the covers. I'll be waiting for you."

He understands. He's not turning away from me, despite the drama of my fucking life. He gets that I've tried to be sunshine for so long, but that today it's cloudy and that's okay. "Yeah, I'll look in on her. Sadie and Chili as well. And then, yeah, I'll come to bed."

Slowly, I withdrew my hand from his. I slipped from the bed, took a deep breath, and eventually exited my bedroom. I checked on Cheyenne who was fast asleep— sharing the double bed with Eb while Twain slept in a dog bed on the floor.

Arthur would likely have a conniption fit about Eb.

So I wouldn't tell him. Sometimes secrets were okay. I'd just told him fucking everything. Instead of running for the hills—or at least back to the shelter—he was preparing to hold me all night.

Sadie and Chili didn't stir, snoozing peacefully in their crates when I peered around the doorframe to see how they were doing.

I double checked the alarms and, finding everything was set, I headed to bed.

To be with the best man I'd ever met.

CHAPTER 21

ARTHUR

"I'm sick of this!" Cheyenne kicked the kitchen chair, and it fell over with a bang. Out in the family room, Sadie yelped. Cheyenne looked stricken. She called, "Oh God, sorry, baby. I'm so stupid. I can't do anything right." She knelt, scrabbling at the chair to get it upright.

"Hey, hey." Brooklyn came back from the front door, where he'd been returning an adorable pair of Corgis to their owner. "What's wrong?"

"Everything." Cheyenne rubbed her eyes. "I feel like a prisoner. Harvey's out there, somewhere, doing God knows what. And in a week, the judge might send me back to my parents."

I tried to be optimistic for the girl who was starting to feel like my own little sister. "There's been no sign of Harvey for two days. The cops have his license number now, and he's wanted for attempted kidnapping by every law enforcement group in California. Surely he's just washed his hands of you and headed back to his safe zone in New York?"

Brooklyn and Cheyenne were both shaking their heads before I was done. "If Dad had sent Denver, then yes," Brooklyn said. "He'd write her off, same as they wrote me off, not worth the trouble. But Harvey's different."

"He holds a grudge," Cheyenne noted.

"Yeah, and he can't stand losing." Brooklyn forced a smile. "We'd have been better off to let you hit him on the head with your cane. That he maybe could accept. Instead, he lost to a ten-pound dog, a teen girl, and an elderly lady with a cell phone. I don't think he'll leave until he wipes out that memory." He glanced at Cheyenne. "Which is why you can't go anywhere without one of us."

"I *understand* why, I just hate it. I'm going stir-crazy and there's only so many times I can scrub the kitchen floor."

Xandra wandered in and twined around Cheyenne's ankles. She picked up the cat and hid her face in soft, cream-colored fur. I eyed her hunched shoulders, thinking about how often I'd done the same, losing myself in the comfort of a purring cat. Didn't make the world go away, though.

How long will this go on? "Harvey has a job and kids, you said? He can't just hang out here forever."

Brooklyn shrugged. "No, but...one thing that community's good for is mutual support. He probably has his mom watching the kids, and his job will wait for him."

"Maybe you and Cheyenne should go away for a while. Stay with someone else till he has to give up."

"Stay with whom? I don't have the friends you do. Anyhow, I can't take time off from my business. My regulars need care daily. If they have to do daycare somewhere else, even for a week, they might not come back."

I wanted to offer to run the business while he was away,

but the shelter was stretched too thin for me to do both. My phone rang. *Neil.* Speaking of the shelter. I answered, "Yeah, what's up?"

"The insurance adjuster's here with the plumber, looking at where we had that water leak. He has some questions for you, and if you can't do it now, he says it'll be a couple of weeks before he's back this way."

"Crap. All right. Tell him I'll be there in twenty. Maybe twenty-five. I'll need to call for a ride."

"You got it. Sorry to drag you back in when you just left." Neil cut the call.

"I can drive you," Brooklyn offered. "Except no, that leaves Cheyenne home alone." He hadn't driven me anywhere since the encounter with Harvey. "Maybe she could drive you and hang out at the shelter, and bring you back."

"Yeah!" She perked up, setting Xandra on the floor. "I haven't seen the shelter. That would be cool."

"You could come too," I suggested to Brooklyn. "Show her around while I do the boring insurance and plumbing."

"Sure."

Cheyenne grinned at him, then her smile slipped. "Can we leave all the babies alone here? What if Harvey comes and tries to kidnap Sadie as a hostage."

Brooklyn and I glanced at each other. *Is Harvey that crazy?* I raised an eyebrow and Brooklyn gave me a tiny nod. *Well, crap.* I suggested, "Ask Roger to keep an eye out?"

"Oh, good thought."

Brooklyn and I had both liked his other-side-from-Mrs. Bollinger neighbor when Roger came to introduce himself yesterday. He'd apologized for not being around when we'd needed him. He was ex-military, about forty, and he'd heard about the Harvey mess from someone he knew in the sheriff's department. He'd promised he was keeping an eye out, and swore that Harvey wouldn't tangle with him. Roger's air of competence made that sound like more of a fact than a boast.

I said, "We can stop by his place as we head out."

"Ooh, yeah," Cheyenne agreed. "Can we go now?"

"Jeans?" I suggested, looking at her bare legs in shorts. "If you want to play with the dogs."

"Two minutes!" She dashed out of the kitchen, Xandra scampering behind and swatting at Cheyenne's bare heels in fun.

Brooklyn's sigh was heavy, and I pulled him into a hug. "You okay? Don't want to come?"

"No, I do, just not sleeping well."

Tell me something I don't know. He'd had nightmares both nights since Harvey's appearance, ones he didn't want to recount. I hugged him tighter.

"And I hate that we can't just settle into living our lives, that Cheyenne still has to be looking over her shoulder. At least when I left home, I was out. I didn't worry about being dragged back to Dad."

I kissed his silky hair, since I had no reassurance to offer that wouldn't sound banal.

Cheyenne skidded back into the kitchen. "Hey, I thought we were in a hurry."

Reluctantly, I let go of Brooklyn. "Going now."

"Can we take Eb? You said he used to wander round the shelter with you. I bet he misses it."

I'd noticed that as much as Cheyenne adored Sadie, she liked to keep Ebony close to her. Even though he was a marshmallow, there was no doubt some comfort in having ninety pounds of dog at her side. "I suppose so. If you'll watch him while I'm busy."

"Yay!" She ran to get his headcollar and leash. "Come on Eb! An adventure."

Before we hit the road, Brooklyn pulled the SUV into Roger's driveway and jogged up to his door. The man answered, and seeing his alert air and broad-shouldered stability was reassuring. As Brooklyn spoke, Roger turned toward the house and nodded.

"He'll keep an eye out," Brooklyn reported as he swung back into his seat. "Okay, shelter."

I had Brooklyn park along the side and coded us in at the employee door. Cheyenne bounced on the balls of her feet, Eb's leash wrapped around her hand. "This is so cool. How many pets are in here?"

"We have fourteen dogs and nineteen cats right now," I told her. "And two rabbits."

"Rabbits? Like, for pets?"

"Yep."

"Can I see them?"

"Just keep Eb at a distance. He wants to slobber on them, and it makes them nervous." I saw Neil approaching down the hallway and gestured. "Brooklyn, you know where everything is. You can show her the evening-walks routine. Yasmin and Mario should be back there. If she wants to meet any dogs, or give them a quick playtime outside, only let her near the ones with the green stickers, and put Eb in a kennel first."

"Got it." Brooklyn touched my shoulder. "Go deal with your *plumbing*."

I liked the sparkle in his eye and the way he looked less worried here. Neil was waiting, but I paused to watch the rear view of Brooklyn walking away. Someday, we'd both be healthy and unworried and I could properly savor the little zing that looking at Brooklyn always gave me.

Neil cleared his throat, and I turned to him. "Right. Lead on."

The water damage, caused by an in-wall leak from a section of pipe that should've been replaced, was worse than I expected. The plumber put his finger right through a decent-looking bit of drywall with an apologetic glance, showing where it was waterlogged on the inside. The insurance guy, of course, wanted it patched, not replaced. Discussion ensued.

Forty minutes later, we had the estimate hashed out. Naturally, not signed off on. The adjuster would take it back to the office to run some numbers. But I had a hope we could get started on fixing things.

Activity in the shelter had died down while we were working. We'd closed to the public a while ago and, looking at the time, I knew the last feedings and walks should be almost finished. Somewhere outside, someone called a goodbye and a car started. I showed the adjuster and plumber out the front, and relocked the door.

Neil came into the lobby, slipping on his jacket. "All done?"

"Yeah. I think we're fully covered, but it's always a fight. Excuse me, a discussion."

He snorted. "Better you than me. I'm heading out unless you need me. Sawyer has plans for us." He grinned.

"Go get your man." I waved. "Just lock up. I'll set the alarm when we leave."

When he was gone, shutting off the front lights on his way out, I looked around. In the mellow evening light slanting in the big windows, the front of my shelter sparkled, marble tiles gleaming, little flecks of gold reflecting off the chandeliers. The luxury fittings were ridiculous, but I'd come to love every inch of them. The unique feel, the high open ceiling and polished charm, all said that the fur-babies who called this place home mattered. That they were gifts to win, not strays begging for scraps. Illusion, since we were perennially short of funds, but a state of mind I encouraged.

I heard Brooklyn's voice somewhere in back, and Cheyenne's laugh, and warmth filled me. This was the life I'd always wanted. Back when I was the shy, quiet kid, trying to be so good that someone would notice and value me, this was what I'd have dreamed of, if I'd had the imagination. A place like this to bring help to so many innocent pets. A man who took care of me and let me take care of him. A family who needed me, even in the form of a borrowed little sister and a furry pack.

I have it all now. And I needed Brooklyn to know it. I vowed to court him, to show him how much he meant to me. This difficult time would pass, and then I could date the man I'd somehow been gifted by the universe. Take him out to eat, give him little gifts, share my favorite movies, take him to my bed and make him feel like the king of the world. I'd be willing to get shot all over again, if it brought Brooklyn to me.

My cane slipped on the marble as I headed to the back, and I made a mental note that we needed to reapply the non-slip coating. Dog claws were hard on surfaces. I found Cheyenne in the kitchen putting bowls in the dishwasher while Brooklyn checked off names on the exercise list.

"I didn't mean to put you two to work."

"It was fun," Cheyenne chirped.

"Mario had a date, so we told him we'd do the last couple of runs for him." Brooklyn hung the clipboard on the wall. "How's the plumbing?"

"Meh. Needs some work, but we should be covered."

"Did you really live here at the shelter?" Cheyenne asked.

"Sure did. I mean, I guess I do. I will?" I exchanged looks with Brooklyn, but this wasn't the moment to discuss our future. "There's an apartment upstairs, along with the shelter office. Want to see?"

"Sure."

"Eb will probably tow you up there. He left some toys behind."

I led the way into the hall, glancing at the side door to make sure it was locked. Occasionally I'd had volunteers be careless leaving, when they knew they weren't last out for the day. But since Harvey, I'd had a serious talk with them again. *Yep, deadbolt's thrown.*

The flight of stairs ahead of us didn't look as intimidating as it had back on that bad first day when I'd almost crushed Brooklyn, but it was still a steep climb. I took Eb's leash from Cheyenne and let him go free. "Upstairs!"

The big lab galloped up, his feet thudding on the treads, and panted down at us from above. Cheyenne followed him. Brooklyn said, "I'm staying behind you, just in case."

"I've been up and down here this week, to use the office." With Neil hovering, though I didn't say so.

"Even so." He waved me ahead.

Upstairs, I showed Cheyenne the office and then my apartment. She tilted her head. "It's cute, I guess, but seems small to have three dogs and a cat."

"They get to spend time downstairs and out in the exercise areas, so it works fine."

"I bet they like Brooklyn's house better."

"Don't nudge," Brooklyn told her.

"Just saying. Hey, Arthur, when you move in with my brother, you'll need a caretaker for the shelter. Maybe I could live here once I'm eighteen."

Brooklyn snorted. "You're not moving out while you're in high school."

"Afterward."

"You're going to college."

Cheyenne's chin tilted up in a defiance I was already familiar with, so I deflected, "We should head out. Sadie will want her dinner."

That made her laugh. "*Twain* will want his dinner. Sadie's not that pushy."

"Yet."

"You want to bring anything *home* with you?" Brooklyn asked me. The emphasis and his eyes staring into mine made me certain he'd used that word deliberately.

Just you. That's all I need to be home. "Nah. I brought clothes yesterday. Let's go."

We made our way down the stairs, Cheyenne holding onto Eb. Between the railing and my cane, I was steady enough. *Go, me.* Eb pulled on his leash a bit as we got to the bottom, whining. Maybe he wanted his dinner.

Then, as we approached the side door, Harvey stepped out of a side hallway, a small but deadly looking gun pointed at us. "Well, lookie here. I was just planning to collect the crippled motherfucker, and I hit the trifecta."

Cheyenne yelped and shrank back. Brooklyn and I moved in unison to get in front of her. I heard Eb panting hard, nervous and unsure, probably smelling my fear.

"How did you get in here?" I asked inanely. "The doors are locked."

"But they weren't three hours ago." He gave a feral grin. "Your people don't really pay attention, do they? So many places to hide." The smile slipped from his face. "Okay, change of plans. Phones out and on the floor, everyone. Now! Do it!"

Brooklyn and I eased our phones out of our pockets. I

debated the chance to hit the emergency button but he was watching us closely and that gun, though held in his left hand, didn't waver. When we'd set our phones down and straightened, he eyed Cheyenne. "Yours too, girl."

"I've never had a phone." Her voice was admirably steady.

"Don't bullshit me. I bet your dear brother got you one, first thing. Cough it up. Now!"

She hesitated, then pulled out the burner we'd got her and laid it on the floor.

"Right." Harvey looked us over, seeming to be thinking.

Three of us and one of him. Without the gun, I might've tried to see if my childhood baseball skills worked with a cane, but I didn't dare.

"Okay," he said. "Outside. Crip-guy first and then Brooklyn and little Cheyenne will stay right close to me."

At least he wasn't going to just murder us out of hand and drag Cheyenne off, but we were still in deep trouble.

Brooklyn said, "Leave Cheyenne here. I'll go with you. Do whatever you want."

Harvey barked a laugh. "Why? You're no use to me. I'm no queer and you always were a weakling. Move it!"

I turned to the exit, opening the deadbolt as slowly as I could. The alarm panel had an emergency button too, but I had no excuse to reach for it and the muzzle of Harvey's gun was now aimed squarely at Cheyenne. My heart pounded and I felt dizzy. Fear or vertigo? *Fuck no, not now.*

"Outside, one by one."

I pushed the door open and stepped out into the cool Gaynor Beach evening. Dusk was falling, but the last colors still brightened the sky.

Brooklyn followed me, and then Harvey shoved Cheyenne out ahead of him. She'd dropped Eb's leash but the big dog stuck to her far side, his ears down. He wasn't any kind of attack dog. Probably just as well with a gun in the mix.

"Out front. The gray truck. Walk that way." Harvey gestured with his chin.

The pickup parked at the far side of the lot had California plates on it, but otherwise looked like the one Harvey'd driven off in. Maybe he'd stolen the license plates somewhere.

I walked toward the truck, one slow step at a time, leaning on my cane harder than I needed to so I'd seem weak and useless.

I am weak and useless.

Surely there was something I could do, but I couldn't think of what. My heart pounded but the dizziness didn't worsen.

"Stop there." Harvey worked to pull his key fob out of his pocket and pop the locks. I saw that his right hand was wrapped in a stained, makeshift bandage and felt a fierce satisfaction that at least Sadie had sunk her teeth into the motherfucker. *I hope I get my turn soon.* Fury was turning my vision red. How *dared* he come into my shelter and try to kidnap a child? I would *end* him. I'd never been a violent man, but the handle of the cane dug into my clenched palm.

Harvey looked back and forth between the truck and us. "Sit down, both of you," he snapped. "On the ground. And hold that dog or I'll shoot it."

I grabbed Eb's leash and eased myself down to sit on the edge of one of the planted curbs. Even six inches might make a difference in how fast I stood up. Brooklyn sat on the pavement beside me.

Harvey nodded. "I'm leaving now, me and my fiancée. I'm taking her back to her daddy, all lawful, and we'll get married with his blessing. No liberal California court gets to come between a man and his daughter, and the wedding her daddy wants for her."

All lawful. I wanted to choke, to shout that this was kidnapping and he'd go to prison for life. But if he thought he had nothing to lose, he might kill Brooklyn and me after all.

He nudged Cheyenne, urging her to move with his heavy boot against her ankle. "Over to the truck, Chey. You two stay put there. You try to come at me, and I'll gut shoot you. Girl, get in on this side and slide over."

Cheyenne shot a terrified look at us over her shoulder, then climbed in the driver's side of the pickup. I saw her scoot over and struggle with the other doorhandle, trying to get back out, but Harvey must've done something to disable it. He got in beside her, slammed the door, and started the engine. Both his hands were on the wheel and I didn't see the gun, as he pulled forward out of his space, turning...

Brooklyn was muttering, "Fuck, fuck, fuck!" beside me.

I fumbled in the rock bed, and as the truck moved faster, I found a fist-sized rock and threw it with all of those remembered baseball skills. I hit the windshield in front of Harvey, spiderwebbing it with cracks but not breaking through. Harvey swerved and stomped on the gas.

Then I saw Cheyenne grab his bandaged hand off the wheel, open her mouth wide, and bite down on the bandage, her eyes wild, her jaw clenched on him.

Harvey screamed, loud enough to hear where I was scrambling to my feet. *Infected dog bite. Go Cheyenne.* Cheyenne was whipped back and forth with the force of his attempts to get free, but she hung on with hands and teeth.

Harvey took his other hand off the wheel to punch at

her and as he twisted, his foot must've come down on the accelerator. The pickup leaped forward, plunged up over the curb, and smashed into the shelter through the big front window. Glass crashed. Stucco cracked and fell. I saw the airbags deploy as the truck slewed to a stop.

"Cheyenne!" Brooklyn bolted toward the accident. I tried to follow as fast as I could in a shambling run.

Harvey's door opened and I held my breath but he staggered out without his gun, blood running down his face. Brooklyn ignored him, working his way toward Cheyenne around the other side. After a glance at Brooklyn and another at me, Harvey began to run for the street.

Oh, no, you're not disappearing again. I was *not* putting Cheyenne through more days of being terrified about where Harvey was. I tried to run after him, but even with the crooked, hurt-ribs way Harvey was moving, he was faster than me.

I looked down at Eb, trotting at my side, ears half-cocked as if he wasn't sure what the game was. He'd been originally owned by a college student who gave him no discipline and lots of unfortunate tricks. But maybe one of those could save us now.

I pointed at Harvey and said in a happy, let's-play tone, "Ebony! Tag! Tag him!"

Ebony woofed and leaped forward. As I called, "Tag! Tag!" he chased down Harvey. Harvey spun at the sound of paws closing behind him and raised an arm in front of his throat, his other hand ready to intercept a head aimed to bite.

But Eb didn't attack. Instead, he leaped forward off his hind legs and planted both front paws high on Harvey's shoulders, stiff-legged with all his weight behind them.

"Tag" meant "knock him over." His past owner's idea of a joke on his buddies.

Harvey bowled over backward hard. His ass and shoulders hit the concrete and I saw his head bounce.

Good. See how you like a concussion.

I called Eb urgently. "Eb, come! Come!" His usual follow-up to "tag" was a thorough face-licking and I didn't want him in Harvey's reach.

Eb lollopped back to me, ears up and tail waving happily. "Good boy," I told him, hustling forward. "Good job."

When I reached Harvey, he'd rolled over face down and was groaning, scrabbling to get up. I planted my cane in the middle of his neck, right at the base of his skull, and leaned on it heavily. He cursed, but collapsed flat and froze, his face pressed against the pavement.

"Don't move," I said through gritted teeth. I wanted to hit and hurt, smash his skull, break his spine. I leaned down a bit harder. "I don't know if I can pop your skull off your neck like this, but I'm willing to try."

"Fuck you." His voice came garbled. "F-fuck. You took my woman. Gonna die."

"Move an inch and if this fails, I'll let the dog rip your throat out."

"Fuck you, motherfucker." But he didn't move.

Suddenly, an alarm sounded from the shelter, wailing loudly. *Fire?*

Brooklyn panted up to me, his arm around Cheyenne. "Something's smoking."

"Shit!" I looked over my shoulder at my pride and joy, full of vulnerable animals. Then down at Harvey. "Cheyenne, are you okay?"

She grinned at me with blood on her teeth. "My arm hurts, but I have his gun." Sure enough, in her hand, she held the pistol, her casual grip seeming competent. *Teach your kids to use guns and you may regret treating them like crap.*

"Point it at Harvey," I told her. "Shoot him if he moves. Brooklyn, get Eb and take care of Cheyenne."

"What?" Brooklyn stared at me, his face pale. "Where are you going?"

I knew what I was doing was crazy, but I couldn't help myself. The siren wailed in my ears. The dogs barked hysterically in the back. I rushed toward the damaged window as fast as I could, my leg trying to trip me as I climbed over the damaged wall. Inside, I could smell smoke, and something along the wall sparked in bright flickers.

Fire extinguisher! We had a dozen, all through the facility, and overhead sprinklers too. *Why aren't they going off?*

Even as I had that thought, the sprinklers let loose with a torrent of water. I stumbled, slipping on the wet floor, and found the nearest extinguisher.

The sparks of light beside the broken window seemed smaller. *Drop the cane. Pull the pin. Aim at the base—where? There. Squeeze. Sweep.* Foam shot from the extinguisher, hitting the wall. I adjusted my aim, sweeping back and forth. Water soaked my hair and ran down my face. I kept going till the extinguisher ran dry, my chest heaving with my breaths.

When no foam left the hose anymore, I dropped the extinguisher, squinting. I didn't see flames. The air was thick with moisture and tinged with smoke, but not unbreathable. Outside, I heard a siren approaching.

Time to get out.

Ya think?

The recklessness of what I'd done made me stagger, but as I looked at the spot where flames had flickered and saw only foam and black char, while the dogs went nuts in the back, I couldn't be sorry. The siren hit a crescendo outside and stopped, although I could hear another farther away. As I turned, scooped up my cane, and tried to walk, a firefighter in full gear burst through the broken window opening and rushed to my side.

He grabbed my arm. "This way. Get out!" His muffled voice sounded pissed off. I let him support me on one side and deployed the cane on the other as he hustled me toward the back, away from the damage.

"The dogs!" I said as he half-dragged me down the hall.

"You first. Here." We reached the side door and there were my phone, Cheyenne's, and Brooklyn's side by side on the floor.

"Did you call 9-1-1?" I asked. "I mean, the cops. He tried to kidnap her."

The firefighter cursed as I slipped out of his grasp to pick up my phone. "Outside, sir. Now! Worry about the rest later."

I hit the emergency button, but let him haul me out the door, away from the building, and around toward the front. A cop car came screaming down the road toward us and peeled into the lot, so I guess my call was unneeded. I shut off the voice of the dispatcher, sticking the phone in my pocket. The cops leaped out of their car and ran toward Brooklyn, Cheyenne, and Harvey.

Fifty feet away, the firefighters were shooting water through the broken window into my shelter.

Better than fire. Keep the babies safe.

"Wait here," my rescuer said, letting go of my arm and sprinting to help his buddies.

I wasn't about to do that when Brooklyn and Cheyenne could be still at risk from Harvey. Ignoring my screaming leg, I trudged in their direction. As I approached, I could see that luckily, one of the two officers had been among the cops responding to Harvey's first kidnapping attempt. She had her cuffs on the right person, as Harvey snarled and cursed on the pavement.

"…can be used against you in a court of law," she was saying as I approached. The other cop stood over the gun which lay on the ground, and was speaking into his radio.

Brooklyn must've caught sight of me out of the corner of his eye, because he dropped his arm from around Cheyenne's shoulders and charged my way. "Arthur! Dammit! You bastard!" He lunged at me, catching me in a hug so ferocious I almost fell.

"Hey, hey, I'm okay," I wheezed.

"You could've died!" He squeezed me again, then shoved me away. "What the hell were you thinking?"

"That there are fourteen dogs, nineteen cats, and two rabbits in there, and seconds count." I peered over his shoulder. The firefighters were still working, but they didn't seem excited, and no one was chopping holes for more hoses. I breathed a sigh and prayed that we were safe. "I couldn't let them burn."

"Fuck!" Brooklyn yanked at his hair. "Yes, okay, it would be tragic to lose any of the fur-babies. But Arthur, I'd trade all of them in a heartbeat for you. If you die, who's going to save the two thousand cats and dogs you'll help in the years to come?"

"The shelter would find someone. I'm not irreplaceable." I knew that.

"You are to me." Brooklyn stepped close. The sunset colors lit his eyes to green and gold, wide and scared in his perfect face. He put his hands against my bearded cheeks and held me still, looking so deep into my eyes I thought he might see my soul. "You are irreplaceable to me. If you died, it would rip my heart out. Don't do that to me, Arthur. Please."

I met his gaze, and for the first time in my life, I felt truly special. Truly loved, not an afterthought, not a second choice. Brooklyn's murmur of, "You're my heart. There's no one in the world like you," filled up that dark, bleeding space inside me that had been carved deep through years of not being enough for the people I'd desperately cared for. Filled it and overflowed.

"I love you," I said. "I won't do that again." And then, because I couldn't resist. "Of course, with luck, the need won't arise again."

Brooklyn stared at me, then cursed and kissed me, hard and passionately. When we broke apart, he said, "I love you too. And you're still a bastard. How can you joke about this?"

I looked over his shoulder at the flurry of emergency personnel swarming the parking lot. *Laugh or I'd cry?* But even though I was still terrified, the emergency seemed to be under control.

An ambulance had arrived, but it was Harvey they were loading. Cheyenne stood close to a cop, who had her arm around the girl. The firefighters were talking more than firefighting, while guys in two different uniforms began striding our way.

And here in my arms was the man I'd somehow, unexpectedly, wonderfully, when I'd given up hope, come to love. So I kissed him one more time before I said, "You take Cheyenne, who probably needs a doctor, and the cops. I'll take the animals and the firefighters. Meet back at your place?"

"Dammit." Brooklyn nodded and gave me the gift of his smile, complete with lopsided dimples. "I'm not done yelling at you. But yeah. Deal. I'll see you at home. Take care of yourself, though."

I'd have quipped, *always do*, but Brooklyn would've scorned that for the lie it was. Brooklyn was the guy who really cared what happened to me, and he deserved only the truth. So I simply said, "You too. And Cheyenne," before turning to meet the guy in the turnout gear to find out how my shelter full of furry critters stood, while Brooklyn walked forward to meet the cop.

CHAPTER 22

BROOKLYN

"I THINK THEY SHOULD'VE GIVEN YOU A RABIES SHOT." I plopped next to Cheyenne on the couch in the family room, glad to stop moving after hours of hell.

Chili launched herself onto the couch next to me and nuzzled my arm.

Eb sat at Cheyenne's side. On the couch.

Twain and Sadie lay on their beds—pressed together—fast asleep.

Arthur sat in the recliner with his feet up, an ice pack on his leg, the heating pad ready to take over, and Xandra resting on the top of the chair as she occasionally kneaded his hair.

Naturally, I wanted him next to me on the couch, but keeping the leg elevated was a requirement. Also, Cheyenne needed me close.

Dogs on the couch? We could go over the rules again tomorrow.

I hadn't missed how excited Sadie had been to see Cheyenne. Hell, almost as excited as Chili had been when she spotted me.

"Sadie doesn't have rabies." Cheyenne appeared absolutely indignant. "And she didn't bite me."

"True." I grinned. "But Harvey might've. You had blood exposure." I had to joke—even with dark humor. Although…I hoped they'd test him for blood-borne diseases because it actually wasn't funny. *Crap.*

"I owe Sadie treats from now until the end of time." Cheyenne managed a smile. "If she hadn't bitten that asshole first, and if it hadn't become infected, then my chompers might not have been so painful. Blech."

She'd washed her mouth repeatedly in the hospital—along with being checked out from head to toe. Air bags could cause serious damage. She'd been so hellbent on escaping that she hadn't done up her seat belt. Had the airbag hit at a different angle, I might not have her beside me right now.

I grasped her hand.

The doorbell rang.

Arthur, dear man, tried to get up.

"I can go." Cheyenne offered, but the uncertainty was clear in her eyes. Harvey might be in jail, but if Denver had decided to follow, then…

Nope. Couldn't go there.

I ordered Arthur to stay put, disentangled myself from Chili, and headed for the door. Midnight was late for visitors, but practically all the lights in the house were on.

Arthur had only been home half an hour, since dealing with the chaos at the shelter. The smashed front had been boarded up, the power turned off at the main pending an inspection, and a security guard was onsite, thanks to one of the cops who knew someone. They'd talked about evacuating the animals, but decided that as long as there was no live electricity, the risks were minimal. Arthur said some of the animals were a bit freaked out, but they'd settle better in their familiar cages and runs.

He'd wanted to stay all night as reassurance, after the cops and firefighters were done.

Then that Neil guy had showed up, stuffed him in a cab with promises to keep an eye on his babies, and sent him home to rest.

I owed Neil a whole bunch of homemade cookies.

Tomorrow, my boyfriend could deal with all the cleanup and inspection and assessing the damage. And the insurance.

Again.

I checked the peephole, then grinned as I opened the door. "Wynn."

"Hope I'm not too late." His eyes read uncertainty.

"Not at all. A welcome sight." *Unless you're coming to tell me that Cheyenne has to go back. Hell, I might just take her and run to Canada.*

I closed the door and beckoned him to follow me. "Soda? Water?"

"I'm not staying that long, but thank you. I heard what happened, and I wanted to check in, see if there was anything I could do."

"That's mighty kind of you." We walked through to the family room. "Won't you sit?" I pointed to a wicker chair with a comfy cushion on the seat. *Thank God I have that. Otherwise, he'd be on the couch with the pile of pooches.*

"Sure. Thanks." He lowered himself into the chair.

God, I hope there's not too much fur. Oh well, he's wearing jeans.

His gaze honed in on Cheyenne. "How are you?"

She touched the bruise on her temple from the airbag. "Could've been worse." She managed a smile. "Eb might've tagged me instead of Harvey."

273

Wynn's gaze shot to me, then switched over to Arthur. "Tagged?"

Arthur shrugged as he swapped the ice pack for heating. "A game his previous owner taught him, leaping on people. I'll need to unteach it, *again*—because having a ninety-pound dog knock you to the ground isn't a good thing."

"Harvey?" Wynne grinned. "So that's how he cracked his head? I heard they diagnosed him with a concussion, although I didn't get a full report. HIPPA privacy, you know. I assumed that was the airbag."

I said, "Probably both. Too bad it didn't knock some sense into him." I'd heard him howling about false arrest, illegal imprisonment, and how his militia was going to come and save him, even as they strapped him into the gurney. When the cop asked me if he was serious, I said about the first two, certainly. About the last? I couldn't see community members driving across the country to break down the walls of the jail. Even people as...special...as my former family and acquaintances wouldn't run *that* afoul of the law.

"He's facing damn serious charges." Wynn's gaze settled back on Cheyenne. "The custody case is now a slam dunk. We already have them on tape promising to force you to marry Harvey. Now I heard he admitted your father sent him after you. Or, at the very least, provided all the information about where to find you. Your parents knew the kind of man they were sending, and they didn't care. Judge Mathas will take all that into consideration. I know her, and she takes child-endangerment seriously. Brooklyn's the only person who's had your welfare at heart through all this. She'll pick your brother."

A tightness in my chest loosened a little. I'd been so fucking worried. Yes, things looked good enough to be cautiously optimistic. But that was a far cry from *slam dunk*. Wynn might be confident, but I'd wait until I had the papers in my hand before celebrating.

Wynn leaned forward. "I'm also going to suggest counseling—perhaps for all of you, but definitely for Cheyenne. Not just because it will look good, but because I truly believe you will benefit. You've been through a hell of a lot."

She stiffened.

Since I'd retaken my place on the couch, I was able to reach over and grasp her hand. "Yes. Whatever we need."

"Dr. Josiah Braithwaite counsels children and young adults—"

"I'm an adult." She jutted out her chin.

"I believe his practice is toddlers to twenty." Wynn held her gaze.

I don't want to know why a toddler might need therapy. "If you text me the doctor's information, I'll be happy to make the call."

"Give the receptionist my name, and she may be able to expedite—this isn't the first time I've called in a favor."

As a lawyer in a small town, he probably saw a lot. Possibly more than I could've ever dealt with. "Thank you."

He nodded. "Are you going to be okay? I mean, okay is relative…" His gaze traveled over all of us, but settled on Cheyenne.

She gripped my hand. "I'm safe."

"You are."

"I'm never going back."

"No, highly unlikely."

"Then yeah, I'm okay. Although that was scary shit." She cut me a glance. "Mom and Dad would flip their lids at the idea of a shrink, but hey, if they hate it, maybe that's a good sign. Talking to a professional wouldn't be the end of the world."

I offered an encouraging smile. "Nope. Not at all."

"Then I'll leave you be." Wynn rose.

Cheyenne released my hand and popped up. "I'll see you out and lock the door behind you."

It didn't surprise me that Cheyenne wanted to check the door locks herself tonight. Even knowing Mrs. Bollinger and her cell phone were on one side while trusty Roger was on the other, it'd be a long time before I left a door unlocked, even just to step outside a moment. Probably longer for Cheyenne. The shock of finding Harvey looming up inside a safe space would linger.

They exited the room.

"So, she's staying." Arthur said the words quietly.

"Yep." I eyed him, spotting the uncertainty. "So are you. You think I can do this by myself?"

"Of course you can. You're Brooklyn West—you can do anything, have anyone—"

"Stop that bullshit right now. I want you. Like a forever kind of thing. So we'll need to figure out how to bring the rest of your stuff from the shelter—"

"Just like that?"

"Yeah, just like that." Cheyenne popped her head into the room. "Since the pooches have all had a run outside, I'm going to shower and then go to bed." She eyed us. "I get Eb and Twain. Eventually, when she's more comfortable, I want Sadie in my room. That fourteen days will be up soon."

Not that soon, but I'd done precisely nothing about trying to rehome her. Because, despite Arthur's menagerie, we had room for one more. I was certain, with my boyfriend's tutelage and Cheyenne's patience, that the little dog could gain enough confidence to co-exist with strangers. She was beginning to attach herself to Cheyenne. Just as Chili had become my shadow, I could imagine Sadie becoming Cheyenne's, and then we'd be okay.

Cheyenne added, "I want a home with all the dogs in it."

"You're going to get tired of the clouds of dog fur." Arthur said the words with a smile, but I recognized worry.

"Nope." She popped the *p*. "Fur's fine. Furry clothes, pillow, not a problem."

"Dogs aren't supposed to sleep on the bed." I met her gaze.

She blushed just a bit—a sure sign she knew she was in the wrong.

"But I guess tonight can be an exception." Whatever she needed to ward off the nightmares. "We'll need to get you into school next week. Or at least earning a GED. And college or a trade isn't optional. If you're staying here, then —for now—you're in school."

"But soon I'll be living at the rescue shelter and helping take care of the animals." She twirled a lock of her hair in her fingers. Another sign she was uncertain.

"All things we can discuss in the future." I gave her my brightest smile. "The point is, you're staying in Gaynor Beach. This is your home. We're a family, Cheyenne. The three of us." I shot a glance at the man I already loved more than life itself. No way was I letting him go anywhere other than our bed. And soon. We were both exhausted.

"A family." Cheyenne repeated the words.

"A family." Arthur said them with a lot of feeling—like he was starting to accept this.

I could love Arthur and not have to hide anything. My sister was mature enough to know what would be going on inside my bedroom. I dreaded to think how soon she might bring a boy—or girl or enby—home, putting me in the parental position. But I'd deal with my own neuroses at the time. Hell, if I was back home, I'd be married with at least one kid and another on the way. Probably more if I'd married Rachel. I could stand up and take the responsible adult role.

"You'll always be my little sister."

She rolled her eyes. "Good night." She eyed the collection of pets, from Xandra on the back of the recliner to the herd of dogs. "Eb, Twain." She clicked her tongue.

Twain sleepily rose from his bed and stretched.

Eb jumped down from the couch, stretched, and sauntered over.

Chili, as if sensing the moment, scooted off and strutted across the room. She tucked herself into Twain's bed—clearly enjoying the warmth—and rested her nose mere inches from Sadie.

Who cracked an eye, decided all was right with the world, and went back to sleep.

I figured we were good leaving the two dogs free in here.

Both had their crates where they could hunker down if they needed the comfort of their own space. Sadie hadn't shown any destructiveness so far, and she was calm with a dog friend around. As things stood, they clearly felt each other was enough.

Cheyenne was nearly out of the room before she pivoted and hurried back. She made her way to Arthur and pressed a kiss to his cheek.

His shock was priceless.

I rose and pulled her into an embrace. She still felt slight in my arms, but a comfort in a way I'd really never had in my life as she hugged me back. Now I had two people who would hold me tight. Two people who needed me as much as I needed them. That kind of reassurance meant everything.

She pulled away first, clicked her tongue at the dogs, and then took off.

Eb and Twain followed—clearly pleased with however things would go.

Arthur lowered the recliner footrest. He flicked off the heating pad while I snagged the ice pack.

He rose, tested his leg, then reached for his cane. Stretching stiffly, he met my eyes, then deliberately ran his gaze down my body. "Soon."

"Not until the doc clears you. I'm well aware tonight will set you back."

He frowned.

I stepped into his space and kissed his cheek above that wild beard. "Come to bed? I need to hold you tonight. Also, forever."

Xandra leapt from the back of the recliner and headed toward the bedrooms. She quite liked the room that Arthur had used for what…a day or two? Now, she could rule it.

"Yes?" I murmured against Arthur's skin.

He grasped the back of my neck and guided me to him for a proper kiss. "Yes, to a forever thing. Yes, I'll come to bed." His eyes held promise, despite a rueful edge of knowing we'd have to wait. Then his expression softened and the heat faded, leaving only the promise of love.

I'd hold him to that promise. And eventually ensure we made it a *forever thing* in every way possible.

EPILOGUE
ARTHUR

TWO MONTHS LATER

THE FRONT LOBBY OF MY SHELTER GLEAMED AND sparkled, with added glitter from the colored lights and ornaments hung high on the walls. The racks of leashes and dog toys and treats had been pushed back against the wall to make room for tables draped in seasonal red cloths. Elbow-high tables, because this Holiday party was pups-included, and keeping the food up meant less ease of grazing for the furry contingent.

Probably not zero, which was why chocolate, grapes, and onions were off the catering menu.

Ebony, at my side, slanted up a pitiful look and licked his lips, as if I hadn't given him six homemade treats off the dogs' table already. "Liar," I murmured.

Turned out Mrs. Bollinger had been cranky from loneliness, and after becoming a hero for running off Harvey, Cheyenne's frequent visits had won her over. She was around here somewhere with the mini-poodle she'd adopted, and the candy-cane liver snaps for dogs were her contribution.

"Doing okay?" Shane appeared at my side, Mimsy draped around his neck like a fur stole. He knew crowds were not my favorite thing.

"I am now. This is all friends." Last night, we'd done a fundraiser party for the shelter, open to all the community. Neil had outdone himself, with auctions of pet portraits and training sessions and hand-knit sweaters that brought in a good chunk of change. Brooklyn donated a couple of first-week's daycare vouchers, which hopefully would get him some repeat customers. We were making ends meet, but he was still growing his business reputation.

"*Lots* of friends tonight, though." Shane gazed out over the crowd. "*Most* of whom would've told me if they got shot." He raised an eyebrow at me.

I had to laugh, which was no doubt his intention. "You're not still holding a grudge?"

"I'm getting over it, since at least you told me right away when the bad guy ran a truck through our front window and set the place on fire."

"A small truck. A very limited fire."

"You—" He broke off. "Are you teasing me now?"

"Maybe a bit."

He grinned, then slipped Mimsy to the floor. "Hey, I taught her a new trick. Watch. Mimsy, bonbons!"

The cat slinked off between partygoers' legs, ignoring various dogs, until she reached a small table holding a bowl full of fancy wrapped candy canes. With a smooth leap, she landed on top, selected a cane, grabbed the wrapper in her teeth and trotted back. Shane held out the crook of his elbow, and she jumped up with her prize.

"Looks like blue raspberry. Good choice, Mims."

But before Shane could take it from her, a tanned hand

reached around him and snagged the candy. "Thanks, Mimsy." Shane's boyfriend Theo peeled the wrapper and stuck the end of the cane in his mouth, his blond curls lit like a halo in the sparkle of the lights.

"Hey. I taught her to steal for me," Shane said in mock displeasure. "You get your own thief cat."

Theo laughed, then turned to me. "Has he chewed you out again for keeping him in the dark?"

"For the fiftieth time since you guys got home? Yeah."

"He means it with love," James's smooth, deep voice said from behind me.

"Nah, I mean it with irritation." Shane tilted his head at Theo. "We've been here, done that. Mimsy did her show for the kids. Ready to go get horizontal?"

Theo's gray eyes darkened and he nodded. "Yeah. Might as well. Relax, I mean."

"You're not fooling us, kids," James called after them as they headed to the door, before turning to me. "How are you holding up?"

"I'm okay." James was one of the few who knew that I still got the occasional headache or dizzy spell, mostly set off by stress. "Last night was stressful. This is fun. Is Colin here?"

"With Widget, yeah. And the kids. Which is why I have about six seconds to say Merry Christmas and great party, before I have to get back to them."

"Those three still a handful?"

"We're out of the 'behave like angels so we can stay' phase, and into the 'test the foster parents to see if they really mean it' phase."

"Bless you and may God have mercy on your soul," I intoned, meaning the first bit with all my heart.

"Thanks." James gave me a quick, rough hug and strode off into the crowd.

Cheyenne, coming up beside me, eyed him as he went. "He's tall. Taller even than Brooklyn. I bet that makes the foster kids feel safe."

I wrapped an arm around her. "I bet it does." Cheyenne didn't mention Harvey much, and she was working with her therapist, but when she'd turned eighteen, the topic of moving out into the shelter apartment never came up. The idea of living alone, with no one but Sadie for company and protection, didn't seem to appeal to her. And honestly? Brooklyn would've worried himself sick. Me too, probably.

I had a young guy up there now, living rent-free in exchange for nighttime shelter duties, while he worked on a plumbing apprenticeship. Wouldn't hurt to have a plumber who owed me a favor in a couple of years, and he was a good kid. When he couldn't find a place that would've let him have his dog, he'd slept on the street with her, till Shane spotted him.

Speaking of good guys… "Where's Brooklyn?" I asked Cheyenne. But then my eyes were caught by a familiar dimpled smile. "Oh. There."

My man loved parties. He was so great with people. Last night, while I gritted my teeth and tried to work the room, he'd shone as master of ceremonies at the auction. Brooklyn amazed me. With his family history, he'd have had every reason to be guarded, but he put himself out there and made friends everywhere he went.

Right now, he was swooping a familiar giggling toddler through the air, the boy secure in Brooklyn's hold. James's brother Danny looked on with a smile, while his fiancé knelt and reassured their shy five-year-old daughter. Little Thomas seemed thrilled with his Brooklyn-ride, chubby brown arms waving as he babbled, "Trubby. Trubby!"

Or maybe he was psychic, because at that moment

KAJE HARPER & GABBI GREY

their husky, aptly named Trouble, pulled her leash out of Danny's fingers and bolted across the floor. A couple of people swayed, their knees hit with fifty pounds of fluff-covered muscle. A couple of others grabbed and missed.

I turned to see where she was going, and there, coming in the second door of the front foyer, was Mama, flanked by two of the goddesses of James's tribe, his sister Gracie and her girlfriend Jezebel.

I flinched, expecting disaster as the half-trained husky was about to collide with the older Black woman with a heart condition. But before any of us could intercept, Gracie bellowed, "Trouble! *Sit!*"

We could almost see that husky's eyes get big, and then her butt hit the floor, three feet from Mama.

Mama laughed, that rich, warm chuckle that had saved me from feeling so alone a time or two, even as it made me long for family of my own. "Good dog," she said, then looked around as Gracie snatched up Trouble's leash. "Where's that Arthur? There you are! You've been far too much of a stranger lately. I haven't seen you for months."

And something sweet as honey rolled through me, with Brooklyn ten feet away turning to meet my eyes, and Cheyenne under my arm. Here was my own family, the people I loved, mine to introduce to one more person who would love them too. Mama's heart was big enough to include even hangers-on like me. In a way, she and James and Shane and all the friends I'd made here had taught me to be open to being loved.

That had always been the hard part for me—not taking care of others or caring about them, but letting them do that for me. Accepting that they wanted to.

I called, "Brooklyn. Let me introduce you."

"And bring that grandbaby of mine with you." She waved. "Hey, Thomas!"

The toddler stretched his arms toward her, and Brooklyn came over, holding the boy easily on his hip. I was reminded he had grown up with younger siblings. I guided Cheyenne forward too. "Mama, this is my boyfriend Brooklyn, and his sister Cheyenne, who's living with us."

"I heard about that." Mama met Cheyenne's gaze. "You did well, girl, getting away from people who wanted to own you. Nobody gets to own us. And if they ever give you trouble again, I've got some big strong boys who'll back you up. If that's not enough, I'll give those parents of yours a piece of my mind myself."

"Ooh." Danny eased Thomas out of Brooklyn's hold and passed the baby to Mama. "Pulling out the *big* threats."

"You bet," Mama retorted to me. "Smart folks know who to listen to."

"Yes, Mama," I agreed meekly.

She chuckled and then asked Brooklyn and Cheyenne a few easy questions, nothing fraught about home and history, just how they were settling in. But when she was done, she eyed me over the toddler's black curls. "So, Arthur, your man here seems to be good with babies. I always wanted to see you with some little ones of your own."

"Hey, Mama," James said. "Don't push. Don't you have enough grandbabies yet?"

"No such thing as enough," she replied.

"We haven't talked about it." I exchanged looks with Brooklyn.

"No rush. Just sayin'." Mama bent to hear little Hallie, who tugged at her skirt. "Cupcakes? Of course I need one." She let the five-year-old pull her across the room like a galleon under sail, guided by a tiny tugboat.

"Maybe you should talk about it," Cheyenne said to Brooklyn. "While I'm still around to babysit." She stared off across the room, then took Eb's leash from me. "Oops, there's someone I want to talk to. Enjoy your heart-to-heart."

Brooklyn and I watched as she strode across the room toward a petite, long-haired Black woman whose self-possessed air suggested she was perhaps a year or two older than Cheyenne. Reaching her target, Cheyenne said something and then had Eb sit and hold up a paw.

"Hmm," Brooklyn murmured, watching as the other woman bent and gravely shook Eb's proffered foot. "What do you think?"

"I think Cheyenne will tell us when she wants us to know." I suddenly needed to get some alone time with this man. Because Cheyenne also wasn't wrong. Maybe we should talk. "Can I show you my etchings?" I gestured toward the hallway, drawing him away from the crowd, then pointed up the stairs when we reached them.

"I thought Liam lived up there now."

"He does, but there's still the office. Come on."

Brooklyn raised an eyebrow but took my outstretched hand and followed me up, a trip I could finally make with ease. I unlocked the office at the top, guided him in, and closed the door behind us.

The party below came to us as a muted babble. I hadn't turned on the lights, and through the window at the end of the room, we could look out across the neighborhood. We drifted over there, standing shoulder to shoulder, looking at the dark night outside. Many of the homes had holiday lights up, and the scene glittered with red and blue and green and gold. Although also... "Is that an inflatable octopus with a silver-headed cane and a Santa hat?"

"Our kind of people," Brooklyn chuckled.

I turned to face him. "So. Mama's way out ahead of the game, but we haven't talked about it. Do you want kids one day?"

"I don't know," he said slowly. "When I was with Becca, we discussed it, but the idea scared me silly. I don't know if that was because I knew we didn't have the kind of solid foundation kids need, or I assumed someone who grew up like I did would be a terrible dad."

I had to kiss him, fast and soft. "Well, Cheyenne should sure have set that second fear to rest. You're great with her."

"Not the same as with a baby."

"Probably harder."

"What about you?" Brooklyn patted my chest, then gave my beard a tiny tug. "You have excellent dad energy with all your fur-babies."

"Yeah. I guess I didn't think I'd have anything left to give, with all the dogs and cats I cared for."

"I hear the past tense in there. What about now?"

"Now? I'm not ready. Not any time soon. But I saw you with that little boy, and something in my chest clenched. You *are* great with kids—with James's foster kids, Danny and Rob's little ones. You meet Kevin on his own terms as a young teen. So maybe, someday, I can imagine wanting kids, if I had you at my side to share that life with."

"Okay. So we put that firmly on the *maybe* shelf. Good talk." He kissed me as I laughed.

"Right. At least neither of us is a no, so we know where we stand. And there's one other thing I want to discuss." It was probably too soon for that as well, but we'd been living together for over two months. Every day, we fit together better, in bed and out of it. We'd had a few fights, mostly about me failing to let him know when I was running late, or him assuming I'd say yes to some social invitation when my batteries were low. But we talked through it, and the make-up sex was awesome.

I put my hand on his chest, over his heart. "I grew up in a conventional family," I said. "Midwest country life, uncles, aunts, cousins, church on Sundays, weddings and funerals, farming and hunting and fishing and all. When I decided not to go home after college, and to embrace being out and queer, I thought I was leaving all those conventions behind."

"Well, you left behind the hunting and fishing," he noted. His smile was soft and fond.

"Sure did. But it turns out, I'm more conventional than I thought. Or at least, I want some of the privileges." I lifted my hand to set my knuckles on his stubbled chin and run my thumb over his pretty lower lip. "I want to call you my husband. I want a wedding and my ring on your finger. If you don't, I'm not going to go off in a huff. Or get mad, or even sad—"

"Shh." He leaned forward and kissed me. "Stop trying to accept a no before I say it, and ask me."

I swallowed hard. There he was, this kind, outgoing, handsome, loving boy-next-door who'd survived hard times and come out of them without losing his smile, and here I was. Stocky and long-nosed and wild-bearded, though he'd told me not to cut it when I asked. Distractable and awkward, except with my fur-babies. Almost forty, and still without money in the bank.

"I don't have a lot to offer," I told him, "except everything I am. I love you, and I want to spend my life with you, and make you happy. Will you marry me?"

"You're offering me you, and that's the biggest gift in the universe." He kissed me again, hard. "Yes. Absolutely yes."

"You're sure?"

"Hm, let me see. I was the one who dragged you home with me, who held your pets hostage so you would stay, who gave you a bratty younger sister who would never let you hear the end of it if you left. Am I sure? Hell, yeah."

We grinned at each other, there in that darkened office, the glow of the octopus Santa a colorful backdrop.

"Next question," I said, not quite seriously. "Do we let Cheyenne plan this wedding, or do we secretly elope?"

"Oh my God, she would kill us." Brooklyn choked. "She'll want to do the party up right."

"Party. Yeah. About that. There's no rush, right? We can wait a month. Six months. 2042 has a nice ring to it."

Brooklyn gathered me into his arms, and I leaned against him. His strength still surprised me sometimes, the way he could take my weight and make me feel so safe, so wanted. He kissed my hair, then eased the band off my ponytail and ran his fingers through the long strands, tugging gently. "No rush. Whenever it feels right to us."

"Spring is lovely in California."

"So it is."

I laid my head on his shoulder, luxuriating in the feel of his hand stroking my hair. "There's nothing I'd rather do in spring than call you my husband."

"I'll put it in our calendar," he agreed.

We stood there a long time, arms around each other, rocking a little back and forth. Until a muffled crash and bark from downstairs broke us apart and called us back down to the wonderful, fur-filled, family-building life we shared.

ABOUT THE AUTHOR
KAJE HARPER

I get asked about my name a lot, but it's not something exotic. "Kaje" is pronounced like "cage" – it's an old nickname; my pronouns are she/her. My books are primarily M/M romance, often with added mystery, fantasy, historical, SciFi, paranormal... I also have a few Young Adult stories.

After decades of writing just for fun, my husband convinced me I really should submit something, somewhere. My first professionally published book, *Life Lessons*, came out in May 2011. I have a weakness for closeted cops with honest hearts and teachers who speak their minds, and I was delighted and encouraged by the reception Mac and Tony received. I now have a good-sized backlist in ebooks, print, and some audio, including Amazon bestseller *The Rebuilding Year* and Rainbow Awards Best Mystery-Thriller *Tracefinder: Contact*. A complete list with links can be found on my website "Books" page.

All my social media links can be found at https://linktr. ee/kajeharper

And if you like **free short stories**, check out the weekly Sunday Stories on my FB Group - **Kaje's Conversation Corner** - https://www.facebook.com/ groups/208207893795147/

ALSO BY KAJE HARPER

Hidden Wolves (realistic werewolves)

Complete - 7 novels, 3 short works

Unacceptable Risk (Book #1)- **FREE**

Necromancer (urban fantasy)

Complete - 7 novels, 3 spinoffs

Marked by Death (Book #1)- **FREE**

Changes series (M/M/M mystery)

Changes Coming Down (Book #1)

Changes Going On (Book #2)

new

Changes on Ice (Book #3 – MM asexual)

Tracefinder (paranormal thriller)

Tracefinder: Contact (Book #1)

Tracefinder: Changes (Book #2)

Tracefinder: Choices (Book #3)

Finding Family (contemporary)

The Family We're Born With (Book #1) – free novella

The Family We Make (Book #2)

Rebuilding Year (contemporary bi awakening)

The Rebuilding Year (Book #1) **FREE**

Life, Some Assembly Required (Book #2)

Building Forever (Book #2.5)

Life Lessons (mystery, single parenting)

* Also in audio and in KU *

Life Lessons (Book #1)

And to All a Good Night (short story #1.5)+ *Getting It Right* (#1.8)

Breaking Cover (Book #2)

Home Work (Book #3)

Compensations (novella #3.5)

Learning Curve (Book #4)

Through All the Years (short story #4.5 on my website)

Stand-alone FREE Novels:

Into Deep Waters

Nor Iron Bars a Cage

Stand-alone Books and Novellas:

Over 20 including

Cowboy Dreams – royalties from 2025 go to Ukraine charity

Stand-alone FREE Short Stories:

Like the Taste of Summer

Show Me Yours

Within Reach

Shooting Star

Audiobooks:

Into Deep Waters – Narrated by Kaleo Griffith

The Rebuilding Year – Narrated by Gomez Pugh

Life, Some Assembly Required – Narrated by Gomez Pugh

Building Forever – Narrated by Gomez Pugh

Life Lessons – Narrated by JF Harding

Transparent Is a Color –Narrated by JF Harding

A full list with blurbs, and download and buy links can be found at:

https://www.kajeharper.com/books

ABOUT THE AUTHOR
GABBI GREY

USA Today Bestselling author Gabbi Grey lives in beautiful British Columbia where her fur baby chin-poo keeps her safe from the nasty neighborhood squirrels. Working for the government by day, she spends her early mornings writing contemporary, gay, sweet, and dark erotic BDSM romances. While she firmly believes in happy endings, she also believes in making her characters suffer before finding their true love. She also writes m/f romances as Gabbi Black and Gabbi Powell.

ALSO BY GABBI GREY

Want more Gabbi Grey?

Check out her Love in Mission City series, set in beautiful British Columbia.

The first book is

Ginger Snapping All the Way (Love in Mission City Book 1)

Other books in the series:

Stanley's Christmas Redemption (Love in Mission City Book 2)

The Beauty of the Beast (Love in Mission City Book 2.5)

Sleigh Bells and Second Chances (Love in Mission City Book 3)

A Daddy for Christmas 2: Foster (Love in Mission City Book 3.5)

Rayne's Return (Love in Mission City Book 4)

Gideon's Gratitude (Love in Mission City Book 5)

Love in Mission City: The Boyfriend Gamble

Love in Mission City: The Four Seasons

Love in Mission City: The Boyfriends Duet

Love in Mission City: The Shorts

Puppy Pride

Rayne Check

Archer's Awakening

Leo's Lust

A Daddy for Christmas 3: Lorcan

Thought You Were the One

Love Without Reservations

Rocktoberfest

Axe to Grind

Grindstone's Edge

Voice to Raise

Vancouver Film World

Catch a Tiger by the Tail

Solstice Surprise

Valentino in Vancouver

You See Me

Sun, Surf, and Surprises

Ginger in the City

Caressa's Homecoming (Bound by Love Book 1)

Cole's Reckoning (Bound by Love Book 2)

Young Adult

Didn't See You Coming

Audiobooks

Hugh (Single Dads of Gaynor Beach)

Anthony (Single Dads of Gaynor Beach)

Love Furever (Friends of Gaynor Beach Animal Rescue)

Husky Love (Friends of Gaynor Beach Animal Rescue)

A Furever Home (Friends of Gaynor Beach Animal Rescue)

Ginger Snapping All the Way

Stanley's Christmas Redemption

Sleigh Bells and Second Chances

Rayne's Return

Gideon's Gratitude

Rayne Check

Archer's Awakening

Thought You Were the One

Love in Mission City: The Shorts

My Past, Your Future

If Only for Today

Catch a Tiger by the Tail

Solstice Surprise

An Uncommon Gentleman

A Sensible Gentleman

Didn't See You Coming

Want a free short story? The story is set in Gaynor Beach, California where there are plenty of single dads and puppy rescues! You can sign up for my newsletter so you can keep up with all the great stuff I'm doing as well as pictures of my own pooches, Ally and Finnegan.

Hemingway's Happy Day

·

Newsletter sign-up: https://sendfox.com/gabbigrey

Website: https://gabbigrey.com/